ABOUT THE AUTHOR

Maddie Please was born in Dorset, brought up in Worcestershire and went to university in Cardiff.

Following a career as a dentist, Maddie now writes full time, and lives in Devon with her exceptionally handsome and supportive husband.

The Summer of Second Chances

MADDIE PLEASE

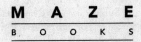

A division of HarperCollins*Publishers*
www.harpercollins.co.uk

Published by AVON
A Division of HarperCollins*Publishers* Ltd
1 London Bridge Street
London SE1 9GF

www.harpercollins.co.uk

This paperback edition 2017

First published in Great Britain in ebook format by HarperCollins*Publishers* 2017

Copyright © Maddie Please 2017

Maddie Please asserts the moral right to
be identified as the author of this work

A catalogue record for this book
is available from the British Library

ISBN: 978-0-00-825729-3

Set in Minion by
Palimpsest Book Production Limited, Falkirk, Stirlingshire

Printed and bound in the UK

For my husband Brian, who never doubted me.
With all my love.
Thank you.

PROLOGUE

It was quite incredible really, when I considered what a long time things took to do as a rule. Meeting Ian and moving in, supporting him as he built up his business, entertaining people who drove me nearly mad with boredom, getting contracts, the crazy nit-picking of flaky homeowners. These things took months, sometimes years. To lose it all took no time at all.

I lost my partner, my home, a lot of my friends and my peace of mind – not necessarily in that order – and yet, only a few days had passed.

We had shared the usual formulaic Christmas with Susan picking at her food as though I was trying to poison her. And then Ian had started on about the bloody New Year's Eve party we were having.

He'd rolled his eyes at his mother who was sitting opposite me.

'I had to persuade her, you know, Mum. Lottie hates New Year's Eve,' he said. Quietly, as though I was simple and couldn't hear him.

'I don't!' I said. 'That's so not true.'

I would have said it more emphatically with words like bollocks or crap attached, but Susan has been known to leave the room when I swear so I didn't. It was Christmas after all.

'She says it's just one more day,' Ian continued. He sent me a mischievous grin to show he was teasing me. I pulled a face at him and tried to kick him under the table.

Susan put down her knife and fork and peered over her glasses at me.

'You're very young, Charlotte. Perhaps you think there will always be one more day.'

Oh God, I knew what was coming.

Susan sighed and shook her head.

Yes, here it was.

'I would give anything to have one more hour with Trevor. One more day.' She bit her lip, shook her head and struggled on bravely. 'If I had known he would be taken from me so soon.'

And after the party, wallop! One bloody shock after another, everything getting worse and worse until I came to dread waking up each day because I knew something else horrible was bound to happen.

And then the day came when I packed my clothes, my jewellery box, my grandmother's clock and as many of my belongings as I could fit into my car – the only thing I now owned – and handed back the keys to the house to an anxious solicitor who looked like Rodney Trotter's younger brother doing work experience. I could almost imagine Susan's glee as she closed one claw-like hand over them with an evil cackle. I'd always known she had never really liked me, but now she could make her feelings more than clear. She blamed me for what happened, and this was the perfect revenge.

CHAPTER 1

Snowdrops – a friend in adversity, consolation, hope

I reached Holly Cottage – my sanctuary – just before the late January sunshine faded into the grey-green hills of Devon. I had lost just about everything familiar to me; my partner, most of my friends, my job, the home I had loved. I pulled into the gravelled drive, turned off the car engine and opened the window. The silence was deafening. I took my seatbelt off and listened for a while; I realised it was the first peace I had encountered for a very long time. Hardly anyone knew where I was, that was the marvellous thing. And that was the way I wanted to keep it.

The road, if you could call it that, meandered up past the house and then tapered off as though it had lost interest into an unmetalled track with grass growing down the middle. Holly Cottage looked as though it had been dumped on the grass verge on the brow of the hill with views over the rolling countryside. It was like a child's drawing of a house; stone walls, a slate roof, three upstairs windows and two downstairs, either side of a black front door. I had only travelled about forty miles, perhaps it was just my state of mind, but as I got out of my car, the air seemed livelier, different. I took a deep lungful of freedom and felt a bit shaky.

This was it, then, all pretence was gone. For the last few years I had lived in happy ignorance in Ian's five-bedroom house surrounded by a half-acre of garden. I'd been anticipating a summer holiday in the Dordogne in a customer's *gîte*. I hadn't even known, much less cared, who my electricity supplier was. In hindsight, I had been beyond naïve; I'd thought nothing would ever change. Now I was going to live in a borrowed two-bedroom cottage with nothing much to recommend it but the view. How the hell did this happen?

But of course, if I was honest, I knew exactly how I'd ended up here. I'd trusted Ian, trusted him completely. And then everything had come crashing down. If it hadn't been for the kindness of Jess I don't know what on earth I would have done. I parked in front of the black door and remembered the conversation that had changed my life.

Jess had pouted for a moment, running a hand through her blonde hair.

'Of course, Holly Cottage!'

'Oh, I don't think…' Greg said, his brow furrowed in thought.

'Please, don't, I'm not a charity case just yet, you've been so great these last few days. A lot of my friends…'

I didn't finish the sentence. I stood up and wandered around their conservatory, clearing my throat, pretending to look at their garden. Really I was trying to control my easy tears. A lot of my so-called friends had silently disappeared from the scene, as though Ian's sudden death and my destitution might be infectious. To be honest, I didn't want to talk to anyone any more, I couldn't bear explaining everything over and over again. So I had got used to ignoring my mobile. I didn't log on to my laptop to look at my emails.

Jess turned in her chair, the wicker creaking.

'Lottie, you'd be doing us a favour, honestly you would.'

Her enthusiasm grew the more she considered it.

'It's only a little place. I bought it just before I married Greg. I used to work in a club in London. Greg calls them my wild years but they weren't really. I lived on Uncle Ben's Rice in a ghastly place in Peckham. I saved all my tips for two years. Very generous some of them were.' Jess widened her blue eyes at me. 'Oh nothing dodgy, so don't worry.'

I looked at Jess with astonishment and new respect. She might look like a complete airhead but obviously she wasn't. I was the nitwit here, with no financial sense at all, no career, finding myself at thirty-four broke and without prospects.

'It's all furnished; you wouldn't need to take anything. Just your clothes and your bits and pieces. We could help you with that, couldn't we, Gregsy? The van, you know.'

Her husband grunted and shifted in his chair, evidently not thrilled with the way things were turning out. Jess didn't seem to notice; either that or she was ignoring him.

'It has been rented out for three years but the tenants have just gone, owing money of course.' She gulped as she realised the tactlessness of her words. 'Sorry, didn't mean to say it like that. I'm not sure if I want to rent it out again or sell it. But either way it needs an upgrade. It's right out in the country, the other side of Exeter, but less than an hour away. It's a bit out of the way but really pretty. Ideal for you, in fact.'

I didn't look at her. I tried to gather my thoughts.

'How much would it be?'

Greg opened his mouth to speak but Jess interrupted him.

'Nothing. All you need to do is give it a clean up, do the clever stuff you do with curtains and wallpaper and have a good flick around with a paintbrush. You're ever so good with the interior décor sort of thing. Much better than me, that's for sure. I know I need to spend a bit of money on the place. You'd be doing me a huge favour.'

'Oh, *Jess!*'

'No really, you would, wouldn't she, Greg?'

Greg made some non-committal noises and looked back at his phone. I could tell he wasn't very happy about this.

'That's settled then,' she said, pleased.

'It's not settled at all,' I said. 'I can't just use your house for nothing. I can't accept, it's too much.'

'It's not too much. You really would be helping me out. We've been friends for ages, and you were so lovely to us when we moved here. I know you can do this sort of thing in your sleep. Picking out colours and stuff. You could do it for a living, you know.'

'I don't know about that,' I said, trying to look modest.

I'd spent such a long time doing Ian's house, picking fabrics, sourcing furniture, choosing colours, and I'd loved every minute.

'Yes, you could, like that programme on TV where people have to upgrade rooms and paint crappy old furniture to make it look nice again. You could do that. We both said you should apply, remember?'

'Yes, I know—'

'Then stop arguing with me. Look, it can't be rented out as it is.' For the first time she looked serious. 'Greg's brother lives down there. We don't have an awful lot of contact with him but he does have a key in case of emergencies and he sent me an email last week. About the Websters. They did a moonlight flit and left the cottage in a bit of a state. I was going to pay someone to get it cleaned up and put some of Greg's men in there to decorate it but if you do it, it's a win-win situation, isn't it? This is just so "meant to be".'

Jess gave me an artless smile, one that I bet never failed to succeed. I gave her a hug.

'Well – thank you, Jess.'

I felt quite tearful and we stood and looked at each other for a moment, both of us a bit emotional.

Greg glanced up from his iPhone. He looked less jovial than usual.

'I'll tell Bryn to expect you any time this week, shall I?' Jess continued. 'And if he's not in I'll leave a message on his answerphone. He always picks those up.'

I began to panic. I was being either helped or pushed, I wasn't sure which.

'Who's Bryn?'

'My little brother, God help me,' Greg muttered. 'I've got to go and check my emails.'

'Don't be like that, Gregsy,' Jess said, twirling her blonde hair between slender fingers. She watched as Greg went off to his office and turned back to me. 'They fell out a few years ago but Bryn's really nice once you get to know him. Just big, tall and a bit scary. Like a bear. But I know he's not half as bad as he seems.'

This was far from reassuring.

'Maybe this isn't such a good idea after all…' I said.

Jess patted my hand. 'Course it is. Think about it. It's an adventure. A change of scenery. A bit of excitement. Just what you need.'

'Don't tell anyone where I am,' I blurted out. 'I don't want anyone to know.'

My head was aching. So was my heart. I had loved the house I had shared with Ian so much. I had been proud, but we all know pride comes before a fall. And what a fall.

I had decorated and planned every room in the years I had lived there. I had chosen things. The colour of the walls, the flooring, the towels, the lighting. Everything was perfect. Or it had been. It wasn't now, was it? And it wasn't mine either.

I stood outside Holly Cottage, lost in thought. Just about everything I had taken for granted had gone wrong. Now I had to take this chance and focus on the future because I certainly couldn't change the past.

I got out, locking the car behind me although, to be honest, it didn't feel as though there was a living soul for miles. I wandered around to the back of the house, my heels catching between the broken paving slabs. I wondered if the 'huge and bear-like' Bryn was around to watch the homeless idiot arriving. Might he be lurking in the shadows under the trees down the lane? For some reason I pictured him standing, shoulders hunched like Lurch from *The Addams Family*, knuckles dragging on the ground. Fortunately there was no sign of him. But he had left the back door key under an upturned bucket in the porch as Jess had assured me he would. The key stuck for a heart-stopping few moments and then turned in the lock with an unwilling squeak. I let myself in to the hall.

The stale scent of wet dog, mingled with something even more unpleasant, hit me. The smell of damp carpet, neglect and, unmistakably, fish.

I left the door open and made my way into the sitting room, one hand over my nose. The room was flagstoned with a large rug over the top, which was soaking. Someone had flung a plastic bucket plus water into the middle and my shoes squelched as I took a hesitant step into the room. They had also enhanced the décor by chucking around a few shovelfuls of ash from the fire. The walls were pale and marked with squares of grime where pictures had been removed. Underneath one windowsill the paper had been pulled off altogether and someone had drawn stars in pink and purple felt tip pen on the wall.

The smell was stronger here, pungent and eye watering. Trying not to gag, I pushed back the curtains and opened both the sash windows. The crispness of the evening air was welcome. I hurried back outside for a moment to refresh my lungs and then went upstairs to explore further, finding a small bathroom and two bedrooms.

There was evidence in the expensive wallpaper and the sisal carpet that this place had once been very pretty, but now it was neglected and extremely dirty. There were stains on the floor and muddy fingerprints around the china light switches, and someone had been free with wax crayons on the walls of the landing.

In the corner of the bathroom was a huge web, the spider still busy in the middle with a struggling bluebottle. I shuddered. On the mirror, in coral lipstick, was scrawled *Bitch*. It neatly crossed over the reflection of my cold, pale, frightened face.

Jess had wanted me to clean and decorate, that was the deal, but it was obvious this place wasn't just in need of a flick round with the antiseptic wipes and a lick of paint; it needed pressure washing. The stink from downstairs was curling up the stairs so I opened all the windows and re-buttoned my coat.

In the larger of the two bedrooms was a mahogany wardrobe that had once been highly polished and beautiful, but was now scratched, covered with globs of Blu-Tack and propped up with a brick at one corner where one of the feet had been lost. There was a sink in the corner filled with scummy water and dead flies.

'Bloody hell!' I said.

My words echoed around the room.

'What on earth's been going on here?' asked a voice from behind me.

I spun round, squeaking with shock. There was a silhouette of a man in the doorway, his shoulders almost filling the space. I yelped again.

'Well, if you don't want people to walk in you shouldn't leave all the doors open,' he said, unapologetic.

'And you shouldn't just wander in to someone else's house uninvited,' I said, my voice shrill with fright. I flapped my hands at him to shoo him back down the stairs.

He turned and went, his movements unhurried and careful in the confined space of the stairwell. I followed him downstairs and into the kitchen, trying to calm the thudding of my heart.

'What's happened here?' he said. 'It wasn't like this the other day. And what's that terrible smell?'

'How would I know?' I replied. 'I've only just got here.'

'Hang on,' he said and went into the sitting room, ducking his head under the lintel. He searched around for a few minutes and then retrieved a rotting fish wrapped in newspaper from behind a radiator.

'Jesus!' I clamped my hand back over my nose and watched him take it outside into the garden.

He reappeared, framed in the kitchen door. 'I've no idea where that came from. I'm assuming it's nothing to do with you?'

'Of course it isn't. Why the hell would I do a thing like that?'

'OK, calm down. All I know is it didn't smell like this when I last called in. Nor was there a pond on the sitting-room floor. Perhaps the Websters are responsible?'

'The Websters?'

Oh yes the Websters. What had Jess said about them? I should have paid more attention.

'The last tenants. Two years without a problem and then Mr Webster discovered skunk and scratch cards. They left a few days ago. Spent all his money on things other than his priorities. But I know he left his house keys behind when he left. I can't think how he could have got back in. I've been here, Webster had a beaten-up old camper van. Red and white. I'm sure I would have noticed…'

I stood watching him for a moment wondering who he reminded me of.

'It needs a bit of a sort out,' he said, his blue eyes flicking from the piles of junk mail behind the door to the chocolate handprints on the wall. At least I hoped they were chocolate.

'A bit of a sort out?' I said, incredulous. 'Never mind the smell, it's absolutely filthy and disgusting.'

'Ah well.' He shrugged his shoulders. They really were very broad. 'I'm Bryn Palmer, by the way.' He held out a hand and I shook it.

'I'm Charlotte Calder. What do you mean "ah well"? Would you want to live here?'

He stuck his hands in the pockets of his jeans and rocked back on his heels. 'Nope.'

'Nor do I.'

'Well don't then,' Bryn said. He flicked another look around that conveyed his boredom with the whole conversation. 'It's up to you. I thought you needed a place to stay?'

'You mean beggars can't be choosers?'

'Why would I say that? No one is forcing you to live here, are they?'

I struggled with my temper. I was caught between Holly Cottage and a hard place. I had nowhere else to go, at least at the moment. I had considered my Auntie Shirley in Croydon but I couldn't bring myself to make that call. A one-bedroom maisonette with a view of the library car park seemed the very last resort. At least here I had a bit of privacy. And a bed.

'Couldn't someone have at least checked the place to make sure it was at least habitable?' I said.

His dark brows drew together in a frown. I had overstepped the mark, that was obvious.

'Someone? You mean me?'

'Well, it wouldn't have killed you,' I muttered.

'That was up to Jess and Greg to sort out, not me,' he said, 'you're not my responsibility. I'm not here to sort your problems out.'

Bloody cheek, it was as though I was being passed around from one responsible adult to another. Like some sort of delinquent child.

'But you live down here in this godforsaken spot,' I said, dismissing the beauty of the hills around me with a wave of my hand.

He refused to be drawn in to any discussion.

'If you aren't staying I'll have the keys back.' He held out one hand, ready to take them.

I stood, fists clenched, trembling with indecision for a few moments. It was this or sleep in the car. I had no idea about council accommodation for a single woman without children but

I guessed I would be low down on a long list. I didn't want to spend money on a hotel. I couldn't go back; the locks had been changed. I had no choice.

'I'll stay. For now anyway,' I said.

'Fine.' Bryn obviously didn't care either way. 'If you're staying we should get that wet rug out. I could help you do it now, if you like?' he said.

I closed my eyes and tried to calm down. I needed him to help me; I'd never manage it on my own. Not that I'm scrawny or anything but I'm only five foot four, there's only so much leverage I could get.

'Thank you, that would be very kind of you.'

He nodded and I noticed there was a bit of Matthew McConaughey about him, mixed with some other actor whose name I couldn't remember. Plus evidence of a fair amount of time spent in the gym. It was an attractive mixture. Pity his character wasn't so appealing.

I spent the next half an hour helping him shift furniture and alternately pulling at the rug with all my strength and gagging at the smell. Or, perhaps more accurately, he had been helping me. By the time we managed it I must have looked a sight – red, sweating and with my hair falling all over my face. A glamorous episode in anyone's book.

At last Bryn got the offending article out into the front garden, leaving me exhausted and filthy, shoving furniture back into approximately the right place.

'Well, I must be off,' he said.

He was about to leave and I was really going to be on my own. I was suddenly nervous. Perhaps I could keep him talking for a few minutes longer.

'I've brought some stuff with me but is there anywhere I can get some fresh milk or some bread?'

Bryn gave an impatient sigh. 'You can get milk and a few essentials at the post office shop in Bramford St Michael. Back

12

down this hill and turn left. You can't miss it.'

'Towering skyscrapers and retail parks?' I said.

His mouth twitched. 'A fourteenth-century church, a pub and a bus stop on the left. You'll see a row of thatched cottages and the shop is just beyond that. You'd better be quick; they close in half an hour. Unless they feel like closing earlier. Which they sometimes do. If they are shut you'll have to carry on for a few miles to Stokeley. There's a Superfine there that's open until ten o'clock.'

'Thanks,' I said in a very ungrateful tone. With any luck Bryn and I would not meet again. I didn't quite understand why he was here in the first place if he wasn't involved in the upkeep of Holly Cottage. But I soon found out.

He flicked me a slow and rather blush-inducing glance. I could see the resemblance between him and Greg, at least in looks. He had that same energy combined with a strong impression of competence. He was the sort of man who would deal with life not let it deal with him.

'I'll be off then.'

I stepped to one side to let him leave but he walked in the opposite direction, out of the kitchen door, down the small garden and through the gate at the bottom.

'Hey! Where are you going?' I called after him.

'Home,' he said.

I followed him for a few steps and watched as he walked into the garden of the house next door. I realised for the first time that his garden was huge and absolutely crammed with spring growth.

The contrast between that and the untidy mess in what I already considered 'my' garden could not have been starker. Mine boasted a shabby, overgrown lawn, weed-choked borders and the battered remains of an old bath.

Bryn looked at me as he drew level. It was obvious he was trying hard not to laugh at me.

'You live in Holly Cottage, I live in Ivy Cottage. I'm your neighbour,' he said.

'Just when I thought things couldn't get any frigging worse! That's all I bloody need.'

I couldn't help it; the words were out before I could stop myself. Bryn looked at me for a moment, his eyes were very cold and my spirits sank even lower.

'Sorry, it's been a crap sort of day,' I muttered.

'Happy to help,' he said at last.

I turned away and went inside, slamming my door behind me.

CHAPTER 2

Daffodils – uncertainty, unrequited love, deceit

It wasn't supposed to be like this. It really wasn't.

Nine years ago I'd finished my English Masters degree and taken a sort of late gap year working for the local paper as gofer while I wrote my 'bestselling novel'. I had been filling in for someone one lunch hour, selling advertising space, and Ian had come into the office to place an ad for his company; Lovell Kitchens. He had amused me so much that I had agreed to go for dinner with him that evening. He'd then charmed me into meeting for a picnic the following day, then into a relationship, and after six months much to his mother's annoyance I moved in with him.

By the time that happened, my gap year had become two years and looked as though it was turning into a career choice. Ten years older than me, Ian had seemed handsome, sophisticated, funny and charismatic. We had wanted the same things, we enjoyed similar tastes, and he had made me laugh back then. I'd been very lucky. When my university friends started complaining about trying to save a deposit for their first house, I just walked into one.

Ian worked hard, the years had been good to us, and we had a lovely home. Five bedrooms, five bathrooms, a fabulous hand-built kitchen with every possible gadget, and a wood-panelled study for Ian. I'd discovered a talent for interior décor and had brought new style and colour to the house, all paid for by Ian's generous hand. Even in the middle of winter the half-acre of manicured gardens were neat and attractive, mostly thanks to the attention of our gardener. Much to Susan's disgust we'd never married but we enjoyed our lives together. Ian was a generous host and I was a good cook. We'd had some marvellous parties when we first met.

In the past couple of years I suppose we'd just got a bit out of practice, with Ian away so much on business. And for want of something else to do, I'd recently gone back to part-time work. Not for the money, but because I was bored. There are only so many times you can decorate a house and move the furniture round.

We'd made lots of friends who included us in their busy circle of golf, fussy dinner parties and meaningless celebrations. Most of the men were more Ian's age than mine, and many were involved in property development or building, but I was culti-vating a group of my own too. Younger second wives and girlfriends keen to shop and have fun and go on spa breaks. Spa breaks! Wouldn't that be nice now? And best of all, Jess had moved into our village, a sparky high-maintenance blonde with a taste for heels and spray tans and a laugh like Barbara Windsor. We'd instantly recognised a kindred spirit in each other even if I could never rival her for glamour. She was married to Greg, a meaty-looking man, and last year they had returned from several years living in Spain and bought The Grange, the biggest house for miles. Ian had nearly had kittens with his excitement.

After I was sure that Bryn was staying indoors, I found my handbag, took my cigarettes out to the garden and lit one. Always one to conform, I knew I shouldn't smoke in someone else's house; not that it would have mattered under the circumstances.

I felt giddy for a moment; perhaps it was the nicotine. I went to brush some dead leaves off one of the garden chairs near the back door and sat down. It wasn't fair, none of this was my fault, was it? And yet here I was, on my own, miles from anywhere, looking into a future that was uncertain to say the least.

I shook myself; self-pity had no place here, I was going to have to buck up my ideas. I couldn't treat having a job as an antidote to boredom any longer. I couldn't rely on Ian's seemingly bottom-less wallet or acquaintances that had bought me flowers and sent cards when it all happened but now shied away from me in case my bad fortune rubbed off on them.

I walked down to the end of the garden through the thick, neglected grass and tried to see if there was anything apart from rubbish and weeds. A bank of nettles had taken over one of the borders. Something else that I think was honeysuckle was curling bare tendrils around a dirty and unpainted wooden lattice. It was a mess. Perhaps I could do something out here when I had a moment? Perhaps there was more under the rich red soil than was apparent. I went back into the house and picked up all the junk mail that had stacked behind the front door. Nothing to do with pizza delivery or takeaway menus, I noticed. Leaflets about hedge cutting, the local parish magazine, details of refuse collec-tion, a flyer from the local feed merchant telling me about special offers on hen coops and wire netting. Perhaps I would have some chickens.

I pictured myself wandering down the garden with a bowl of kitchen scraps, the hens fat and feathery clustering around my ankles. For some reason I imagined myself wearing an old-fash-ioned wraparound apron over a flowery frock. Oh get a bloody grip! I had moved a few miles over the county border, not into the last century! It wasn't that long ago I was hosting dinner parties in the latest season's fashion. I'd been famous for my huge shoe collection. I hoped Age Concern in Taunton had appreciated them.

When I had finished decorating and styling Ian's house for the second time, I had found a job working part time as a receptionist at the doctor's surgery. I'd been on duty one Saturday morning when I met Greg Palmer. It was also the day I found out we were having a New Year's Eve party.

There were several messages to deal with on the answerphone and a trail of people came through the doors with appointments or wanting repeat prescriptions. The phone rang almost continually. At about ten thirty there was a brief lull and after having made sure Dr Hawkins was occupied with a patient, I went to make more coffee. When I came back to my desk a tall figure was standing there, muffled up in an expensive-looking tweed coat and a cashmere scarf. He fired me a broad, white smile.

'Greg Palmer to see Doctor Hawkins,' he said.

I stabbed at a couple of computer keys. I hadn't worked here long and I was quite capable of getting things wrong.

'I don't seem to have you on the system,' I said at last.

'No problem, princess. I saw the good doctor yesterday, he told me to pop in today to check everything was OK. Just tell him Greg Palmer is here.' He winked and flashed me another smile, utterly confident of his success in circumventing our appointment system. It was a good thing the other receptionist, Daphne, wasn't in my place. She would have sent him packing and enjoyed doing it too.

'OK, I'll tell the doctor you're here. Do take a seat.' I spoke into the intercom. When I turned back he was still there, looking at me with a speculative gaze. He held out a large, tanned hand. A heavy gold bracelet clanked out from under his coat cuff.

'You're Charlotte, aren't you? Charlotte Calder? Ian's partner?'
We shook hands.

'I'm Jess's husband. We're looking forward to coming over on

New Year's Eve,' he said. His eyes, startlingly blue in his tanned face, didn't waver for a second. I had the uncomfortable feeling he might be imagining me with my clothes off.

I must have looked a bit blank for a moment. What bloody party?

'New Year's Eve?'

New Year's Eve was weeks away. What the hell was Ian playing at?

Greg leaned a companionable elbow on the desk, and a blast of his aftershave punched me in the nose.

'Yes, I saw Ian the other day up at the golf club and he mentioned you were thinking of having a party. Sounds good to me, and Jess is always up for a bash. He told me you worked here. I thought I would make myself known. Just popped in for a review of my war wound.' He held out his left hand, which was bandaged. 'I caught myself with the electric carving knife a couple of days ago. I called Simon and he popped out to patch me up. They do say you shouldn't mix champagne and tools, don't they?'

I don't know how he managed to make this sentence sound suggestive, but he did.

'How awful,' I said, trying not to laugh. I shuffled some patient record cards into alphabetical order. 'I bet that hurt.'

'A bit of blood, just a nick on the side of my hand, that's all.' He winked at me again. 'Still, it got me out of doing anything else, so not all bad. Jess is a bit of a madam in the kitchen. She likes things done her way and I'm not very biddable.'

To my relief Dr Hawkins' surgery door opened and his patient hobbled out after him, her ankle heavily strapped up.

'Feet up for a few days, Jill,' Dr Hawkins bellowed at her, 'let Sidney get the meals and feed the chickens. Ah, Greg!' The two men shook hands; smiles all round. 'How's the hand?'

Dr Hawkins ushered Greg into his surgery and the door closed behind them. I dealt with Mrs Guthrie and made her a review appointment for next week. All the time I could hear loud male

19

laughter from behind the closed door I was aware of someone fixing me with a basilisk stare from across the waiting room.

'I was next,' an old man grumbled from under his bobble hat. 'I've got my leg here. I was definitely next. Who's he to go in when I was next?'

'I met your new bf Greg Palmer at the practice this morning,' I said when I got back at lunchtime. I kicked off my shoes and dumped my handbag on the kitchen table. Ian was still in his dressing gown nursing a Friday night hangover, reading emails at the other end of the table. He raised an enquiring eyebrow like a young Roger Moore.

'Bf?'

'Best friend. He said you'd invited him and his wife to a party here on New Year's Eve.'

'Ah yes, I did.'

'What bloody party? Don't you think you should invite me first?' I said.

'Sorry, darling, I forgot to tell you, but strike while the iron's hot, eh? We were at the golf club and got talking. He sounded very pleased indeed. Friendly, wanted to bring some champagne. That's the sort of party guest I like.'

Ian held out an arm, I went to kiss him and then put the milk into the fridge.

'Well, Jess is nice. We've had lunch quite a few times—'

'You didn't tell me!'

'You didn't ask. You've been so wrapped up in work recently. She's fun. A bit loud, very friendly, lots of flashy jewellery, but Greg's a bit of a sleaze ball, isn't he?'

Ian's head came up, indignant. 'He's not! Why would you say that?'

'Too much aftershave, gold man bracelet.'

'No, he's not, Lottie. He could be very important to us right at this minute if only you realised it. He's just bought one of those huge hybrids. A Mitsubishi something. I pretended I wanted to know about mpg. I went and looked it up in *What Car?* He gave me a look filled with meaning. 'He must be loaded. He's sold his business in Spain for a fair old sum by the sounds of it and he's looking to invest in property development over here. We could do very well out of him. If he wanted us to shove in a couple of the new Windermere kitchens I was telling you about it would be a godsend. He's blue-sky thinking.'

'Huh?'

This was not the sort of thing Ian usually said.

'He's thinking outside the box.'

And nor was that. It seemed Greg was having quite an influence already.

Ian opened another email and began to read it.

'What box?' I said, wondering if he knew.

Ian didn't answer for a moment. He stabbed at the keys of his laptop and frowned.

'Look, I'll explain another time. I need to fire off a few emails this morning. There's been a bit of a hiccup.'

'Oh, not work?'

'Isn't it always?' Ian pushed back his chair. 'I'll be in the study.'

I looked at the clock, which incorrectly said twenty-seven minutes past eight. I couldn't reach it and I'd been waiting for Ian to get it down and change the battery for weeks.

'Give me half an hour and I'll sort out some lunch,' I said.

I looked over at him. He looked rather pale and a thin film of sweat gleamed on his upper lip.

'Are you OK, darling?'

'Yes, yes fine.'

He didn't look fine.

'What's the matter?'

He hesitated in the doorway, tapping his phone against his thigh.

'Nothing, nothing. Bloody hell, you do go on sometimes.'

Well, that wasn't fair.

He went off towards his study and I heard him close the door behind him.

I made some vegetable soup and heated up some pitta bread to go with the hummus in the fridge – always Ian's favourite lunch. I heard him go off upstairs after a few minutes and then heard the rumble of the pump as he turned on the water in the wet room. I went to the bottom of the stairs and listened. Usually he sang in the shower, snatches of 'Swing Low Sweet Chariot' if he was feeling particularly cheerful. Today there was silence.

I went back to stirring the soup and flicked another, pointless look at the clock. Perhaps I should get the stepladder out and change the battery myself?

Ian came down after a few minutes, dressed in chinos and a dazzlingly white polo shirt. He wasn't going into work then. His hair was wet and rumpled from the shower, showing up the thinning bald spot he was usually so careful to disguise. His face was grim. He went to stand at the sink, looking out across the frosty garden.

I bit back the obvious question; what was the matter? I knew it would provoke an outburst of some sort. It must be something to do with his company. I knew business had been bad over the last few months with the economic downturn. These days, not many people seemed to want the hand-built kitchens Ian's firm provided.

'Lunch is ready, darling, come and sit down. We were busy in the practice this morning. Nothing too interesting but…'

Ian turned on his heel and stamped past me. 'Oh for God's sake. I don't want any fucking lunch, I'm going out.'

He grabbed his coat from the hallstand and slung it on, one arm struggling down a sleeve.

I followed him into the hallway. 'Honestly, who rattled the bars of your cage?'

Ian patted his pockets for his car keys and didn't answer.

'Why not have something to eat first? It wouldn't take a minute,' I said.

'I've got things to do.'

I put a hand on his arm. 'Look, I can tell something's wrong. What's the matter, darling? Can I help?'

He shook me off. 'No, you fucking can't help.'

'Ian! There must be—'

'Just shut up, Lottie,' he yelled.

'Don't be so bloody rude!'

'Leave me alone. This isn't anything you can help with; you've done enough already. Spending like it's going out of fashion. Holidays. New car. Shoes. God knows how many handbags. Grow up! What did you think would happen?'

'What?' I staggered back in astonishment. This was not like Ian at all.

'And it's me that has to sort it all out, isn't it? You just carry on blithely, arranging expensive parties, frittering away.'

'Hang on a minute. You're the one who wants this party, not me!'

He threw me a furious look and slammed the front door behind him so the air between us shuddered.

'And I've only got seven handbags!' I shouted after him. 'And one of those is a fake!'

I went into the living room and watched him through the window as he unlocked his car, dropped his keys on the drive, picked them up and threw his briefcase into the passenger seat before driving off in a spray of gravel. He turned left out of the drive – he definitely wasn't going to work. I stood watching the road, wondering if he would come back but he didn't.

I went back into the kitchen and sat down at the table, leafing through a pile of catalogues. I'd seen a lovely pair of suede boots in one of them, perhaps if Ian was starting to complain about my spending I'd better not buy them. I sat leafing through some others until I realised an hour had passed and Ian still wasn't back. I went back to look out of the window, worrying, biting my nails, wondering what had happened. What had I done to provoke this sort of reaction? Everything had been all right until… until he got that email. Some business problem. Of course. I'm a lot of things and one of them is nosey.

I went into his study, my bare feet sinking into the thick pile of the new carpet he had insisted he needed, in case he was going to take business contacts in there for a drink or something. The room was stuffy and dark, the curtains nearly closed. I drew them back and let the sunlight in. Dust motes spun in the warm air. I opened a window, letting in the cold afternoon to freshen up the atmosphere.

On his desk were piles of paperwork. Estimates, delivery notes, all fastened together with big bulldog clips. His massive iMac computer was turned off and there was a yellow Post-it note stuck on the side; Bentham Tuesday 11.30. It meant nothing to me. The printer stood silent in the corner. The bin was filled with shredded paper.

Feeling rather uncomfortable, I sidled up to the wire in-tray and casually leafed through the contents. Notes from customers, queries about delivery dates, a few photographs of a kitchen Ian's firm had recently installed. I opened a couple of the drawers but there was nothing other than a bundle of red *Lovell Kitchens* pens, paperclips in a china dish, a ball of elastic bands.

I thought about looking through the filing cabinet and went to open the top drawer, but it was locked and there was no key. I wondered why and I began to feel the first shivers of unease. He was hiding something from me; I knew he was. But why? He always told me everything. Confided in me when he was worried about something, came home to share his successes with me first.

The front door banged and I gave a guilty start. Ian was back. I went out into the hallway to see him shrugging off his coat.

'What are you doing in my study?' he said. 'You know I don't like anyone interfering with my stuff. Poking about.'

I bit down my temper. 'I'm not poking about.' I wished I had thought to bring a duster and some polish with me as cover. 'I do live here, you know. I was just tidying up. I opened the window, it was hot and stuffy in there.'

He went into the study and looked around as though he might have been burgled. He took the Post-it note from the computer screen, screwed it up and threw it into the wastebasket. Then he closed the window and turned to me.

'Lunch?' he said. 'I'm starving.'

He hurried off to the kitchen and I'm afraid I stuck my tongue out at his retreating back. We sat down at the kitchen table and I passed him a pottery bowl filled with soup.

'Nice,' he said after a few mouthfuls. He reached for some pitta bread and dunked it into the hummus.

'Are you OK?' I said.

Ian looked up, surprised, 'Of course,' he said.

He carried on eating, his spoon scraping against the bottom of the bowl, setting my teeth on edge. I winced.

'So have you thought any more about the food for the party?' he said.

'No, not really, I rather thought you had gone off the whole thing.'

'Not at all, I'm looking forward to it,' he said, and shook his head. 'You do have some funny ideas.'

I was confused. An hour ago he had stormed out, berating me for my profligacy, now he was behaving as though nothing had happened.

'I saw Steve when I was out; you know, bald Steve from the granite place. I bumped into him on the industrial estate. I've asked him to our party. I think he might come, although he did mention something about having visitors. You knew he and his wife had split up, didn't you? I think the young brunette he was with might have something to do with it. Very naughty-looking little thing.' Ian chuckled.

I couldn't let it drop. 'So why did you go off like the hounds of hell were after you an hour ago?'

'Oh nothing at all, just a misunderstanding,' Ian said, scooping up the hummus with a sweep of the last pitta, 'all sorted out now.'

I got up to put some more in the toaster. 'You're sure?'

Ian sighed and smiled up at me. He put an arm around my waist and pulled me in against him. 'You're such a worrier, Lottie. Everything is fine. So, any plans for this afternoon?'

'No, not really; I suppose I should get the ironing done,' I said without any enthusiasm.

'Well I know what I'm going to do, I'm going to put a new battery in that darned clock.' He finished his soup and dropped the spoon into the bowl with a clatter. 'I've been meaning to do it. Didn't you realise it's been stuck at eight thirty for weeks?'

'Yes, of course I did. I asked you to sort it out ages ago. I can't reach it.'

'I don't remember that. Anyway, there's a tall man here now, little lady, I'll fix it.'

I stood up and began to clear the table while he whistled 'Edelweiss' and rummaged in the kitchen drawer for a new battery.

Everything seemed fine again. His mood swings were becoming very hard to predict. In the following weeks, of course, it would become all too obvious what the matter was.

CHAPTER 3

Aquilegia – resolution, determination, anxiety

My brief foray into Bramford St Michael's village shop that afternoon had sadly not uncovered a little known haven of locally produced delights, but a dingy place with half empty shelves and a freezer that needed defrosting. I liberated three packets of savoury curried rice, a sliced loaf reduced to 25p, some cheese slices, long-life milk, and an exhausted-looking Cornish pasty. Presiding over it all was an elderly woman with wild, white hair who watched me warily as though I was going to pull out a shotgun. She counted out my change with slow fingers and grave suspicion in her face.

'I'm so pleased you're still open,' I said rather gushingly, wondering if I could loosen her up a bit with my devastating charm, 'isn't this a lovely village. So pretty.'

'...and one makes five and five is ten,' she said, not to be swayed from her task.

'Well, I'll see you again soon, I'm sure,' I said with another bright smile.

'Yes, mebbe we will,' she said in a tone that suggested she'd heard that before.

The village straggled along the river valley, beginning with some modern-looking houses where a few children were leaping about on a trampoline in the garden, and then some older cob cottages, their thatch green with moss. There was a pub, The Agricultural Arms, still with a string of fairy lights outside, left over from Christmas. Beyond that was the church; everything but the tower hidden behind some dense rhododendron bushes.

I drove back up the hill to Holly Cottage feeling even more isolated. Below me the streetlights in the village began to come on and I sat in the car for a few minutes and watched lights appearing in the cottages below me. I went indoors, shivering a bit with the cold and the unfamiliar solitude.

I suddenly remembered that awful night. Ian nursing a large whiskey under the pool of light cast by the standard lamp in our sitting room. He had looked up at me with mournful eyes.

'*What*?'

Oh God. That was the moment. If only he had said something else.

If he had apologised or cried or begged me to forgive him, things might have been different. If he had come up with some pathetic excuse, told me he had been a fool. If he had taken me in his arms and told me that he loved me. That he would never again hurt me.

I had waited for a moment, willing him to say something else, something kind. The seconds ticked past and he didn't say anything. The little instant was gone. My temper flared again.

'What. Is that all you can say? *What*?'

'Well what am I supposed to say? With everyone looking at me as though…as though…'

'As though you're a lying, deceitful bastard? Well should that be a surprise to you? Perhaps it's because you *are* a lying deceitful bastard!'

'Oh don't start, Lottie,' he'd said wearily. 'I'm not in the mood just at the moment.'

'Well nor am I, funnily enough!'

'Look, we're not even married, are we? I asked you to marry me years ago and you didn't want to.'

'And you knew perfectly well why that was! And what the hell has that got to do with it? Just because we're not married? What about our commitment to each other? What about bloody fucking common decency?'

I went into the dingy little kitchen of Holly Cottage and flicked on the kettle. There was no point going over it again and again. It wouldn't change things. I had to move on now, look to the future, do the job Jess had given me; repay her friendship in the best way I could.

I hoovered up the pasty straight from the wrapper, reasoning it would decrease the washing up and also the possibility of contamination in the mould- and grime-ridden kitchen. Wandering around, licking the slick of grease from my teeth, I investigated the cupboards, relieved to see that although they were dirty they were good quality and could soon be revived by some attention from me and a soapy cloth.

In the cupboard under the stairs I found a vacuum cleaner, its collection bag strained to bursting point. There was also a fairly comprehensive collection of cleaning materials, something that the previous tenants had not thought worth taking. Or using, let's be frank. I pulled out several bottles of cleaning spray, some crisp dusters and cloths, and a new mop and bucket and felt a rather peculiar thrill of excitement. Perhaps I was losing the plot. I arranged these treasures on the kitchen table (blue Formica, in a retro, cute way, not a this-table-is-really-old way). Tomorrow I would stop being so negative. I would get a good night's sleep and make a start on revamping Holly Cottage.

That first night I sat in front of the fire in my warmest coat, gloves and Ugg boots, watching the flames lick around the logs. There was no TV and mine hadn't arrived yet, but that wasn't much of a loss as far as I was concerned. Ian had indulged in the most expensive satellite-viewing package and for years nearly ninety pounds had gone out of our account every month and still most nights his parrot-cry had been 'there's nothing on worth watching!' This was a statement with which I couldn't argue.

There was only so much sport, *Top Gear* and *Man v Food* I could bear to watch. When Ian discovered re-runs of *The Professionals*, I abandoned hope and went back to my fledgling writing career. My concentration span didn't seem up to a full-length novel any more so I'd turned to writing short stories. I'd been reasonably successful too, won a couple of competitions, and although my total earnings were barely into three figures, it was something I enjoyed.

We had also spent hundreds of pounds every month on the gym I occasionally used although I was more likely to be found in the bistro with a white wine spritzer than on the treadmill with a bottle of water. Then there was Ian's membership of the Golf and Country Club where he had a pewter tankard behind the bar and the steward would greet him with, 'Usual, is it, Mr Lovell?' every time we went there. Ian loved that.

It had been a mild winter so far but after a few hours with all the windows open the house was freezing, hence the coat and gloves. The room still held its faintly fishy smell courtesy of Mr Webster's leaving present, but at least with the fire going it was bearable. I sighed, and then, rather approving of the sound, sighed a few more times.

I suppose I might have stayed there all evening sighing and feeling sorry for myself except I was still hungry. I got up and shuffled to the kitchen, my Ugg boots finding the going decidedly sticky underfoot.

I heated up some soup and ate a packet of crisps (leek and potato and cheese and onion respectively, so three of my five a day) and then I went upstairs, fumbling with the light switches, trying to work out which one worked which bulb, wishing I had thought earlier to make up the bed. There were two bedrooms, one with a big window at the front and the other with windows at the front and back of the house. I chose the bigger bedroom for no other reason than I preferred the wallpaper. It was pale blue and cream, tiny flowers with flecks of gold at the centre. I had brought some sheets and a duvet with me. Some of my possessions were stashed in my car, the rest were going to arrive when Greg had a spare hour to drive them over in his van. I hadn't really wanted to bring too much of my stuff into the house until I had cleaned it. That had been one of my better decisions.

I made up the bed, stripped off my clothes and got in. It was freezing. Where were my pyjamas? In the boot of the car? Oh no, I remembered they were in the roof box. That was one of my bad decisions. I got back out, put my socks, knickers and a T-shirt on and tried to think about being warm.

I suddenly remembered with pinpoint clarity lying on a beach in Greece three summers ago, my hot skin almost at one with the hot sand under my towel. We had decided on a last-minute week away. Ian had been sitting in the shade at a table under a vine-laden pergola. Tapping furiously at his laptop, muttering about work and cursing the economy. Perhaps he had been doing it even then, feeding our money into the ether in a never-ending stream.

I opened my eyes and the memory faded. I was just aware how absolute the silence was; how dense the darkness. Ian would have hated it.

'Can you see me?' I shouted up into the dark ceiling. 'You wouldn't have liked this, would you? The dark and the cold and the bloody quiet, what do you think, Ian? Is it funny? Does this serve me right for refusing four times to marry you? Would it have made any difference if I'd said yes, Ian? Well I suppose I wouldn't be homeless, would I? By the way, your poor mother is devastated. Didn't think about her either, did you?'

The irony of my situation took a few seconds to sink into my tired brain.

'You stupid bloody bastard.'

I wasn't sure if I meant Ian or myself.

The following morning, contrary to the popular saying, things didn't look better they just looked grimier. The winter sun shone feebly through the filthy windows, highlighting the dirt. I constructed a hideous sandwich with some of the 25p loaf and the cheese slices and made a mug of tea. I opened the kitchen door and peered outside, hoping my new neighbour was not around to torment me. There was no sign of him.

Outside, the day was brightening up. A bright sapphire sky over a soft folding landscape of hills and hedges. The only sounds were birdsong and the breeze rattling through the bare branches of a silver birch tree at the end of the garden. I stood in the doorway and sipped my tea wondering why Ian and I had never thought to move to the countryside. It was so peaceful, so beautiful. But then Ian had been determinedly town bred and I was a sheep, following him and his plans without thought.

I ate my sandwich, marvelling for a moment at its complete lack of flavour or texture. It was quite a relief to finish it, but I treated it much as an astronaut might approach a freeze-dried meal, as a way of consuming calories to sustain me through the morning. And then I went down the garden and had a cigarette, wondering whether I should give them up now that I needed to be a lot more careful with money.

I rolled up my sleeves, scrubbed the scum off the draining board and ran a sinkful of hot water laced with a generous slosh of disinfectant. I then spent an industrious hour emptying and washing the kitchen cupboards before organising my equipment and crockery into them. There didn't seem to be much room. The trouble was I was used to a vast space in which to cook, with a six-burner stove, a double oven and a large American fridge-freezer. Here there was a fairly straightforward collection of units and appliances around a small table and four chairs. This would also serve as my dining room. I was going to be seriously short of space and there was still Greg's van full of my other stuff to fit in at some point.

I thought back with tears prickling my eyes to the huge extending oak table and ten leather chairs that had filled the dining room at home and then reminded myself that wasn't my home any longer and it never had been. I had given the table to the women's refuge; they needed it and I certainly didn't. I was being pretty pathetic. This would do just as well if it were clean. I carried on scrubbing. To my surprise I discovered it's hard to feel sorry for yourself when you are concentrating on unidentifiable grime. There was a strange pleasure to be had from finding what colour the worktops really were.

After a while the kitchen began to look a great deal better and I rewarded myself with a cup of instant coffee.

I had scrubbed the four kitchen chairs and put them outside the back door to dry so I took my coffee upstairs while I had a good look around. Jess had said it needed cleaning and it certainly did, but it needed more than that. It needed some TLC. And also, courtesy of someone's careless cigarette habit and chewing gum disposal, new carpets. The bedroom I regarded as mine for the time being was potentially lovely with a whitewashed ceiling, old roof beams diving down into the floor in a way that suggested the cottage was far older than I had originally thought. There were painted built-in cupboards and two leaded windows that framed a fabulous view down the valley. I opened the window, making several woodlice homeless in the process. In the distance I could see the river sparkling in the sunshine, and the wind was cold but somehow exciting, as though it was bringing me a fresh start and new energy. Under the trees snowdrops were beginning their optimistic journey, bringing hope for the spring and the first potential of another new year.

Completely unexpectedly I began to cry. Why was I here? Why had Ian rushed off that night? I was frightened without him, that was the truth. I was used to him being there, used to his energy, his drive, the sheer noise of him. His crazy enthusiasm, his irritated muttering about customers as he worked his way through his correspondence.

When he was at home he usually had some paperwork to check or emails to read at his end of the kitchen table. Sometimes he would read me snippets from women who couldn't decide what they wanted.

Should I have worktops made of black granite or white Corian? Shaker-style doors or high gloss? Cream or Faded Cashmere?

Tell me what you think, Mr Lovell? Which do you think would suit me best?

'It's your money,' he would shout at the screen, exasperated, 'it's your fucking kitchen, it's not that difficult, just make your bloody mind up!'

And then he would look up and catch my eye and grin.

I wiped away my tears and sipped my coffee. The other bedroom was wallpapered in a leafy William Morris print and looked out over the lane. The vandalised wardrobe was probably Victorian mahogany and too large for the room, but, inside, it was fitted out with named compartments, each with a little engraved brass plate. Gloves, socks, ties, collars, braces. Just gorgeous. The wood was glossy and patinated with age. Why would someone stick pictures all over it with lumps of Blu-Tack? Who knew.

In the bathroom I had cleared away the worst of the debris, sprayed limescale cleaner over the scummy shower screen and the toilet and left it to work. The floor was dirty and covered in dried mud but the little leaded window opened onto the garden and there was the promise of a rose that had climbed around it, ready to blossom later in the year.

I went back down the claustrophobic stairwell, my feet careful on the narrow treads. Ian would have hated this more than anything. He couldn't bear enclosed spaces, low ceilings, dark rooms.

I wondered if I had the energy to finish emptying my car. I was hungry again and I knew there was a box of food in there somewhere, it was just a pity I hadn't thought to put it somewhere accessible.

Sod it! I suddenly remembered a box of fish fingers going in, which would undoubtedly have defrosted by now. I pulled off my rubber gloves and found the car keys.

Outside it was warmer than it had been for days. The sun was brilliant, the sky cloudless. Of course that meant that the inside of the car was getting warm too. I pulled a couple of bags and boxes out from the back seat of the car and dumped them on the drive, hoping to find the box of provisions. I didn't realise until that moment how disorganised I could be. It also struck me for the first time that a box of spoiled food was a complete waste of money.

'Need a hand?' said a familiar voice.

I turned to see Bryn, standing in his front garden. I think he might have been weeding. Possibly he was planting something or he could have been putting down rat poison. I think he was wearing a pair of ripped and filthy jeans but I know for a fact he didn't have a shirt on. And I couldn't take my eyes off him.

I stood open mouthed for several seconds, a slow blush developing. I could feel it spreading from the backs of my knees right to the top of my head it was that bad. I must have been puce. It was quite possible that my hair was blushing too.

I babbled something unintelligible and Bryn walked towards me, stepping carefully over his newly planted borders. I'd heard about six-packs but I'd never been that close to one in my life. He pulled on a black T-shirt that he had draped over the front gate. I felt a pang of disappointment but realised it was probably just as well. He was wearing serious-looking CAT boots, something I have always had a weakness for, so that didn't help. They were quite large too, which made me think of various rather rude comments.

'I said, do you need a hand?' he said.

35

'Um,' I turned away and looked in the car, 'yes please, if you don't mind. There's a lot of heavy stuff here.'

I grabbed the first thing I saw; a small overnight bag that a six-year-old child could have safely wheeled to the door and he took it and stood waiting for me to find him something else.

I kept my gaze steadfastly fixed in the boot. *Don't look at him. Keep calm. Don't look at him.*

I spotted the cardboard box that I had filled with food from the freezer and then forgotten about.

'I could take that in, if you like?' Bryn said, his voice unnervingly close behind me.

The embarrassment of having to admit my ineptitude was too much.

'No, no, that's OK. I'll manage,' I said, wishing he would go away.

I tugged at a few over-stuffed black bin liners and managed to spill a pair of my (joke Christmas present from Karen) days-of-the-week knickers onto the driveway. The pair with *Magic Monday* stared up at us. And of course it was actually Monday.

'I hope you haven't got Thursday on,' Bryn said, straight-faced, 'that would never do.'

I gave a weak laugh and stuffed them into my pocket, then reapplied myself to the cardboard box of frozen food. As I dragged it from the car the bottom, soggy with thawed ice, dropped out and my stash of fish fingers and potato waffles (secret vice for when Ian was away) scattered all over the ground.

'Mmm, delicious,' he said.

'Oh God,' I groaned.

To his credit Bryn didn't laugh, he reached across and lifted out a plastic crate of tinned food instead and took that into the house. I followed with some carrier bags filled with my last crop of vegetables from my garden.

'Wow, it looks incredible in here,' Bryn said as he put the crate down on the table. 'You've done a great job. You'll have the place ship-shape in no time. Very nice.'

'Gorgeous,' I said, looking at the muscles in his arms. 'I mean, this cottage could be gorgeous. Actually it's been rather enjoyable. Cleaning the kitchen. I didn't think I'd ever say that but – well, I'm rather pleased with it so far.'

'You're working wonders,' he said and I felt a disproportionate sense of pride. I had worked wonders, and I'd done it on my own too, at no cost.

I felt a bit silly and fluttery and quite lightheaded, but that might have been because I hadn't really eaten anything since the grim breakfast sandwich.

He turned round and I quickly began to put things away.

'Thanks,' I said, lining up the tins of tomatoes with some precision so I didn't just stand and gawp at him.

'Any time.'

'I would offer you a cold beer or something but...'

'But you don't want to? It's fine,' he grinned.

'No, it's not that at all, I haven't got any,' I said, flustered.

'I have, if you fancy a quick one?' he said.

I could almost hear the brain cells responsible for double entendres jiggling about like a crèche of unruly toddlers.

'I've got an awful lot to do,' I said.

'Maybe later?'

I began to line up herbs and spice jars and made a lot of *umm* noises. Then I unpacked various different sorts of oils. Olive, vegetable, sesame, walnut...there were quite a few. Plus five different types of vinegar. What did I need that lot for? Did I think I was going to be on *Masterchef*?

'Keen cook, are you?' Bryn said, picking up the champagne vinegar and reading the label.

I took it from him and put it into the cupboard. 'Oh, you know...'

'You could have me for dinner one day.'

The brain cell toddlers jostled about a bit more.

'I mean, you could invite me over.'

Ah. 'Perhaps when I'm settled.'

'I love fish fingers,' he said. He had a wicked grin and very white teeth against his tan.

I opened the fridge door and put a few things inside. The freezer was empty apart from some novelty ice cubes. I hesitated, my head on one side trying to make out exactly what they were. When I realised they were ice boobs I shut the freezer door very quickly, I didn't want him to see them and think they were anything to do with me.

Quick think of something else. Something dull.

Mobile phone contracts. Changing electricity suppliers. Mulching.

'You can't refreeze fish fingers,' Bryn said, 'you'll be ill.'

I turned round. 'I wasn't going to.' My tone was that of a stroppy fifteen year old.

Bryn went out and brought in a couple more boxes that he dumped under the table. From memory they were filled with casserole dishes and some Waterford crystal wine glasses. From the tinkling sound as Bryn put the box down there was now one fewer.

'That doesn't sound too good,' he said, 'sorry about that.'

He opened the top of the box and delved about for a second. Suddenly he snatched his hand out with a gasp and stood hanging on to his arm as blood seeped out between his fingers.

'Sod it, that was a bit of a mistake,' he yelped.

He sat down rather heavily on one of the kitchen chairs and closed his eyes. I watched fascinated as the colour drained from his face.

'Not very good with blood,' he said after a moment, 'especially my own.'

I galloped up the stairs to find the first aid kit that I had, mercifully, unpacked earlier in the day and put into the bathroom cabinet.

When I got back he was bent over, head almost touching his knees, still clutching his arm and obviously feeling a bit wobbly.

'So stupid,' he said, 'sorry.'

I hesitated for a moment, looking at the curls that nestled into the nape of his neck and fighting the overwhelming impulse to wind them around my fingers. To cover up my hesitation I went into brisk and efficient mode and dabbed at him with wet kitchen roll and antiseptic wipes. Once I got rid of the gore we both realised it was just a long scratch from a piece of broken glass, easily solved with a large plaster. Gradually the colour returned to his face and he gave an embarrassed grin.

'Sorry about that. You must think I'm a right idiot.'

'No, not at all, I'm sorry you hurt yourself. It was my fault, not packing things properly.'

He pressed the plaster down hard onto his arm and looked up at me.

'Like I said, I've got some beer in the fridge next door and some cold roast beef. Do you fancy a roll?' he said.

Why did everything seem to be laced with innuendo this morning? It was like living in a *Carry On* film.

'No, thank you. Now if you are feeling better I must get on,' I said, trying to sound brisk and busy. I found the cloth and re-wiped the draining board. Then, as he was still looking at the contents of my cupboards, I began polishing the kettle. Something I am not known for.

He must have realised that I wanted him to go.

'Well if you change your mind, you know where I am. I'll go this way, if that's OK?'

Bryn went out of the kitchen door and loped across the garden in his CAT boots. I ran the cold tap and splashed some water on my face. What the hell was the matter with me? I had no business feeling like this. I was behaving like a silly teenager. Just because a man was good-looking and had muscles and an amazing smile and lived next door. Of course it meant nothing. Well it should.

CHAPTER 4

Rhododendron – deceit, danger

Over the next few weeks I scoured Holly Cottage from top to bottom. There wasn't an inch of grubby paintwork that I didn't clean, not a single scuffmark that I didn't try to remove. The bathroom in particular took several cans of elbow grease. It looked as though one of the previous tenants had enjoyed more than a few adventures with unusual hair-dye shades. Behind the roll top bath were splashes of blue, green and magenta. Impossible to remove but if I was going to redecorate I needed to make some sort of effort. And it kept me busy, that was the most important thing.

I didn't want to think too hard or too deeply about anything. I didn't want to compare my new home with my old one. I didn't want to think about what I was used to and what I now had. Above all, I didn't want to think about the future.

One morning I realised it was nearly three weeks since I had seen Bryn. I wondered where he had gone. Even when I went out into the garden and made a half-hearted attempt at cutting the grass he didn't appear. The mower I found in the shed wasn't up to the task any more than I was. I found that very disappointing, as our gardener had been a wizened old man who produced sleek lines in the turf with apparently no effort at all. I'm no expert in these matters but I think the blades on the mower were bent or something. Perhaps it was the wrong sort of grass? At its best the machine spat clumps of moss over my feet and occasionally lumps of earth. I found an old strimmer in the garage and fiddled about with it, trying to untangle the 'tangle-free' line feed. It wasn't much use at strimming but it was great for flicking gravel painfully against my ankles, so I gave up. Looking at my progress I could safely assume the ground staff at Wimbledon weren't going to come calling any time soon. But somehow the beauty of the countryside was getting a hold on me. I had been feeling I was never going to get myself back on an even keel but the garden kept sending out buds and shoots of greenery like a powdering of hope over the bare branches.

I was used to designing the inside of a house. I had made colours and fabrics work even when Ian had pulled that face and voiced his doubts. Now I began to wonder if gardens could work the same way. Perhaps if that hedge was removed, if those trees were cut back?

Crocuses were beginning to sparkle in the grass at the end of the garden; white and golden yellow and purple – heralds of a new spring that only a few weeks ago I didn't think I had the courage to bear.

I kept darting looks at Ivy Cottage, half hoping Bryn would come out, see how incompetent I was and take over, but the kitchen curtains remained shut; the top half of the stable door closed. Perhaps he was away? Maybe he was ill?

I carried on messing about at the end of the garden for the rest of the afternoon. There was a fair amount of debris to remove from the neglected borders. Apart from the bath there was a collection of foil takeaway trays, a rusted child's bike, the remains of several very large nylon dog bones (that explained the damp dog smell) and a broken basketball hoop buried in the nettles at the end of the patch. There was also a rotting wooden construction, not so much a compost bin as an additional rubbish dump.

I toiled away for a couple of days while the weather was good, and then realised I had only succeeded in moving the debris from the garden where it had been well hidden, to my driveway where it wasn't. Perhaps I needed a skip? I couldn't afford a skip.

I didn't know what to do with all the stuff I had accumulated. Should I put it into the car and take it somewhere? If so, when and where? Bryn would know. And with all those muscles and also the use of his useful pickup truck, he would make short work of it. Perhaps I could take him up on that offer of a beer too. I hadn't really spoken to anyone for nearly a week, apart from the boy in the mobile phone shop who had sorted out a new contract for me, and a friendly cashier called Maureen in Superfine who always seemed to be there in the afternoons. I'd tried going to the village shop in a sort of ingratiating desire to support local industry but they seemed to open and close when they felt like it.

I decided to give up for the day; I needed bread as I seemed to be living on sandwiches and my endless tea and coffee consumption meant I was always in danger of running out of milk.

As I drove into Superfine's car park I wondered why I wasn't cooking any more. I loved cooking; I even enjoyed watching other people cooking on television programmes yet now I was living on tins of soup and cheese toasties. Perhaps I should make more of an effort? Maybe then I would ask Bryn over for a meal by way of a thank you. He would like that. I didn't suppose he had much company either. He seemed to live on his own. I wondered if his arm had healed up OK? Probably; after all it was three weeks ago and I hadn't seen any ambulances pulling up outside.

'Back again, my duck?' Maureen said as she scanned my shopping, weighing my fruit and vegetables and frowning at the scale.

By then I knew all about Kyle, her son in the Navy, and Himself's (her husband's) bad back, and more than I wanted to know about her 'various veins'.

'I'm always running out of milk,' I said.

Her face brightened. 'Got a cat, have you?'

'Well no—'

'My cat gets through pints of the stuff, although Himself says it's not good for 'em. I says to him, well if you'm so clever you tell Fluffy, 'cos I'm not.'

She scanned a packet of chocolate cookies and looked at them admiringly.

'They looks nice. I couldn't have them though. I'm supposed to be losing weight and if I had them in the cupboard I wouldn't get no peace until I'd eaten 'em all. That's fourteen pounds twenty. Having a busy day, are you?'

I handed over a twenty-pound note. 'Well I've not lived here long. I'm doing some decorating. For a friend.'

Maureen rolled her eyes. 'You can come and do mine when you're finished! I've been waiting for Himself to paint the front room for years but it's still not done. The paint will be solid in the tin by the time he gets the lid off. And there's your change, me duck.'

I hesitated. There was no one behind me waiting to be served.

'Are there any jobs going here, do you know? It's just…well you know.'

Maureen sucked her cheeks in. 'No, I don't think so. You'd have to ask at the so-called Help Desk. Not that they will be much help if they can avoid it. Too busy gossiping and complaining and messing about with rotas. But you could ask.'

'Thanks.'

I wandered past the Help Desk where two women in purple suits were busy tapping in barcodes and sighing as they tried to organise a refund for a harassed-looking woman with two toddlers who were rolling on the floor kicking each other. Perhaps another day.

Three days later I noticed the stable door into the kitchen was open again and my heart gave a little leap. Bryn was back from wherever he had disappeared to.

I went upstairs to change into a clean T-shirt, slick on some red lip-gloss and run a comb through my hair. After fiddling about for a few moments I tied my hair back and wiped off the lip-gloss. Then I changed into another shirt and faffed about wondering how many buttons to do up or undo. Then I added some blusher and a smudge of grey eye shadow. And a pink lip-gloss.

I took a look at myself in the bathroom mirror and rolled my eyes. For heaven's sake, my brown hair needed cutting, my blue eyes under the badly smeared eye shadow looked tired. More than that, I looked like a right clown. What on earth was I playing at? I just needed the man next door to come and help me move a bath, it didn't matter what colour my mouth was.

On my way to Bryn's front door I noticed a car parked around the side of his house. A red, soft top sports something and I wondered how he would fit his long legs into that. I went and knocked on the door.

After a moment I heard someone moving about inside. I hesitated, my hand raised, wondering if I should knock again and then the door opened. Not Bryn at all but a glorious redhead in tight jeans and a baggy boyfriend jumper that was in danger of slipping off her tanned shoulder.

'Hi,' she said.

She looked down at me from atop her long legs and gave a dazzling smile that spoke of several thousand pounds and many hours at the orthodontist.

'I'm Bonnie, you must be the caterer.'

Bonnie? She certainly was. But caterer? As if. And who was she? Sister? Girlfriend? *Wife?*

'Bonnie?' I said.

She laughed and tossed her *because-I'm-worth-it* hair about.

'Short for Bonita. Which is a ghastly name isn't it? Do come in,' she said.

Mesmerised, I followed her pert bottom down the hallway and

44

into the kitchen. I had assumed this house was a mirror image of mine but it was bigger. There was a conservatory tacked onto the side and some sort of extension or office in the garden beyond, half hidden by some bushes. I suppose I should have told Bonnie I wasn't the caterer but at this stage I was far too busy being nosey.

I caught a glimpse of a sitting room painted in dark red with floor to ceiling bookcases, a beautiful grandfather clock in the hall and then she took me into the kitchen. It was rather old fashioned with a huge built-in dresser and under the window a Belfast sink with a red gingham curtain underneath it.

'So it's going to be a surprise party,' Bonnie said, leaning back against a newish and familiar-looking granite worktop (probably Sahara Sparkle), 'for about twenty. OK?'

'Well I'm not actually…'

She flicked her hair back. 'Maybe twenty-five.'

'Yes, but…'

'Do you like vegetarians?'

'I couldn't eat a whole one,' I said.

Bonnie frowned rather attractively. 'Sorry?'

'Look I think there has been some misunderstanding.'

She blinked a couple of times and looked at me, waiting for me to explain.

'I was hoping to see Bryn. Is he around?'

'Well no, not until tonight, who are you then?' Her tone was suddenly rather frosty.

'I'm Charlotte – Lottie from next door.' I pointed in the direction of my cottage.

And who are you? And why are you throwing a surprise party?

She suddenly looked very annoyed. It was as though someone had flicked a switch. 'You're not the caterer? Not from Delicioso?'

'No.'

Bonnie gave an extravagant sigh and rolled her large, hazel eyes.

45

'Next door? Oh I see. Jeez. Why didn't you say? I didn't realise… I knew…oh never mind. She was supposed to be here half an hour ago.'

Bonnie did what anyone would have done when they found themselves in this situation and checked her phone.

'Hmm I've missed a call. Bloody crap reception here.'

She listened to a message and sighed.

'Not coming?'

'No.' Her pretty mouth tightened in annoyance. 'Are you sure you're not a caterer?'

'Positive.'

She gnawed at a manicured thumbnail. 'It's Bryn's birthday soon; I thought I'd throw him a surprise party.'

'Does he like surprise parties?'

I'd bet a month's non-existent salary he didn't.

'No, he hates them, but I think they're fun.' Bonnie waved her phone again. 'They can't get here until after the weekend, and that's no good.'

I thought hard about what I could say to get her to tell me what her relationship was to Bryn but I couldn't think of anything that didn't make me sound like a stalker.

'You don't know anyone I could ring do you?'

I shook my head. 'Sorry, I've haven't lived here long.'

Bonnie pouted. 'Delicioso were my last hope. It's frigging impossible round here; it's like the bloody dark ages. I keep telling him to move.'

'Have you tried the Internet?'

Bonnie shot me a withering look. 'Or extra-super-slow-narrow-band as we prefer to call it? You must be joking.'

'Well you could try ringing around.' I made a move to the door. 'I just called to see if Bryn's arm was OK. He had a nasty cut…' I hesitated as I saw her eyes glaze over.

'I've no idea, he has a silly thing with blood, I never take much notice. It just encourages him.'

46

'Ah, well it was some time ago. OK. I just…well perhaps I'll catch up with Bryn later.'

'I wouldn't bother if I were you. He doesn't like visitors. As a rule. He's a very private person. We both are.'

I had the feeling she was delivering some subliminal message but I didn't quite get it.

Bonnie picked up a battered copy of the Yellow Pages with the tips of her fingers and looked at the cover as though it was written in Swahili.

'Not after all the trouble with Mrs Webster next door,' she continued, her voice casually silky. She fired me a sharp look filled with meaning and I shrugged.

'Mrs Webster had a…*thing* for Bryn, I'm afraid. She seemed to think there was something between them. Obviously not, but a lot of women…well let's just say she was punching way above her not *inconsiderable* weight.'

'Ah.'

'Yes, I'm sure you *understand*.'

Open brackets *he's mine so keep your paws off* close brackets.

There didn't seem much to say after that so I made my way back to Holly Cottage, noticing again with a twinge of envy how beautifully kept Ivy Cottage's gardens were in comparison to my own.

There were drifts of new colour along the borders as the first of the spring flowers began to bloom; I could glimpse regimented rows of bamboo canes and a trellis laden with burgeoning something. I wished for a moment that I could sneak in and take a proper look. Perhaps if Bonnie hadn't been there I might have risked it.

I went to the end of the garden and leaned over the fence and was startled when my mobile rang. It was Jess. I had received some texts and a couple of emails but this was the first phone call I'd had for a while.

'At last! How's it going, Lottie? Are you OK?' She sounded just

47

as scatty as ever. I could almost imagine her twirling her hair around her fingers and looking in the mirror for non-existent wrinkles as she spoke to me.

'I've been trying to ring you for days. The signal down there is pants.'

'Yes, fine, I've just been cleaning. I was wondering what to do with the junk in the garden?'

'Greg will take it away. He's on his way over in the van. That's why I'm ringing. He'll drop off your stuff and load up.'

Her voice sounded odd, as though she was putting on mascara as she was talking.

'I don't even know where the tip is. And there's a stinking wet carpet…'

'Oh, Lottie! Stop panicking. Greg will sort it out. He's got that paint for you too. The chalky stuff you wanted. Mouse's Bum and Coco something. Greg says they are grey and beige and I'm round the bend; thirty pounds for a tin when he can get big tubs of trade white for a fiver. His idea of cutting-edge design is woodchip and magnolia. I told him to beak out of it. I know you're going to make the place look fab. I hope you're still up for it?'

'Yes, of course I am. Bring it on. I'm having a great time. '

'Greg might measure up for the new carpets when he gets there. He knows a bloke who will do him a deal. For God's sake don't let him buy brown, he doesn't think there's any other colour. What did you have in your old hallway? With the stripy wallpaper? Do you remember?'

'Can't remember, it was called Pumice, I think.'

I thought back. But all I could remember was that New Year's Eve party.

Greg and Jess Palmer had been the last to arrive that night, bringing with them their own style and dress code. Their arrival almost caused Ian to trample on his other guests, he was so eager to get to them. Greg stood out in a smooth and expensive-looking dark suit and Jess looked like a high-end stripper in red sequins and studded stilettos. Ian wasn't actually drooling but it was a pretty close thing.

'I love this house,' she purred as she slipped off her (at least I think it was fake) fur, revealing gleaming bronzed shoulders and most of her bosom. 'Greg and I viewed a place just up the road when we was looking to move here. We always hoped this one would come on the market, if I'm honest. How long did you say you'd lived here?'

'Nearly eight years, although Ian has been here about ten,' I said.

We were becoming good friends by this point and now Ian had managed to get his hooks into Greg I had the feeling we might progress from just seeing the Palmers occasionally in the paper shop, the gym and the golf club to seeing a lot of them over the next few months as Ian and Greg blue-sky-thought together as to how best to invest Greg's money.

'I love this,' she said, running a tiny hand over my striped grey wallpaper, 'and the lighting too. And I really *love* the colour of that carpet. It's really classy, ain't it, Gregsy?'

'I have a thing about lighting,' I said. 'I hate seeing the light bulbs.'

'You got a great eye for design. You could give me some tips once the en suites are finished. Greg wants to put seagull wallpaper in one and ducks in the other. No, don't laugh, he's perfectly serious. Even I can see that's naff. I only ever do white and cream with lots of gold accents. It doesn't look the same over here though. Not like it did in Spain. More duller. Must be the lack of sunshine,' Jess said.

'Well, the Met Office says we are in for a BBQ summer,' I said.

'Really?' Jess looked hopeful. Her blue eyes gazed at me, lash extensions fluttering.

'They're usually wrong so don't get your hopes up just yet.' I held out a platter of vol-au-vents and Jess reeled away as though I was offering her strychnine.

'Oh dear, no thanks, I mustn't. I get a bit funny about carbs after seven o'clock,' she said, patting her non-existent tummy. She fished about on the plate for a celery baton and nibbled it, shoulders hunched. Her expression of robust enjoyment was one I usually reserved for cake but I suppose we can't all be the same.

'So when are you planning to rent out Holly Cottage again?' I said.

Jess spoke through stretched lips this time, as though she was putting on lipstick. 'Oh I don't know. I'm still not sure what I want to do. I did think of selling it. Anyway. See how we go. A couple of months, maybe?'

'You mustn't let me get in the way of that,' I said.

'Lottie, I'm just grateful you've taken this off my hands. It's no good asking Greg's men to do it, they would just slap up some lining paper, paint it with whatever was left over from another job, shove in some off cuts of carpet and it would look rubbish in no time and I'd be back to square one. Look, I'd better go. I've got heaps to do here. Greg should be arriving with you soon anyway and – um – Bryn's not about, is he?'

'No, I haven't seen him for a while. I don't know where he is. There's someone called Bonnie here though.'

'Bonnie? Why the…Oh, of course, I remember – Bryn's gone to Chelsea. Just as well.'

I frowned. 'Why?'

'Oh nothing. Look, I'll shoot off now, there's someone at the door. And whatever you do, don't give Greg any cake!'

Jess ended the call, leaving me more than a bit confused. Bryn and Greg were brothers, weren't they? So why should it be good that Bryn wasn't there? And he'd gone to Chelsea? What was he doing in Chelsea? He didn't look like a footballer. Did he?

Twenty minutes later I heard the unfamiliar sound of a vehicle driving up the lane and stopping. I peered through the sitting-room window, holding my breath. The view down towards the village was glorious; especially now the local farmer had cut back the hedges. I could see all the way to the church and the sunlight was glinting off the gold-painted weather vane on the top. But even after all this time I still felt the same plunge of dread when the phone rang or people came to the house unexpectedly. Today there was nothing to worry about; it was just Greg in his white van. I sighed with relief and went to open the front door.

'Princess!' he called. 'How's it goin'?' He was quite casually dressed in head to toe Ralph Lauren. Well, casual for him anyway.

'Great.' I went out onto the drive and watched as he unlocked the back of the vehicle. Inside I could see a load of decorating stuff. Paintbrushes, huge tubs of paint, and folded-up dustsheets. Beyond that there were some familiar-looking boxes and bags containing the rest of my clothes and other things I had managed to salvage before the house was sold.

I felt an unexpected pang of irritation. Whatever was in those bags I had managed without perfectly well. Perhaps I was having a change of heart? Maybe it was the shock? I was beginning to enjoy having less clutter. That would make a change after decades of hoarding and wanting stuff. Perhaps now I would learn to embrace clear worktops, sweeping expanses of bare white walls with just one artistic twig in a glass frame. In years to come I would ask people to take off their shoes before they walked on my white carpets and I would talk knowledgeably about the liberation of minimalism.

On the other hand I could see my television and numerous wooden cases saved from Ian's extensive wine collection and my spirits rose several notches. Now that was the best thing I had seen for ages. Well, apart from Bryn with his shirt off but I suppose that shouldn't really count.

Greg came to envelop me in a friendly hug. He smelled of expensive aftershave and cigarettes and I tried to think how long it had been since a man had actually touched me with affection. It must have been months. I also tried to remember when I had smoked my last cigarette. At nearly ten quid a packet I definitely couldn't afford them. Perhaps giving up would be the one good thing to come out of this mess.

'All OK?' he said.

'Yes, fine, really.'

Greg jerked his chin at Ivy Cottage. 'He's not in then?'

'Bryn? No, he's been away for a few—'

'Good, good. Well I'll get this lot unloaded and then we'll have a cuppa, eh? Stick the kettle on, there's a good girl.'

'Can't I help you?' I hovered around him, hands flapping. For one thing I feared for his crisp blue and white striped shirt.

'Nah, piece of cake, won't take me a sec. Jess says you've got some junk for me to take.'

'Stuff I've pulled out from the garden; an old bike, some rotten wood and of course there's a wet carpet. It stinks.'

'Nice one.' Greg turned back to the van and clambered inside.

'Why don't you want to see Bryn?' I blurted out.

I don't think Greg heard me because he didn't answer. He jumped down and walked towards me holding a bundle of canvas dustsheets.

'I'll put all this in the garage, shall I? Talking about pieces of cake, I don't suppose you've got any? Cake? Or I wouldn't mind a biscuit if there was one going. Her Majesty's got me on low carbs. I told you she would. I'd kill for a chocolate digestive.'

'Jess said I wasn't to give you any cake.'

'Miserable cow. But she didn't actually *say* biscuits?'

'No, but—'

'Well, there you are then. Just leave them out and I'll nick a couple when you're not looking.'

I laughed and went to put the kettle on.

I didn't have room for everything in the house so Greg put all my stuff away in the garage, even the expensive clothes zipped into their dry-cleaning bags. I couldn't face looking at them. A silk, beaded evening dress, an Armani suit, a Vivienne Westwood jacket, linen trousers and cashmere cardigans. None of it seemed to have a place in my newly small and unimportant life. I couldn't imagine myself wearing white trousers or silk negligées ever again. Greg gave me a few funny looks and then hung the clothes from a metal tool rack.

'Up to you, you could always flog 'em on eBay,' he said.

'Perhaps I will,' I said.

Or I could take them to a charity shop.

I imagined myself sneaking into Stokeley or Okehampton very early one morning, dropping the bags off in a doorway under a sign saying '*No donations to be left here*'. Would the helpers be pleased to get such garments or exasperated? I had no idea. What if someone saw me and made me take them back? I shuddered at the thought.

I pulled out a tray, made a pot of tea and found two packets of biscuits. Bourbons and Custard Creams. Greg fell on them with an expression I could only describe as ecstasy.

He crammed in a Bourbon biscuit and munched. 'So, how are you managing for money? If you don't mind me asking.'

'Ian and I were planning to go to France this summer, I had money for that in my account and I have some savings; I've been living on them up to now. But…' I tailed off. Perhaps it wasn't the most tactful thing to do, to complain about having no money when they were letting me stay here for nothing.

Greg looked thoughtful. 'Oh well. Perhaps you could…no forget it.'

'What?'

'Nah.'

'Go on.'

'Get a job?'

'I've already been into the local supermarket to ask about a job. There's a doctor's surgery in the next village too. I've left a message with them.'

'That's the way. Nil cardamom and all that.'

Perhaps I needed to try a bit harder.

Greg finished his tea and helped me take down the curtain hanging across the front door. Then he applied himself to moving the paint and the rollers in from the van.

I took up the thread of the conversation while we had coffee an hour or so later. Greg offered me a cigarette and I pounced on it with a cry of joy. He lit it for me and I took a deep drag, spluttering slightly. My head reeled with the nicotine rush. It didn't seem quite as great as I remembered.

'Anyway, I still have my jewellery. I can always sell some of that if the going gets tough.'

Greg blew across the surface of his drink and narrowed his eyes.

'You'd only get scrap value. It's never as much as you think. Unless of course Ian was in the habit of buying you Fabergé eggs? Or vintage Rolex watches?'

I pulled a face. 'Hardly.'

I looked down at my emerald ring; I'd called it a commitment ring, not wanting to go as far as engagement ring despite the fact that Ian had proposed. It was a pretty thing and I clenched my fingers protectively over it. Surely I hadn't come to that just yet? I had some pearls and a diamond pendant, bought to celebrate our first and fifth Christmases together respectively. I had various expensive things; even a bracelet in a turquoise Tiffany box, souvenir of our Christmas trip to New York. Was it only a few months ago? It felt like a lifetime.

God it had been marvellous. He'd really gone over the top. A hotel suite with fruit and flowers and an incredible view over Central Park. Ian had proposed yet again – it was like a running joke between us, he would ask me to marry him and I would come up with some damn fool excuse to make us both laugh. Let's wait and see what happens with the Trump administration, I said. This time Ian tried to persuade me with the bracelet from Tiffany. I could remember his face so clearly as he gave it to me. Happy, proud, pleased with my delight. What the hell had he been doing? Stringing me along like that while all the time…

I remember having cocktails in the Waldorf Astoria. Margarita for me; Long Island iced tea for Ian. I closed my eyes. I could remember it all so well, the scent of money and perfume on a damp November day. I wonder now where the cash to pay for that had come from. A gambling win or just money siphoned off from the business?

I have been trying to get hold of Mr Ian Lovell for weeks. I wonder if you can help? I know he has been abroad on business recently; New York, wasn't it?

Now I was on my own, living in rural Devon with my life in bits.

I felt giddy for a moment; perhaps it was the nicotine. I shook myself; Tiffany bracelets didn't keep the cold out or the rain off.

I opened my eyes to see Greg watching me.

'I'd better be off soon. Are you OK?' he said. He took another Bourbon biscuit.

'I'm OK.'

'Cheer up, no one's going to prison, remember?' And he winked at me.

No one's going to prison. Greg and Jess had come to see me a couple of days after Ian had died, bringing me a cake and a casserole I couldn't eat. They found me crying over a bundle of letters and final demands I had found in Ian's study filed erroneously under '*Expenses*'.

'I know you shouldn't speak ill of the dead but Ian was a right sod to leave you with this to deal with. It's a right dog's breakfast. What the hell was he doing? This is serious, you need professional help,' Greg had said, 'this isn't just a couple of quick phone calls. Is the house in both your names? This building society letter is only addressed to Ian.'

I sat slumped over the table and thought for a moment, trying to remember. Never had I felt more stupid.

'No, it isn't. He already lived here when we met. He said it was better to keep it in his name, I don't know why. Something to do with tax?'

'That's baloney, and if anything it makes it worse.'

'Greg! Stop it!' Jess said.

'Well it's true. I can't dress it up. If these debts are real, and the house isn't in your joint names, then the creditors will come after it.'

'Come after me?' I had a vision of more large men on the doorstep.

'Come after the house. What's it worth? Seven fifty? Eight?'

'I suppose so.'

'They'll expect to sell it to recover their money then. There must be some equity in it.'

'I had a phone call from the bank yesterday, talking about a mortgage. I didn't think Ian had a mortgage. It was paid off. I *thought* it was paid off. Ian told me it was. He'd had some money when his grandfather died and then the business took off. He said everything was great.'

'Not according to this.' Greg waved a letter at me. 'Ian must have re-mortgaged to release some equity. It's not illegal.'

'But he should have told Lottie!' Jess said, indignant on my behalf. 'I mean if I found out you were keeping stuff like this from me, I'd have your bloody nuts in a mangle.'

Greg winced. 'Yes, I bet you would. By the looks of things he's in…sorry I mean he *was* in one hell of a mess. I would guess he did the worst thing possible, and that's ignored the problem. I mean, we all hate HMRC but there are a lot of small local traders after their money here. I know this one.' Greg waved a second letter at me. 'He's a good bloke, a plumber. He did our en suites, works like old stink. This sort of bad debt could take him under.'

I pressed my hands to my mouth.

'I want to do what's right, even if it's too late.'

Greg paused and looked at me for a few moments before he cleared his throat and continued. 'Are there any more letters like this?'

'I don't know. Probably.'

'You need to find out. You've got to know exactly who you are dealing with and how much.'

'What then?'

He shuffled the letters into some sort of order.

'Like I always say; when you're going through Hell, keep going.'

Greg had then taken me to see a friend of his who was a financial advisor. The reassuringly named John Strong who had looked at me from under his beetle brows and tapped a pencil against his chin.

'The best tactics with financial issues are absolute clarity and prompt communication, particularly with the Inland Revenue, two things Mr Lovell didn't employ.'

Well that was true. I'd already spent an hour with Simon Bentham at the Nationality Bank and been told much the same thing.

'Do you believe he had other reserves?'

'You mean hidden bank accounts? I don't know,' I said, slumping back in my chair.

I found the courage to voice my greatest fear.

'Am I going to go to prison?'

He smiled at me. 'No, Miss Calder, put that from your mind. It's obvious to me from the paperwork I have seen you were not a party to any sort of deception. If you were, then you were a pretty incompetent fraudster. Your signatures on the paperwork for the payday loans are poor forgeries. Possibly deliberately.'

'Would Ian…'

Again, the thoughtful tapping of his pencil on his chin before he answered me.

'Quite possibly. Elements of this look fraudulent not just

desperate bungling. Money siphoned off from the business and not declared. There is the unmistakable whiff of cash payments in several projects. I'm afraid he didn't cover his tracks very well. And of course HMRC are the very last people you want to tangle with.'

'No, he wasn't very clever, was he?' I whispered.

The mystery of where hundreds of thousands of pounds had gone was only solved when a local bookmaker and the owner of a casino had added their bills to the growing heap on John Strong's desk.

Apart from some large holes in the company accounts that he had tried to cover up, Ian had been a compulsive and untalented gambler. He had fallen into the classic trap of trying to cover his losses with the ever-elusive big win. Sometimes he had won. The new carpet in his study was probably linked to a bet on the Brazilian Grand Prix. The last holiday we had in New York came after an unexpectedly successful night out in a casino. But ultimately, he had lost.

At this point I moved from the classic early stage of 'confused grief' and moved on to 'anger'. How could Ian have done this? How could I not have realised? Why didn't he tell me? Could I have helped him? All those times when he had been quiet and distracted, I had assumed he was fretting over some kitchen plinths or concealed lighting. I hadn't known Big Kev O'Callaghan from the Galaxy Casino was after him.

CHAPTER 5

Primrose – modest worth and silent admiration

I'd always enjoyed painting and decorating, even the tedious bits like sanding down and glossing the woodwork. Ian hadn't and so it was something I had mostly done alone. I began work on Holly Cottage that afternoon. I cleared the hallway, switched on Radio Devon so I could learn about the traffic jams I wasn't caught in, and found some old clothes and trainers to wear. It was a lovely day so I opened all the windows too. The air was fresh and clear bringing with it the faint scent of newly mown grass. I began to feel quite peaceful and in control of things for once. Decorating was just as therapeutic as I remembered; the steady rhythm of the roller covering the old paint with new. I'd opened one of Greg's huge tubs of trade white to use as an undercoat. If I was going to do this, I would do it properly, as though it was my own home.

I think the previous paintwork had once been one of those 'hints-of' shades that only look interesting on the colour charts but always look the same once they are applied to a wall. Smoothing out the little bumps and blemishes, leaving a white, blank surface that no grubby fingers had touched, I began to have quite philosophical thoughts about this being a metaphor for life.

I would obliterate my rather dull past and begin anew. This was going to be a turning point. I would learn from my mistakes and move forward. I would never trust any man again. If I had been a character in *EastEnders* I would have bumped fists with one of the Mitchell brothers, climbed into the back of a black cab and left for a fresh start in Manchester.

I had always prided myself on being a precise and careful decorator. Ian once told dinner guests that I was able to paint a room without the need for dustsheets and I had blushed modestly and agreed with him. People had been so disbelieving that with a little encouragement I think Ian would have got out some paint pots there and then to prove the point.

This time, as the hallway was small, it didn't take me long to finish the first coat on the walls and with a sigh of contentment I stepped down from the stepladder to admire my handiwork – straight into the open tub of trade white. It was a move worthy of the Chuckle Brothers. Not that it was funny.

I stood on one leg, wailing my distress, trying hard to keep my balance and looking for some way to get out of the tub without making one hell of a mess. Perhaps I should have put the paint roller down first? Anyway I wobbled and fell, twisting as I did so like a circus clown looking for laughs from the audience. How I managed to then fall over backwards, tipping the roller tray I was holding all over my chest I'll never know. I couldn't have managed such a perfect prat fall so neatly if I had tried. The shock kept me silent for a few seconds, and then as the cold emulsion seeped through my T-shirt, I let out a howl of distress. I panicked. How was I going to get up without getting gallons of paint all over the flagstone floor?

For a moment hysteria got the better of me and I imagined myself expiring there in the hallway, my foot wedged into a paint tub, paint all over my tits, unable to free myself. Would this be reported in the national press as a calamity of epic proportions (*tragic girlfriend, 34, found dead in decorating tragedy*) or the most hysterically funny way to die? I had no wish to find out and feeling like a beetle on its back I started to squirm. The mess was going to be stupendous.

'What's the matter? Are you all right?'

I froze. Knees and hands in the air. No. Please not that.

'Are you OK? I heard you shouting.'

It was Bryn, of course. He had come up the garden path and was looking over the stable door into the kitchen. He could see me.

'I'm fine,' I said, as casually as I could. 'I always do this when I'm decorating. It breaks the tedium.'

Bryn leaned his arms on the top of the stable door and began to laugh. My humiliation was complete.

'Oh God, I wish I had a camera,' he said, wiping the tears from his eyes.

'Trust me the only thing saving you from a savage and painful death is the fact that you *haven't* got a camera,' I said through gritted teeth.

'I've got a phone though.'

'Don't you bloody dare!'

'Can I come in and help?' he said, struggling to keep a straight face and failing.

I waved an airy and paint-splattered hand. 'No, I'd prefer to stay here for a few days until I died of thirst and embarrassment. Yes, of course you can come in, you idiot!'

The next few minutes were some of the most undignified of my life. It wasn't helped by the fact that Bryn kept laughing and my paint-smeared hands kept slipping out of his as he attempted to get me to my feet. He straightened out one of the spare canvas dustsheets so that I could get to the garden without dripping white paint all over the house. And at last I stood, feeling ridiculous, almost crying with shame on the lawn. All I needed was for someone to push a custard pie in my face.

'Do the doors fall off your car too?' he said, gasping for breath he was laughing so hard.

'Ha ha, very funny,' I said with the minute amount of dignity I had left.

'I think you'd better strip off your clothes out here,' he said.

'I'd rather *die* than do that in front of you,' I snarled.

To be fair Bryn looked as though he was trying very hard to stop laughing.

'What's going on? Why are you doing that?'

With an exclamation that sounded like the beginnings of a rude word, Bryn spun round.

'Shi...Bonnie! What are you doing here?'

Oh *wonderful*.

Bonnie, alerted by the noise, had come out to see what was going on. She leaned over the fence looking at me in some bewilderment as though I had daubed myself with paint on purpose. Of course she was immaculate in a mint green dress and crisp white cardigan, her Audrey Hepburn sunglasses perched on top of her head.

'It's nothing,' I said airily, 'slight mishap with a vat of moisturiser.'

Bonnie looked at me, her face faintly puckered. She was trying to frown but it was hard to tell. I think there might have been some recent Botox involvement that prevented it.

'Is that paint? It's going to take ages to get that off,' she said at last.

'I'll be back in a moment, Bonnie. I have a pressure washer?' Bryn offered with a snort of laughter.

I closed my eyes. 'No, thank you, now please could you go away?'

'Bryn, darling, I've just brought some lunch,' Bonnie said. She flapped a hand at him to catch his attention.

'I'll be right there.' He sounded a bit terse. He turned to me again. 'Sure you'll be OK?'

'I can't find the words to tell you how not OK I am,' I said, 'maybe I'll try later.'

'I'll come out after lunch, and if you're still here—'

'If I'm still here you can shoot me.'

'Take care,' he said before he went back into his house and closed the kitchen door behind him. As I watched I saw him tactfully close the gingham curtains.

I waited for a moment and then stripped off my clothes, gathering them up and shoving them into a bin liner and the dustbin before I could even think about local recycling rules. Then I dashed back into the house, locked the doors and went up for a serious scrub in the shower. After that I closed all the curtains and sat in my dressing gown drinking Ian's wine.

I calmed down by immersing myself in the soothing balm of afternoon-TV land and watched as a happy Alpha Couple who didn't ever seem to have arguments over colours or curtains beautified their home on a limitless budget.

They found the perfect sixteenth-century oak chest in a skip. They inherited a four-poster bed rumoured to have belonged to Queen Anne. A friend gave them an eighteenth-century Venetian mirror as a wedding present. Well it beat towels, I supposed.

They cooed over horrible feature walls without once falling over, sticking things in their eyes or embarrassing themselves. A tall, blonde presenter with an enormous bosom and perfect teeth accompanied them. She didn't seem to do much except smile and admire everything they did. When she jiggled up to their front door a year later to see how they were getting on, the Alpha Couple shyly presented their new-born twins. I did a lot of sighing that afternoon, I can tell you.

I woke on Sunday morning with the headache I deserved.

I hadn't really had any alcohol for weeks and a bottle and a half of thirteen per cent Barolo in one evening was perhaps overdoing it a bit. At least I had managed to get to bed and not fallen asleep on the sofa dribbling into the cushions. I had last seen the Alpha Couple home improvers bonding over a faux-ruined folly that a team of jolly builders – who always turned up on time, didn't churn up the lawn until it resembled Middle Earth after the Orcs had been through, and were never seen drinking tea, smoking or ploughing to the bottom of the biscuit tin like all the builders I had ever known – were constructing at the end of their immaculate gardens.

I lay very still for a moment making that revolting dry-mouth smacking noise that one doesn't make when one has company. I knew that the moment I moved, the headache lurking somewhere in the room would make a leap for me. Eventually the need for rehydration won out and I got out of bed, untangled my dressing gown and dragged it on. As expected the headache launched itself off the curtain rail and latched its mean little talons onto my scalp. I staggered downstairs, drank a pint of water and spent the next thirty minutes looking for aspirin and whimpering. I eventually found some in the bottom of a cupboard, covered in a shredded packet of digestive biscuits and mouse droppings. I was perplexed; I loathe digestives and I never buy them. Perhaps the Webster family had left them? But I would surely have seen them and thrown them out? Weird. Where had they come from? And mice? Oh wonderful.

I sat with a cup of tea on the sofa, not daring to open the curtains. It was nine thirty. By ten thirty I felt a tiny bit better and went to make myself some toast.

Outside the kitchen the day was painfully bright with cheerful sunlight and I could hear birds shouting loudly in the garden. I made toast and Marmite and more tea and stood looking out of the window. I didn't bother with a plate, and felt quite daring eating it off the breadboard. Ian would have had a fit at such sloppiness. He had liked things to be precise, meals to be eaten at the table, the right wine poured into the right glasses.

I remembered what it was like when we were preparing for our last party. As predicted, my part in the proceedings had found me wrapping prunes in bacon, constructing vol-au-vents and messing about with various canapés for two days. I had polished the cutlery, cleaned the bathrooms and hoovered the whole house while he twittered round me with helpful suggestions. Everything was gleaming. The house was immaculate. Ian was happy.

In the afternoon of New Year's Eve Ian went down to the cellar and brought up enough alcohol to flatten several rugby teams, let alone the small group of middle-aged guests we had invited. He organised the drinks on the kitchen worktop, red wine on the left, white and champagne in the wine fridge, spirits and mixers on the right. Then he began to arrange the wine glasses into neat battalions; shortest at the front, tallest at the back. He was humming 'Auld Lang Syne' at this point, so I could only presume he was cheerful. In half an hour his work was done. Twelve hours later he was dead.

In between bites of toast I picked white paint out from under my nails. I wondered if I had managed to shift it from the rest of me, but as the possibility of someone seeing my boobs any time soon was nil, I didn't worry too much about it.

I opened the back door, blinking at the brilliance but enjoying the freshness of the air. In the distance I could hear church bells. Sunday morning. Of course. Perhaps I should go to church and pray for my headache to go. I looked down. On the doorstep in front of me was a large tub of white paint with a note on top weighed down with a stone. I frowned, was this someone's idea of a joke?

Thought you might need this? Hope you're OK, Bryn.

Hmm. I didn't quite know how to take that. Was he being cruel or kind?

I went upstairs to get dressed and thought about continuing with the decorating. Whilst I was debating whether to start on the kitchen or the living room I got back into bed and fell asleep.

I woke to the sound of someone hammering on my front door and in my shock and confusion fell out of bed. I gave a moment's thought to the possibility of finding work as an extra with Mr Tumble on CBeebies and then dragged myself to the landing window. Bryn was outside. He looked up at me and grinned. He looked clean and strong and vigorous. His washed-out blue shirt matched his clear eyes. I bet he'd never had a hangover in his life.

'Are you OK?' he said, 'I was worried.'

'Oh, no need, I'm fine, just, you know, cleaning. Housework.' I made some half-hearted dusting motions on the windowsill with a pair of socks I found there. What day was it? What time was it?

His grin widened as though he knew I was lying.

'I wondered if you'd like some coffee?' he said. 'Bonnie's gone at last. I'm at a bit of a loose end.'

'Yes, OK, why not. I'm due for a break. I'll be down in a minute,' I said, checking my non-existent watch and trying to sound careless. The last thing I remembered was the church bells. Had Bonnie gone to church? Or was that yesterday?

'Come round to mine,' he said and loped off across the garden to his front door.

When I caught sight of myself in the mirror I knew why he had been grinning. I was grey faced, my hair sticking up as though I'd stuck my finger in a light socket and there was still paint on my neck.

I didn't look like something the cat had dragged in. I looked like something the cat had caught, knocked about a bit, sneered at and left on the doorstep. Oh well too late now. I hauled on some clothes, tried to quell my over-enthusiastic hair and went downstairs.

Bryn, dressed in shorts and the aforementioned soft blue shirt, was sitting in his garden looking like something off a book cover. I let my mind wander.

Handsome hunk finds true love with short, destitute but well-meaning klutz.

Hmm, he would have to get rid of his tall, beautiful girlfriend first.

He had set out a tray of real coffee, a cafetière no less, under a pergola covered with unfurling greenery. He stood up as I approached and pulled out a chair for me. He had even put blue and white striped cushions out. I felt as though I had stumbled into a Boden photo shoot.

Handsome, single, housetrained, polite but lonely hunk…

'Help yourself. I've got some chocolate chip cookies if you fancy one? You look tired,' he said, 'bad night?'

Handsome, single, housetrained, extremely tactful but desperately lonely millionaire…

'Oh, I'm OK,' I helped myself to a cookie and nibbled round the edges. 'I've been busy with stuff all morning. Laundry, dusting, you know that sort of thing. I suppose I should be thinking about lunch soon, not sitting here eating cookies.'

Bryn looked at his watch. 'It's quarter to four.'

I gave a slow blink. 'It can't be. Is it?'

'It can and it is. All that housework obviously made the hours fly.'

I looked away hoping to find something in the garden to admire and talk about to cover my confusion. And boy, there was a lot. I know practically nothing about gardening but I could tell Bryn was an expert. I had lived next door to him for quite a while now and knew almost nothing about him except vaguely thinking he might have been a footballer.

'Your garden is wonderful,' I said.

'Thank you, it's my one passion.'

Wow, a man who made real coffee, bought decent biscuits and wasn't fanatical about real ale, football or trains.

I drank my coffee and ate two more cookies while he told me how he had planned his garden.

'I need to mow the grass,' I said, 'but the mower's a bit weird. I don't know if it's me or it.'

'I'll mow it for you if you like,' Bryn said.

'No, I don't mind doing it, I just can't seem to get the blasted thing to cut properly.'

'I'll take a look at it. I expect the blades are a bit misaligned.'

'Thanks, if you don't mind?'

The afternoon was still warm enough to be outside and a couple of early bees were buzzing in the borders behind me. I closed my eyes against the sun and quickly opened them. If I did that I was in real danger of falling asleep.

'Sorry, am I boring you?'

'No, not at all, I'm just a bit tired.'

'All that housework?'

I pulled a face. 'Bit of a hangover, if I'm honest.'

'I thought so.'

'Am I that obvious?'

He grinned and topped up my coffee. 'Let's just say I recognise the signs.'

'I was so embarrassed about yesterday. You must think I'm a right idiot.'

'I left the paint for you in case you didn't have enough. I hope you didn't mind?'

I sneaked a look at him; he was fighting back a grin.

'And I don't think you are a right idiot. It was rather endearing. But it was also very funny.'

I sighed. 'I suppose so. But no one else would have done something so stupid.'

'Only someone as athletic as you,' he said, 'anyone else would have really hurt themselves.'

I gulped my coffee and help my breath for a moment to stop myself choking. No one, not a friend, teacher, relative or passing acquaintance had ever in my life called me athletic.

All of a sudden tipping paint all over myself sounded rather clever after all. What had he called it? Endearing.

CHAPTER 6

Hyacinth – jealousy

We sat in the garden for a while. We drank Bryn's excellent coffee, talked about gardening and ate cookies. It was very restful and soothing. Perhaps I should have made more of an effort to be entertaining. But I didn't have the energy. And really there didn't seem to be the need. Just as I finished the last cookie and the sun was beginning to dip towards the horizon, Bonnie made another appearance.

We both sat up a bit straighter when we heard her sporty little car purring into the drive and then we listened in silence to the slam of a car door and the brisk crunch of her footsteps on the gravel path. Was it my imagination, or did Bryn seem just a little less relaxed?

'Oh!' Bonnie didn't sound terribly pleased to find me in the garden with her boyfriend but she managed to hide it quite successfully. 'How lovely to see you again. It's Caroline, isn't it?'

She swung her Audrey Hepburn sunglasses from one hand. She looked sensational, wearing a yellow fifties-style dress with a gold belt that showed off her tiny waist and the type of shrug that normally only looks good on a six year old. She had also managed to do that chic thing with a silk headscarf that Audrey used to do when she was whizzing round the Côte d'Azur with

Gregory Peck in an open top car. When I tried doing it I looked as though I was selling pegs.

'Charlotte,' I said.

'Of course, Charlotte. I hope Bryn has been looking after you?' She went to stand behind his chair and rested her slim hands on his shoulders. Short of attaching a label around his neck she could not have been more obvious. I saw sparks of annoyance in her eyes and I stood up.

'I'd better be off,' I said.

'Oh, must you?' Bonnie pouted prettily and, still watching me, unwound the silk headscarf from around her throat and shook out her Titian ringlets. Her rather spectacular earrings jangled and sparkled in the sunlight. They were probably cut from the Koh-i-Noor diamond and presented to her by the Sultan of Brunei.

She saw me looking at them and preened happily, sweeping her hair back behind her ears.

'Oh don't go, I was going to open some Prosecco to celebrate.' Celebrate? What? A massive lottery win? Their engagement? Her Prize for the Perkiest Tits in England?

'Gosh, I've got such a lot to do. Laundry, stuff, you know.'

I took a couple of steps away and fell into a flowerbed, crushing what I later discovered was a Regal pelargonium. Bonnie hid a smile with one hand, while Bryn pulled me to my feet. His fingers were warm and strong on mine.

I reminded myself, and not for the first time, that a) Ian had only recently died and b) Bryn was taken. I hurried back to my garden, hoping that the bright laughter I heard a few seconds later was not directed at me.

Inside I did some desultory tidying, wiping toast crumbs and Marmite off the worktop. Did I want to start painting? Did I want to read? Did I want to write something? No, not really. None of the above.

It was Sunday evening and suddenly I was reminded of the

Sundays of my childhood when nothing good ever happened except finishing maths homework. I sorted a bit of laundry and folded some clean tea towels. Then I ate a packet of cheese and onion crisps and a bar of chocolate. It struck me that I was existing on a diet of 'not much' mixed with 'rubbish'. I flopped down on the sofa and turned on the TV.

Enormous Bosom Presenter was back and this time she was steering another pair of home improvers around a dilapidated Cotswold mansion near Burford and flashing her teeth. They had an excited discussion about the cheapness of the house for the area. Only one point two million. Bargain! The home improvers looked a little worried as they only had a budget of one point five million and the house needed a new roof. In the blink of an eye Enormous Bosom Presenter had negotiated a massive reduction of the price and the programme ended happily. By then I was slumped into the uncomfortable curves of the sofa shouting abuse at the screen and eating a Crunchie. Nice.

How did a young couple afford an incredibly expensive house like that, I wondered? When the world of mortgages and house purchase was becoming more and more difficult for people. I didn't imagine I would ever be in a position to afford to buy a house. I expected to be renting forever. Serve me right for feeling so superior to my university chums.

I imagined myself in years to come living in ghastly places with mould growing on the window frames and neighbours upstairs having noisy fights. Everything about my recent life had seemed so sheltered and my relationship with Ian so secure. We had been a team, surely? I remembered how we had worked our way around the room at our party, networking, keeping Ian's dull workforce happy, wine glasses topped up.

And my word they were dull. First came Phil from Ian's Accounts department, festive in beige cardigan and cords and just as tedious as I remembered. His equally colourless young wife, Emma, stood

71

wiping her spotless shoes on the doormat for several minutes while Phil plucked at my sleeve, wanting to regale me with the uneventful story of their journey and the excitement of a burst water main at the bottom of our lane, which was causing a mini flood. Ian picked up on my agonised eye rolling signals and scooped them up and away into the drawing room while I dealt with the steady stream of arrivals.

Next Karen and her husband, Bruce (resplendent in a Santa-strewn Christmas jumper) arrived, trying to conclude a heated squabble about whether it was going to snow and what constituted a white Christmas. They are enormous fun and nothing suits this couple more than a good argument.

Trudy from Ian's HR department brought her grubby-looking fiancé, Ken, and both stood nursing drinks and casting glowering glances at Ian. There was no sign of someone called Julian from the IT department, so perhaps he was elsewhere attending to some techno-crisis. No sign of Steve from the granite place either. Perhaps he was busy with the naughty little brunette? I caught Ian's eye and he blew me a kiss. I grinned, and then realised that Trudy from HR was watching me, distinctly stony faced.

I remember Sophie, a local friend of mine, having a lively conversation with Karen and Jess about the ongoing political scandal concerning a cabinet minister and a pole dancer. I went to join them for a few minutes but then I saw Ian waggling his eyebrows at me across the room and he jerked his head imperceptibly towards Greg Palmer, so I moved on.

Greg was standing by the fireplace talking to Karen's husband, Bruce, his wine glass lodged between our Christmas cards, and his face lit up when I hove into view.

"Ello 'ello 'ello! A tasty treat!' he said, taking a vol-au-vent and looking down the front of my dress. 'That's what we all need.'

'It's lovely to see you, Greg. How's the hand?'

'Doctor Hawkins did a good job. No ill effects at all. Funnily enough I saw him in the pub the other day. He asked after you.'

'Really?' That was nice to hear. 'Give him my regards when you see him again. I hope he had a good Christmas, he told me he usually hates it.'

'I will. He seemed quite cheerful actually. For once he stopped to talk.'

'He's been like that since his wife died. His three daughters descend with their children as soon as the schools break up every term and boss him about until it's time to go back home. It can't be much fun for him.'

Across the room I caught another meaningful glance from Ian.

I don't know what he was expecting me to do. I returned his stare for a second and Ian pulled an agonised face. He was obviously expecting something of me.

'And how are you enjoying living in The Grange?' I said.

'Fine, fine. Of course it's needed a lot of work, looks like the last people to live there redecorated back in the 1940s. There were a lot of bare floorboards, old rugs that sort of thing. And no en suites at all!'

He raised his eyebrows at me to emphasise the depths of the squalor.

'I've always hated en suites actually,' I said, my second bucket of wine making me bold, 'why would you want a toilet in the corner of your bedroom?'

Greg laughed. 'Good point, but Jess insists on it so we're having two put in. You must come over one evening and have a look around. See what we've done. You too, Bruce.'

'I'll tell Karen. She loves a good nose around other people's houses,' Bruce said and then he wandered off to talk to someone else.

'Count me in,' I said. 'I'd love to.'

'Your husband has some *interesting* ideas,' Greg said, rescuing his drink from the mantelpiece and taking a large gulp of his wine. 'Thinks there might be some prospects in the village. The Old Forge is up for sale for a start.'

'That's been empty for quite a while,' I said, trying to sound wise and knowledgeable, 'rising damp and the roof needs replacing.'

Greg put his glass down and reached for another canapé, holding my hand steady on the platter as he did so in a quite unnecessary way. I think he was just one of those men who can't help themselves. He steered me round a little, darting cautious glances over my shoulder. Then I realised what he was up to.

'God this is good. If you stand there Jess can't see me eating this stuff,' he said, 'she's trying to get me off carbs. New Year, new stick to beat me with.'

We chatted for a few minutes while Greg availed himself of my tasty treats at high speed.

'You've got a lovely-looking garden. I saw some of it the other day when I called in,' he said, brushing pastry crumbs off his tie.

'You called in?' This was news to me. I wondered why Ian hadn't mentioned it.

'Ian invited me up for coffee. I think you were at the hairdresser. Who does your garden?' he continued.

'We have a gardener who spruces things up once or twice a month. It's something I'd like to get into though.'

'Really? Well done you. I like a lady with lots of hidden talents. My brother is a gardener. He has a place near Exeter, his plot was quite spectacular, the last time I saw it anyway. His house is a bit of a shambles, but the garden? It was divine.' He kissed the tips of his fingers to show his admiration.

'Marvellous.'

For all his brashness I was beginning to like him.

'Ah well.' I looked at my now empty platter, Greg had been shovelling in mushroom vol-au-vents with surprising speed during the course of our conversation. 'I'd better go and get some more food and mingle otherwise I'll be in trouble!'

'I wouldn't want to get you into trouble,' Greg said predictably, wiping his mouth.

74

I went out to the kitchen and Ian followed me.

'What did he say?' he hissed.

I put my platter down and went out of the kitchen door to have a crafty cigarette. I seemed to be the only one smoking. And to be honest I quite liked that. It was one of the few things that made me different, daring.

'Oh just general chitchat. Said you had some interesting ideas.' I lit up and took a deep drag. The nicotine hit my blood stream in a delicious fizz. God, I loved smoking. I was supposed to be quitting in the New Year as usual. Time to make the most of it while I had the chance.

'Really? What else?'

'He talked about gardening. He said he had been here. Why didn't you tell me?'

'Oh, I don't know, it slipped my mind I suppose. That Jess looks like she goes to the gym pretty regularly, doesn't she?' He slapped my bottom playfully. 'You might consider going with her a bit more often. You could do with toning up.'

'You're bloody rude sometimes, you know.'

'Only joking, gorgeous. Did he say anything else about me? About us working together?'

'Do you want me to pass him a note for you at playtime?' I took a last drag and stubbed out my cigarette on the wall. The night was very cold, almost as though it might snow. I went back into the kitchen, refilled my wine glass and passed the bottle to Ian.

He topped up his glass and emptied it in one go. He should probably slow down on the drinking. He was already slurring his words.

'I need shomeone like him, don't you undershtand. I need a bit of a what d'you call it, cash injection.'

'Well, I'm not going to ask him to bung us a few quid!' I said.

'I din't mean that. Did he mention The Old Forge?'

I turned and reloaded my platter. 'Yes, he said it was for sale and I said it had been empty for a while because it had rising damp.'

'And?'

'And the roof needed replacing.'

Ian made an exasperated noise. 'I didn't mean that. What else?'

'He went on about en suites for a bit. I said I didn't like them.'

Ian was aghast and rocked against the table. 'For God's sake, whose shide are you on? You din't?'

'He just laughed and said Jess liked them so they were going to put in two.'

Ian went over to the freezer and pulled out the bottle of vodka he kept in there for emergencies. He poured himself a slug and knocked it back. I made a mental note to dig out the aspirin for later.

He put the bottle back under the frozen peas and turned round.

'Does he need a new kitchen?'

'What?'

'Does he need a new kitchen at The Grange?'

'I don't know. Ask him yourself.'

Ian refilled his wine glass. 'I can't. You ask him.'

'Don't be ridiculous.'

Ian caught hold of my arm and a couple of cocktail sausages rolled off my platter onto the floor. I went to pick them up.

'You don't undershtand, Lottie…'

'Can I do anything to help?' It was Sophie, tottering in the doorway, an empty wine glass in her hand.

'Fab party, Lottie; Greg Palmer is a scream, isn't he? Who is that Trudy person? She is well weird. God I'm pissed.'

Ian looked at me, slightly wild-eyed. It was only later that I realised why.

'Lottie—'

I thrust the platter into his hands.

'Take those and mingle, Ian, I'll be out in a minute.'

Ian weaved off and I saw Trudy following him across the room with a determined eye on him and the sausages.

Sophie hugged me, more for support than anything, and reached past me for an open wine bottle.

'How are you, hon? Is this white or red? Oh well, who cares?'

She sloshed some of Ian's finest Barolo into her glass and took a sip.

'Fine, I wish I could take these shoes off, my feet are killing me.' I looked down at my new stilettos. Two hundred quid and I could hardly walk in them.

'Oh just take them off, no one will notice. They're all too busy looking down Jess's cleavage anyway. She's nice though, isn't she? You've gotta like her. She's been telling me about some nail artist she knew in Spain, could do flags of all nationalities.'

'Really?'

'True as I'm standing here.' She swayed a little and hiccupped. 'God, I'd better eat something or I'm going to pass out before we get to midnight.'

Sophie grabbed the sausages I had rescued from the floor and chewed.

'What time is it anyway?'

I looked up at the kitchen clock, amazed that at last it told the right time.

'Eleven thirty; Ian better get the champagne ready,' I said.

I began to load up my tray with some prohibitively overpriced mini cheesecakes and filled chocolate shells and then went out to circulate again. Someone had turned the music up; the conversation was noticeably louder as a result. I noticed Ken deep in conversation with Bruce. As I passed them I earwigged.

'...yes, but do you see, in the end the carburettor gets completely clogged and then you have to think about a re-bore. A mate of mine...'

Ah, I had forgotten Bruce was a petrol-head, it seemed he had found a kindred spirit. I moved on.

Karen was standing by the fireplace reading our Christmas

cards. She turned and relieved me of two chocolate cups. Then she looked around the room for a few moments.

'I can't see her now but tell me again, who is the strange, dumpy woman who keeps following Ian about?'

'Trudy Stroud from HR,' I said, looking around for her.

'Yes, I remember. She has all the social skills of a wombat. Not that I know many wombats. I tried to talk to her and she looked at me as though I was mad. Totally ignored me. These chocolate things are really good, did you make them?'

'Don't be daft. As if. They're from that new deli in the Summergate.'

'Scrummy! I keep meaning to go there, and then the electricity bill comes in.'

I looked around for Ian but he was nowhere to be seen. I worried for a moment he might have cornered Greg and be designing him a new Windermere kitchen on the back of a paper napkin. After a few minutes I saw Greg across the room talking to Sophie, who was laughing like a hyena and hanging on to his arm, and Emma who was doing neither of those things. Instead she was standing with a glass of something rather orange in her hand and 'responsible, designated driver' emanating from her like a miasma.

Greg looked up and caught my eye. 'Nearly midnight, Cinders,' he said, tapping his large and very impressive gold watch. 'I put a couple of bottles in the fridge.'

I handed my platter to Karen. 'I'd better find Ian. Perhaps he's gone to the loo?'

I went out into the hall, feeling quite merry and more than a little unsteady on my feet. It was nice to be a part of a celebration for once, not just watch other people enjoy themselves. I was glad Ian had thought of this party, it was going well and the house had never looked better. I'd chucked out last year's gold and green decorations and bought a load of new ones in peacock shades accented with silver. Everyone had admired them. We weren't the type of couple to collect decorations with sentimental connections and we didn't have children so there were no woollen robins or loo-roll angels.

I kicked off my shoes and wandered about in my stockinged feet, my toes throbbing, still looking for Ian. I wanted to be there to kiss him as midnight chimed, give him a hug, admit I'd been wrong about the wisdom of this party. He wasn't in the downstairs cloakroom, or the kitchen. I even looked in the utility room although it wasn't a place Ian knew much about.

Someone had switched the television on in the sitting room, and I could hear a female celebrity hyperventilating about the New Year and shouting how everyone should be in London tonight and if they weren't then they were either stupid or dead. It sounded as though she was either already plastered or on something prohibited. Karen was asking where her glass was. Bruce was telling her to look in the hall. Jess was laughing; that rapid-fire, honking laugh that almost shook the windows. The volume of noise was increasing as people began to be more excited. If he wasn't careful, Ian and his champagne would be too late.

And then everything went spectacularly wrong.

CHAPTER 7

Foxglove – insincerity, deceit

The following day I was well over my hangover, Bonnie's red car had gone from Bryn's driveway and I felt much better and more confident about things.

I decided that from now on I was going to be relentlessly optimistic and cheerful. I read a magazine interview once with an admittedly not very successful actress who believed that positive thoughts make all sorts of good things happen. Almost as though money and starring roles and Fortnum and Mason hampers could be attracted magnetically towards you. Like a personal Hadron Collider for treats. Shortly after that I remember her being declared bankrupt, but it was worth a try.

I had a quick shower and admired the cobweb-free bathroom. I had at last scrubbed the final bits of graffiti off the mirror and only the very faintest of greasy marks still remained if I looked at it from a particular angle. Something I decided I wouldn't do. After all, I was looking at everything in a positive light from now on.

I had breakfast and washed up in such a chirpy frame of mind that I might have expected bluebirds to fly in through the kitchen window to put the plates away. Then I spent a couple of careful hours glossing the woodwork in the hall.

While I did so I enjoyed pleasant daydreams involving cruise ships, trips on the Orient Express and airplane flights where I was instantly upgraded to first class by a smiling flight attendant with a bottle of champagne in her hands. Never having done any of these things, it all took a lot of imagining. Particularly when it came to the smiling flight attendant.

By the time I finished painting, I realised that somewhere in the background of all these daydreams there was a man. Extremely tall and very broad shouldered. Sometimes he was casual in jeans and a dazzling white T-shirt. Occasionally he leaned against the ship's rail in evening dress while the dark sea slipped away behind him into a glorious sunset. On the airline flight he wore a polo shirt and chinos and occasionally reached over to hold my hand and kiss my immaculately manicured fingertips. With a guilty start I realised it was a man who looked a lot like Bryn. It certainly wasn't Ian.

I put the pictures and hallstand back in their places and cleared up. I really needed to get out of the house. I was dreaming up an unhealthy obsession with a virtual stranger. I knew nothing about him other than he liked gardening, might be a footballer and had a girlfriend who was younger and a million times more attractive than I could ever be. I went to find my handbag and car keys and drove away from Holly Cottage and into Stokeley. If I could only find a café where I could sit amongst other people.

I drove around looking for a parking space. Or more accurately two parking spaces together so I had a sporting chance of fitting my car in without any embarrassment. It was Monday so it didn't take long. I was lucky and parked without incident or an audience near the market square.

I found a café nearby where perhaps for the first time in the year there were a few tables set outside. The sunlight was dappling through the trees, the tables had blue checked cloths and a few ladies, muffled up in padded coats and warm scarves, were drinking coffee out of large china cups and chatting. There were a couple of cheeky sparrows hopping about between the tables pecking at crumbs. A tortoiseshell cat was impersonating a loaf of bread on a windowsill. The whole scene was decidedly French.

As I got out and looked around, my new mobile began rattling into life. One text after another pinged into the inbox. I hadn't realised how far off the mobile network I had been or how long it had been since I had been in contact with anyone. The boy in the mobile phone shop had managed to keep my old phone number and there were over forty texts. There were several missed calls and about ten text messages each from Sophie and Karen. Most of the others were from my sister, Jenny. This was not and could never be, A Good Thing.

They all said much the same in various degrees of irritation. Where was I? What had happened? Why didn't I reply? *Where was I?*

I was suddenly very hungry. Before I could talk myself out of it, I ordered a coffee and a doughnut. My sister always had that effect on me. For all my life she, and by default I, had been on a diet. Pavlov's dogs had nothing on me. Jenny. Bing! Doughnut.

I looked for the jam entry point, took a bite and replied to Jenny's latest message.

Sorry, had no signal. I'm fine.

Within five seconds my phone rang.

'Hi, Jenny.'

'Hi, Jenny? Is that all you can say? Hi, Jenny? I've been having a terrible time,' she said. 'Where are you? Are you all right?'

'Sorry, I'm fine. I just had a bit of a bad spell. Well things have been a bit crazy here. Everything got a lot worse.'

'What things? Where are you?'

'I'm in Devon. I'm helping a friend renovate a cottage. I had to—'

'I made the mistake of phoning Susan. I know she's lost her only son and I'm terribly sorry for her but she's a nightmare. On and on and on moaning and complaining. How Trevor put up with her for so long is anyone's guess.'

Jenny began a disjointed and lengthy ramble about what Susan had said and what she had said and who had slammed the phone down first. I carried on drinking my coffee and enjoying my doughnut.

'You're eating, aren't you?' she said suddenly. 'I can tell.'

I swallowed and choked a bit. 'Oh, you know. Late breakfast.'

'What do you weigh?' No time for fond sisterly chitchat then. Straight to the jugular, that's Jenny.

'Twenty-seven stone three and a quarter pounds.'

'Very funny. I bet you are the size of a house, you always turned to food when you were miserable.'

'I'm not miserable!'

'Well you should be. Ian dead and you homeless –'

'I'm not homeless, don't you listen?'

'– and your sister ill.'

I paused. 'Ill? What sort of ill?'

'Ill. Aches. Pains, allergies. I had tests for coeliac disease and then they considered IBS—'

'I thought he was a Tory politician?'

'That's I.D.S., don't be facetious,' she snapped.

'So are you OK now?'

'As well as might be expected.'

'Seriously, Jen, are you OK?' I wiped the sugar off my chin with a guilty hand.

She sighed. 'Oh just old and tired.'

'Nonsense, Jen, you're as strong as…' I couldn't say *a horse* as my sister's dental configuration is a tad equine and she's very sensitive about this '…as strong as Adele out on a hen night with the Kardashians.'

Jenny clicked her tongue at my levity. 'I'll have you know I'm on drugs now.'

'Legal or otherwise?'

83

'Don't be flippant. I'm under the doctor, as Auntie Shirley would say. And it's nowhere near as much fun as it sounds. For cholesterol.'

'Most people your age are these days,' I said. 'When I worked at the surgery Doctor Hawkins scattered those pills around like confetti. That and blood pressure tablets.'

Jenny gave a shocked gasp as though I was psychic. 'I'm on them too!'

'Well, there you are then, nothing out of the ordinary.' A thought struck me. 'Jenny, it's lovely to hear from you but this call must be costing you a fortune. Are you still in Texas?'

'No, I'm staying in Croydon for a few days with Auntie Shirley. It really is the dullest place on earth. She sends her love, by the way.'

'Croydon? Taking a break from all that sunshine?' I began to feel a tremor of unease.

'No, I'm back for good. Trent –' her latest fiancé '– is history. I had to come back because my visa ran out. It's a long story. He brought me back on the *Atlantica* as a treat but then Trent had to go back to Texas and, anyway, for various reasons it was never going to work. So I'm back in dear old England and here I shall stay.'

'Don't make me laugh. You swore you'd never come back.'

'Nonsense. I would never say such a thing. I was hoping to come and stay with you but I had to phone Susan because I couldn't get through to you and she told me you had upped and left after effectively murdering her son. Can this be true? I mean, I wouldn't have blamed you and no court in the land would have convicted you.'

'Jenny!'

'Well I know. Don't speak ill of the dead. So when Trent went back to Texas I came to see Auntie Shirley, but I'll be honest, she's driving me mad. I wouldn't mind paying for a hotel but she won't hear of it. But I think she's getting a bit fed up of me now. *Jennifer, don't forget to turn off the heater in the bathroom. Jennifer, you've put the milk carton in the wrong recycling box*. I'm on her sofa bed and I haven't had a decent night's sleep since I got here. This place is Bedlam. If it's not cats fighting in the wheelie bins, then it's police sirens. And now she's started timing my showers.'

'Auntie Shirley is just careful with money.'

'That's putting it mildly. Do you know the highlight of her week? She likes to go to some ghastly little supermarket just before they close and snap up some ready-meal bargains. God knows how much unexpected horsemeat I've eaten in the last week. I swear there were bits of hoof in last night's lasagne. So where are you?'

'I've told you already, Devon. I've borrowed a two-bedroom cottage from a friend in exchange for decorating it. You're welcome to come and stay but I have no storage space so it's no use bringing a load of stuff.'

'Oh, you know me, I travel very light.'

'This from a woman who once went on an eight-day cruise with fourteen pairs of shoes.'

She huffed a little. 'You do remember the strangest things.'

'And I mean it when I say I'm decorating.'

'But I'd *love* to help! I've always been very handy with a paint-brush, don't you remember?'

'I remember you painting your bedroom walls up as far as you could reach and then leaving it for two years.'

She made an impatient noise. 'What's the matter with you? You must remember the happy times, Lottie. Right, I'll be with you the day after tomorrow. I've hired a car. I have no idea how to work the satnav so you must send me your address and clear directions. Ooops, I'd better go. Shirley has been getting the washing from the line and she's coming back in. The towels here are like cardboard. I told her she should get a tumble dryer. Would she listen? No.'

After she had rung off I ordered another coffee as the first one had gone cold. I think I would have preferred a large gin but it wasn't even midday. I would have liked another doughnut too but the imminent prospect of my sister pinching my waistline put me off the idea.

Then I rang Sophie and had a long and very honest chat with her, reassuring her I was OK, promising to keep in touch with more diligence. It was lovely to realise that people did care about me; I wasn't on my own.

I hadn't heard from Ian's mother, Susan, since the funeral. She had sent me two very long and angry letters after Ian died, one detailing my many shortcomings as a human being and the other giving me a fortnight to clear out. It turned out that Ian had made Susan his sole beneficiary when he had his will drawn up many years ago and he had never thought to change it. So that was the end of that. As the 'most recent girlfriend', as Susan described me, her pen dripping with venom, I had no right to stay in Ian's house and I should push off as soon as possible, taking all my odious effects with me. But she acknowledged if I wanted to come to the funeral then she couldn't stop me. She didn't want any interference, she was paying for it, and she had chosen the time and place. She would choose the flowers, the music, everything.

Funerals are awful things. One hears of some wakes turning into a joyful celebration of the deceased's life. People getting merry and swapping funny stories that lighten the gloom until eventually it turns into a right old knees up. Well I've certainly never been to one like that and Ian's most definitely wasn't one of those.

There was a business-like service at the crematorium where we were hustled in and out past the plastic flower arrangements by harassed-looking staff. I think they were concerned that we might overrun and our party of mourners become tangled up with those for the next dear departed, Terrence Harold Hunt.

As we came out to the strains of 'Jesu Joy of Man's Desiring', the Hunt gathering was already assembled around the litterbins, smoking and shuffling their feet. Terrence himself was waiting at the end of the long driveway under a pile of white roses in a horse-drawn hearse that made our fleet of grey limos look very tame indeed.

A couple of hatchet-faced men cast glances our way and we nodded and grimaced at each other for a few seconds. Then we were bundled off in our Daimlers to the Golf Club for the wake where Susan sat in state in the Captain's ceremonial chair because no one was brave enough to tell her not to, and everyone thought of nice things to say to her about Ian.

People were very kind but I felt like a bit of a spare part, to be honest. I lurked at the back of the room, nursing a warm sweet sherry and a plate of tasteless canapés. The only high spot of the proceeding was when Ian's cousin Pamela sought me out. She took a meandering path towards me that hinted she was several sherries ahead of the rest of us and flopped down into the chair next to mine, kicking off her shoes.

'This is a turn up,' she said. 'I'm supposed to be going on holiday. Tomorrow. Canaries. Last-minute thing. No idea if I'll get packed in time. End up going like this.' She plucked at her black pleated skirt with nicotine-stained fingers.

'That sounds nice,' I said, 'a bit of sunshine.'

'Cruise,' she said, hailing a passing waitress and swiping two dry sherries off her tray.

'We were always going to go on a cruise, but we never got around to it,' I said.

'Terrific fun. Floating hotel. Wake up each day in a different place. No cooking. Food at all hours. Entertainment. Should go. Crew always good fun. Young men. Uniforms.'

She gave me a knowing wink, it seemed she was speaking in alcohol-punctuated shorthand. She knocked back the first sherry, swallowing noisily, and put the empty glass in front of me. She probably remembered at that point why we were all together and her face collapsed into sorrow.

'Terrible thing,' she said, her forehead creased into furrows. She reached over the table and patted my hand. 'Terrible.'

'Yes, it's been a dreadful shock, especially for Susan.'

Pamela shook her head and sipped at the second sherry.

Her husband, always referred to as The Bastard, had scarpered many years ago, leaving Pamela to bring up her two daughters in a careless, alcoholic haze that had been unexpectedly effective. Both were doctors.

Her lips puckered around her glass into a thousand lipsticked creases that spoke of a lifetime of tobacco addiction. I wondered if I would end up looking like her, pickled and kippered by a lifetime of boozing and fags.

'Poor old auntie,' she said at last. 'I expect she'll be next, poor old thing. Sad really. Or maybe it will be Fat Uncle Richard.' She nodded her head and I followed her glance.

Susan was talking to a red-faced man in a straining suit. Fat Uncle Richard, to differentiate him from Tall Uncle Richard who was standing at the bar with a pint of Guinness.

'Or more likely it'll be my cousin Roly, the way he's carrying on,' she said with emphasis, angling her eyebrows towards a worried-looking man of about sixty who was scurrying after his much younger wife as she went outside for a cigarette with someone I believe was her husband's nephew. 'Ah well, and how are *you*?' Pamela said, leaning towards me, her head wobbling. 'I mean, how are you *really*?'

'I don't know,' I said, 'it's all been so sudden.'

'Well of course it has! Of *course*. I expect you'll get married again though. You're young. Attractive.'

This was insensitive even for her and I drew in my breath in horror, hoping that no one had overheard her. The thought of this nugget being passed on to Susan was too awful.

'Well you will,' she said defiantly, perhaps realising that she had overstepped the mark. 'Young, pretty woman like you. Course you will. And maybe next time you'll find someone your own age. Ian was always very *old* and he was younger than me. Know what I mean? When all us cousins got together he always wanted to organise chess tournaments. The rest of us just wanted to nick food from the larder and play hospitals.'

Pamela gave a throaty laugh that rattled across the room, incurring a searing look of disapproval from Susan that crackled in our direction like a blow from a lightsabre.

'I think that's the last thing on my mind actually, Pamela,' I said rather stiffly.

She finished her second sherry and put the glass in front of me. She gave me a long, slightly unfocused look.

'I'm off outside for some fresh air,' she said, code for another cigarette. She heaved her cavernous handbag onto the table and rummaged around inside it for a few minutes, eventually coming up with a gold lighter in one hand and a fresh packet of Lambert and Butler in the other. 'Coming?'

'I've given up,' I said. It wasn't true and to be frank I was desperate for a cigarette but I didn't want to call attention to myself, and I couldn't face walking across the room with Pamela under Susan's watchful eye.

Pamela rolled her eyes and tutted. 'Well, you're no fun any more, are you? But I will say this, take it or leave it. I knew Ian all my life; I won't have a word said against him. Mustn't speak ill and all that. He was a nice enough bloke. Solid. But dull. Boring. No one was more surprised than me when I heard what he'd been up to.' She thought about it for a moment, her mouth pursed. 'Well I suppose you probably were *more* surprised, but I was jolly surprised.'

'Yes,' I said.

'Still, like father like son, eh?'

'Pamela!'

'Oh dear me, yes, Trevor was always after the girls, bit of an octopus from what I've heard…none of the younger waitresses here would serve him in the end.'

'Pamela! Susan will hear you!' I hissed.

'I'm sorry but I speak as I find. And drink? Trevor was a terror. I told you ages ago, it was only because he played golf with the Chief Constable that he didn't lose his driving licence.'

Trevor, Ian's father, had died ten years ago. Two years before Ian and I met so I never actually clapped eyes on this paragon of manliness.

The image of Trevor as both a drunk and a philanderer sat uneasily next to the accepted wisdom that Trevor had been splendid in every way. Handsome, a generous and loving husband, a wonderful father, a talented golfer who might have achieved greatness. According to Pamela, Trevor's major handicap had not been his golf swing but his lengthy affair with the steward's wife.

Of course, we don't mention that.

I looked round, terrified Susan would overhear this blasphemy and strike us both dead.

'And I will say this,' Pamela took a deep breath and then dithered for a minute, 'what was I saying?'

'I've no idea.'

'Right, well, dear, I'm off for a fag. I wouldn't stay any longer than you have to. Auntie Susan's set for the afternoon. She won't want you deflecting the attention from her. I'd go home and put my feet up.'

I let out a long relieved breath. The idea was very appealing.

Pamela leaned over and kissed me on the cheek, enveloping me in a fug of alcohol and cigarette smoke. She hesitated, picked up my half-drunk sherry and downed it then grabbed her handbag and tottered off.

I took her advice.

CHAPTER 8

Purple iris – faith, hope, inspiration, friendship

My sister, Jenny, arrived at Holly Cottage in a rather jaunty yellow hatchback and a filthy temper. She had got caught up in Exeter's one-way system and had spent some time literally driving round in circles looking for the right exit from the roundabout that enlivens the centre of the city. Having chosen one she then blithely ignored the rest of my guidelines until she found herself halfway up Whitestone Hill and had to stop and ask for directions.

She eventually pulled up in the driveway just before five. She got out and staggered towards me rather theatrically as though she had been taking part in the Paris–Dakar rally.

'What on earth possessed you to come and live here?' were her opening words.

I went to hug her. She was very slim, chic in a cream dress, and she brought with her a familiar drift of Chanel perfume.

'And hello to you too, Jenny.'

'When you said you were living in Devon I thought you would be in one of those jaunty little seaside towns with views across to the lighthouse. You know, a village filled with salty old sea dogs telling tales of running before the tide on the outer banks.

Like that place where Martin Clunes is the doctor. Shirley is very keen on him. She's got the boxset. I've bought some adorable Capri pants and two Guernsey sweaters. I was going to buy some deck shoes too. Good job I didn't, it looks like I need wellingtons. This literally is the back of beyond, isn't it? I've often wondered where it was and what it looked like.'

'When you've quite finished bad-mouthing my home, would you like to come in? Cup of tea?'

Jenny pulled her suitcases out from the back of the car and turned to face me, her mouth pursed like a cat's bottom.

'Don't be ridiculous. I'll have a large scotch and water.'

We lugged her bags into the house, where they effectively blocked the hallway, and then went into the kitchen. I began filling the kettle.

'You won't, you know, I haven't got any scotch.'

Jenny went and rummaged in her holdall and came back with a bottle of Laphroaig.

'Ta dah!'

'You shouldn't be mixing alcohol with medication,' I said.

'Oh, what do you know, Miss Sensible? You sound just like Auntie Shirley.'

She found a glass, helped herself to a hefty slug of whisky, topped it up with water, opened the kitchen door and went outside.

After a moment she came back in, her eyes bright.

'Well, I spy with my little eye something beginning with Hunk. Who is that *gorgeous* chap next door? He's doing stuff in the garden, about six two, built like a brick outhouse, no shirt.'

'Oh, that's just Bryn. My neighbour,' I said, resisting the impulse to go outside and look at him too. We would have looked a right pair; a couple of sisters standing ogling the same man.

'Oh, that's just Bryn, my neighbour,' Jenny mimicked, a wicked grin across her face. 'Swipe right! Ding Dong!'

* * *

It was wonderful to have some company for a change but I soon began to suspect this new domestic arrangement was not going to work. My sister was used to more wardrobe space, shops and general excitement. The cuteness, the silence, the isolation of Holly Cottage was too much for her. It was like putting a hungry cat in a carry case with the expectation of taking it to the vet for neutering.

We had just finished breakfast one morning and were about to resume decorating when she suddenly reached the *I can't not say anything any longer* point.

'I don't know how you can stand living here! The broadband is a joke, there's no phone reception to speak of and it's *so* quiet,' she said. 'Beautiful, of course. A philistine could appreciate that. But there's nothing to do here, is there? Unless you're a farmer.'

'Or a writer,' I countered rather self-importantly.

'And how is that coming along?' she asked a trifle waspishly. 'I haven't noticed any literary activity since I've been here.'

'I sold a couple of short stories last year.'

She made a dismissive noise. 'Well that won't buy the baby new shoes, will it? Why don't you write a bestseller?'

I rolled my eyes at her. 'Gosh, that's a good idea, Jenny. Why didn't I think of that?'

My sister always had trouble registering sarcasm.

Her face brightened. 'Erotica. That's all the rage now, isn't it? And I noticed on board the *Atlantica* there was a bookshop and there were a lot of novels about cake or vampires. Perhaps you could write a bestseller about a girl who falls in love with a vampire?'

'It's been done.'

'Really?' She frowned and then started laughing. 'Porn then? A porn star who falls in love with a vampire and they open a cake shop called the Fondant Fancy-a-Bite.'

'Not if I was starving.'

She pouted at my lack of enthusiasm, levered the lid off the paint and began to stir it.

'But it would be funny! A whole new genre – vampire/porn/cake-lit. You could call it Vampoke.'

Bored, she chucked the paint stirrer wooden spoon down and went to flick the kettle on for her third coffee of the day, spooning the coffee into the cafetière with a generous hand. I wondered if she had any idea how expensive ground coffee was. I went to help her; for some reason she found it almost impossible to work in my little kitchen without making an incredible mess. I assume she was used to Trent's staff clearing up after her.

Jenny stopped stirring the cafetière and looked thoughtful.

'I suppose those years with Ian have knocked all the joie de vivre out of you. The first time I met him he was wearing slacks and slip-on shoes that looked like Cornish pasties. That told me everything I needed to know. By the way, I forgot to tell you, the Harpy wants to see you.'

'What?' I staggered a little and nearly dropped the mugs I was holding.

'The Harpy – Susan, she wants to see you. When I was talking to her on the phone a couple of weeks ago. I was trying to find out where you were, remember? She said she wanted to talk to you.'

'Why?'

Jenny shrugged. 'How should I know?'

'Tell me what she said, then. The last time I saw her was at Ian's funeral where she didn't speak to me at all.'

Jenny poured the boiling water on the coffee and stirred the cafetière, the fragrant steam encircling her face. She breathed it in.

'Wowser, I love that smell. D'you think I'm addicted to caffeine? I was once told I had an addictive personality. A Swami in India… such an attractive man. He had an enormous—'

'Jen! Concentrate. What did Susan say?'

'Um, she said she wanted to talk to you. Something about Truly? Trixie? Trilby?' She shot me a look. 'What's the matter? You've gone a funny colour.'

'I don't want to talk to her and I certainly don't want to talk to her about Trudy,' I said.

Light dawned on my sister's scattergun brain. 'Oh Trudy! Yes, of course. The erstwhile mistress. How odd that she should come up in the conversation. It's almost worth ringing the old bat to find out what she's got to say.'

I shuddered. 'No, thanks. Let sleeping dogs lie.'

'In my experience when you let sleeping dogs lie they do one of two things. Either they get in the way or you invariably step on them,' Jenny said, 'and then they bite you.'

'Oh very profound. And that's three things.'

'Let's go out into the garden and have this,' she said, picking up the coffee tray. 'That neighbour of yours might be out there. What does he do, by the way?'

I considered this question while I pulled out the garden chairs and the metal table and Jenny fussed about with a milk jug and teaspoons.

'Do you know, I have no idea. I think he used to be a footballer.'

Jenny sat down and sipped her coffee, eyes narrowed.

She shook her head. 'No, he doesn't look like a soccer player. I'm just curious to know what he does. I'll ask him next time I see him.'

I seized the opportunity to change the subject and ask the question that was uppermost in my mind.

'So what are your long-term plans?'

I hadn't actually seen my sister for three years. We had phoned and Skyped but after she met Trent she had gone to live at his gated community mansion outside Houston where they seemed to spend their days at the golf club (strange, because my sister's third marriage to Crawford came to grief because of his obsession with the game), wandering around their eleven bedrooms, having lunch with friends and presumably admiring Trent's impressive collections of modern money and classic Pringle sweaters.

'I don't know,' she said, sending me a pitying look, 'obviously

I need to look after you for a while. You're looking very drawn.'

Drawn. What did that mean? I looked tired? Ill? Old?

My sister put on a noble expression. 'I didn't know I missed you so much until I saw you.'

This statement reminded me of *I didn't know I loved you till I saw you rock and roll* and I was distracted enough to try and remember who sang it.

'I'm perfectly OK,' I said at last, rather irritated. Evidently my sister had entered a rare 'caring' phase. For a day or two she would treat me as though I might expire at any moment and encourage me onto the sofa with a blanket over my knees and then she would get bored and revert to her normal behaviour.

She gave me a patient smile. 'I know you. You're just being brave. But you've had to put up with a lot, it's hardly surprising if you look a bit haggard.'

'Haggard?'

She nodded. 'And drained.'

'Haggard, drained and drawn. Thanks, that makes me feel a lot better.'

'Ha ha, sounds like hung, drawn and quartered doesn't it? You need some summer sunshine.' She looked a bit misty eyed. '*Rough winds do shake the darling buds of May, and summer's lease hath all too short a date. Tumpty tum tee tum,* then there's something about death. You've had your buds shaken now you need something else. I know; I've had a brilliant idea! Let's go to Spain.'

'Let's not,' I said, 'let's get the painting finished and let me find some money from somewhere.'

She slumped down in her chair, disappointed with my reaction.

'I've got money. You don't think I left Trent empty handed, do you? I've been squirrelling money away for months, just in case. It's a pity you didn't do something similar really, isn't it? I know, let's go on the Internet and book a last-minute thing.

96

Somewhere like Malta or Majorca. Somewhere that's hot without actually frying your brain every time you go outside.'

'I want to get this painting finished, and get a proper job and a home of my own – and then I might have some money for holidays. Until then I'm lying low and regrouping.'

She thought hard for a moment. 'Well how about if I pay someone else to do the painting?'

'That's cheating and not what I agreed with Jess. I'm trying to feel good about myself. This is the first step.'

'How bloody tedious. Well, just think about it, that's all I'm saying.'

'I have some savings, so you don't need to press cash into my palm, and Jess is letting me stay here for nothing in exchange for my decorating and cleaning skills.'

'But what then? And what have you actually done about getting a job?'

'I've got a few feelers out with local doctors surgeries and I keep meaning to go into Stokeley to go to the supermarket. Oh I don't know. What can I do? I'll take to lying on the sofa, watching afternoon TV and knocking back cheap lager.'

'Don't be ridic— Ooh. Hello! I think he's there!'

We heard Ivy Cottage's back door slam and footsteps on the gravel. Jen twisted in her seat and looked over her shoulder. After a moment she turned back to me and raised her eyebrows in a silent question.

'You go and adios the dishes and I'll get him talking,' she hissed.

Adios the dishes? To say I was embarrassed would be an understatement of titanic proportions. I got up and went indoors before Jen could start up an inane conversation with me so as to attract Bryn's attention. As I began to adios the breakfast dishes in the sink I heard her calling out to him across the garden.

'Howdy, neighbour!'

Howdy? Really?

Then she disappeared through the garden gate and I heard her laughing. A laugh that had probably tinkled through the clubhouse of the Jack Nicklaus-designed course at the end of Trent's grounds. Careless, relaxed. One to show her ease with her surroundings, her absolute willingness to be happy, something I realised I had never managed.

Once I had finished the washing up we were supposed to be painting the sitting room. A space that was temporarily unfit for any sort of sitting. The chairs and sofa had been pushed into the middle of the room and covered with a dustsheet. Greg hadn't replaced the damaged rug yet so for now there was just a bare stone floor. I opened the windows, filled up the roller tray with paint and began work.

Outside I could hear voices. The deep rumble of Bryn's voice counterpointed at intervals by Jenny's bright chatter and gay laughter. I ground my teeth and painted on. After half an hour I heard her come in and start rummaging about in the kitchen. Then I heard the kettle boiling. Hang on! Was she was making him coffee? How much coffee did she need? Starbucks would open up a branch in the village if word got out that she was living here. I heard her opening and closing cupboards and I narrowed my eyes warily. She'd better not be taking my secret stash of KitKats.

Forty minutes later I had finished one wall and was gasping for a coffee myself. I went out into the kitchen, crouched under the window like a burglar avoiding CCTV cameras. I straightened up with indignation. Not only had she taken the KitKats (how the hell did she know to look in the empty Oat So Simple box?) but she had used the last of the milk! A burst of hearty laughter out in the garden only heightened my fury. I peered around the curtains to see where they were. They had wandered into Bryn's garden and were busy inspecting some climbing plant. At that moment Jenny looked round and saw me. She waved.

'Cooee!'

I mean, who actually says *Cooee*? Interfering, terminally embarrassing sisters, that's who.

'Cooee, Lottie. Come and join us!'

I closed my eyes in despair and went out into the sunshine.

Jenny waved at me again and beckoned me over. Bryn was chuckling and doing something in the bushes with a pair of lethal-looking loppers. He turned and grinned at me.

I didn't believe my sister's chatter had been all that amusing so I could only assume she had given him a potted biography of my school, dating and relationship history. She had probably told him how I wet myself on my first day in school. Cheers, Jen.

'Not seen you for a few days,' Bryn said.

His eyes were just as beautiful as I remembered. I could feel my usual blush starting and I tried to think of something – anything – else so that I didn't blurt out something about the impressive size of his tools.

'No, I've been incredibly busy.' I tapped my wrist and looked at my watch to reinforce my busy-ness. Unfortunately I had taken it off when I started painting so all I was doing was looking at my paint-splattered arm.

'Half past brilliant white,' Bryn said, his mouth twitching as though he wanted to laugh.

I gave a sickly grin.

'She's been quite the recluse, Brian –' Jenny said, leaning towards him in a conspiratorial fashion.

'Bryn,' I muttered.

'– and she's had a terrible, terrible time. I was telling you, wasn't I? I came back from Texas at the first opportunity—'

'As soon as Trent could manage without you,' I said. 'That's her latest man.'

Jenny and I exchanged wide-eyed glares.

'Of course, but my little sister always comes first. I was just asking Bryn if he has any children and he *doesn't*. He doesn't have a *wife* either, he's not married, isn't that nice?'

I fought down the twin impulses of stuffing my paintbrush in Jenny's mouth and curling up on the ground and turning to stone like an ammonite.

'It must be nice for you both to get together, Jennifer,' Bryn said.

My sister and I glowered at each other for a few seconds.

'Hmm. Well, we must be getting on,' I said. 'Jenny's only here for a few days.'

I grabbed her by one arm and steered her, protesting and *see-you-soon*-ing, back towards Holly Cottage.

'He owns a shop,' she said as I closed the kitchen door and bolted it in case she made a break for freedom. 'Just the other side of Exeter. He's got two others too. One near Okehampton and the other in Dorchester.'

'So?' I said.

'So he must be loaded. Think about it. Three shops, he owns that house too, I asked him.'

I groaned and hid my face in my hands at this point.

Jenny pursed her mouth. 'You could do a lot worse for yourself. He's well set up, easy on the eye—'

'I expect he's got all his own teeth too! Did you ask?' I stifled a scream. 'I won't be able to look him in the face again. You really are the limit!'

Her eyebrows shot up into her expensively highlighted hair.

'What? What have I done? You're hopeless. You moon around wishing things could be different and longing to meet Mr Right but do nothing to help yourself…'

'I've not mooned around once! And who said I wanted to meet Mr Right? Just because you can't stay single for more than five minutes!'

'You always used to complain how hard it was to meet people when all you did was go out drinking with a gang of girls and moan that all the good men are taken. After Jeremy died, Paul and I were married inside six months. I got Crawford to propose in two weeks. I proposed to Trent the night we met.'

'You're not married again though, are you?'

'You're getting very sour, Lottie. It doesn't suit you. I'm sorry for Ian, of course I am, but I'm far sorrier for you. You aged five years for every one you were with him. You were middle aged before your time. Dull clothes, dull life, dinner parties, it was awful to watch. Him and that old bat of a mother – pah! You're only thirty-four, Lottie. Don't you think it's time you had some fun before it's too late?'

She pulled a face and fiddled with her tiny Cartier Tank wrist-watch as she tried to organise her thoughts.

'Look, I like men, Lottie. I've never had any trouble with men, and nor did our mother. Right up until she died. Don't you remember visiting her at that nursing home? Those doctors adored her. And so did the male nurses. She always got the best room and first go in the biscuit tin. It's something in our genes. Nothing to do with looks it's all to do with attitude. Yes, my marriages didn't last forever. I'm probably impossible to live with –'

'You don't say?' I said, marvelling that I had managed to get a word in edgeways.

'– but they were jolly good fun! Why don't you try it? It's better than dripping about waiting to die.'

My sister does love the sound of her own voice but on this occasion, once I got over my annoyance, I had the sneaking suspicion she was right.

Still, I thought she deserved the silent treatment for a while so I washed my paintbrushes, found my laptop and flounced off to the supermarket to get milk.

In a determined frame of mind, I went to stand near to the customer service desk without actually catching anyone's eye. Two women in stiff polyester suits and matching purple nail varnish were standing there, discussing someone called Josie who had apparently been out on a hen night in Torquay and ended up in Grimsby. From the little I heard, I thought she sounded quite fun, despite the fact that she had both 'let down the team' and apparently 'caught the eye of management'. At last the elder and blonder of the two realised I was lurking.

'Can I help you, dear?'

'I wondered if I could, I mean is there any chance…are there any jobs available at the moment?'

The blonde woman looked at her companion and they pursed their lips at each other.

'Nothing going at the moment, is there, Sandra? Mr Phillips was only saying in the staff meeting yesterday there was going to be a bit of a crematorium on jobs.'

Her companion looked puzzled for a few seconds.

'Moratorium I think you mean, Val.' Sandra turned to me. 'Anyway it's all online these days. Go on the Superfine website. Then you'll find out if there is anything going. If there is – or if there isn't for that matter – you'll have to fill out a form and email it to head office. Then they get back in touch with you when there is a vacancy and then they send you to the area office to do a psychometric test. Then that goes off to Superfine's head office. It takes about a month for the results to come back.'

Val took up the story, tapping the counter in front of her for emphasis with one purple talon.

'And then there's the police check thingy and if that's OK then management – that's Mr Phillips – brings you into the store and you have a day's trial. And if they like the look of you then you have a probationary fortnight with a mentor. I was a mentor for that Caroline, wasn't I, Sandra, d'you remember?' She sucked in her lower lip for emphasis. 'Some of the longest days of my life. You do wonder what goes on in girls' heads these days. Anyway, after that, if it's OK, you can work on the till unsupervised for three months and then they decide if you're up to it, and offer you a contract if everything's fine and you haven't run off screaming.' Val chuckled.

Sandra chortled along with her. 'Like they say, you don't have to be mad to work here but it helps!'

They turned back to me.

'So does that answer your question, dear?' Val asked me kindly.

'Yes, yes, it does. I was only hoping for a job on the till or perhaps shelf stacking?'

'Still the same, dear, I'm afraid. These days it's all about form filling and box ticking. Between you and me I doubt we'd get in these days, would we, Sandra?'

Sandra roared with laughter.

'Oh I see. Well thanks so much,' I said and I wandered off, a bit startled. It was as though I was intending to apply for a job with MI5, not a small chain of West Country supermarkets.

Sandra and Val returned to their character assassination of Josie, who had now phoned in sick. Cue a great deal more head wobbling and eye rolling in disbelief.

I went into the store's café, conveniently next to the clothes, where there was free Wi-Fi and the possibility of half an hour's peace and quiet, and logged on. A few minutes' research and I found everyone at Superfine – We Love Your Food As Much As You Do – was committed to providing customers with an exceptional shopping experience but there were no vacancies at my local store or any stores nearby. I completed the online application anyway because the last few months had taught me that you never knew when things might change.

Then, in light of my sister's comments, I did a bit more surfing and found there were several outstandingly glamorous actresses the same age as I was and at least one major tennis star. I looked at their smiling flawless faces and then looked at my reflection in a nearby mirror. Another woman had been browsing in the racks of clothes and was checking her reflection at the same time, assessing the suitability of some zoo-print harem trousers. We caught each other's eye and both of us looked away embarrassed.

I hope she decided against the trousers, they made her bottom decidedly elephantine.

Jenny was right. I looked drained, haggard, dull, whatever other depressing adjective one cared to use. I wasn't so deluded that I didn't understand about photoshopping but I would bet my last KitKat that Gisele Bündchen didn't own a grey skirt and matching cardigan from the Edinburgh Woollen Mill like I did. Ditto Paris Hilton and Venus Williams.

What on earth had happened to me? Where had I gone? Had being with Ian prematurely aged me? I smoothed the skin on my face and neck and wondered if I should try a Croydon facelift. I dragged my hair back from my forehead and tried to sneak another look at myself.

Zoo-trouser woman was now trying on a neon-orange T-shirt and some black and white zebra-print leggings, an outfit that had nothing to recommend it unless she was looking for fancy dress and wanted to go as a pedestrian crossing.

I drank a cup of tea and ate half my toasted teacake while I thought about things. Would Kelly Brook have chosen to do the same thing under similar circumstances? Of course not! She would have teetered off on her Jimmy Choos with some huge rugby player boyfriend to Patisserie Valerie and nibbled an Exotic Fruit Tart (£3.40. I know because I Googled it) while a conveniently placed photographer took pictures of her scissoring legs and wide white smile.

I slumped in my seat and thought about Bryn. And then I thought about Bonnie and I was consumed with resentment.

Why was I six inches shorter and a stone heavier? Why did she have a cloud of Pre-Raphaelite red-gold curls while I just had plain brown hair? She had a red sports car and Bryn for a boyfriend. I had a four-year-old Vauxhall and my sister in the spare room. Even at thirty-nine and three husbands down, Jenny enjoyed herself more than I did. Life was very unfair.

I started on the second half of my teacake and then thought

better of it and pushed it to one side. My new life of positive action would start today and I knew what I needed to do first. I picked up my mobile and opened the contacts, scrolling down until I found the right one. Then I pressed the button and waited.

CHAPTER 9

Daisies – loyalty

'So,' Susan said, 'you'd better come in.'

It was nearly six months since I had last seen her and she looked terrible. Despite all the animosity that had existed between us, I felt sorry for her. She was never a large woman, but her navy twin set and pleated skirt now hung off her like sacks. There seemed to be nothing left of her except her iron will and perfect posture. Her hair, coloured and lacquered for so many years into a style similar to the Queen's, was now silvery, longer and scraped back out of the way into a clip.

I pressed my cheek to hers for a moment; still the same cold, softly scented skin. Perhaps she had a few more wrinkles and lines, but that wasn't surprising.

She showed me into the sitting room with great formality as though it was the first time I had been there. I remembered so many tedious visits, sitting in the unyielding armchair furthest away from the fire willing away the hours. Counting the plate collection on the wall. Listening as Ian boasted to her of his latest (fictional, as it turned out) deals and successes. Sympathising with her aches and ailments. Trying to keep up with the spiteful infighting of the local WI and their attempts to oust Susan from their midst. Following impenetrable tales of someone called That

Dreadful Gwen and her henchwomen Sylvia and Vivienne. The Mafia was nothing compared to that lot, I can tell you.

Susan settled herself opposite me, there was no offer of coffee so I guessed this was going to be a short visit. We sat in silence for a few moments, Susan pleating the folds of her skirt with thin hands. I could see her wedding ring swivelling around her finger as she did so. Nature abhors a vacuum and so do I; I struggled not to start babbling or asking stupid questions.

Eventually Susan broke the silence.

'So, here we are.'

'Yes, indeed!'

My tone was quite chirpy and inappropriate so I coughed and tried again more quietly. 'Yes. Jenny told me you wanted to see me about something.'

'I have had several phone calls from that woman. From Trudy Stroud.'

'Good grief!'

Susan looked up at the ceiling as though she found me immensely irritating for even speaking. The atmosphere between us was unbearable. It was as though she was holding in an outburst of hurricane strength by sheer force of will.

She pressed her fingertips to her temples. 'Why do you always have to be so noisy, Charlotte? Please just be quiet for once. I have asked her not to but she persists. Crying down the phone at me. At me!'

I shook my head in sympathy but suitably chastened I didn't speak.

'And then two weeks ago she began to ask for…'

'Ask for what?' I whispered.

Susan didn't speak for a moment then she stood up and walked to the window. Outside the garden was its usual, dull, regimented self. Neat rows of bedding plants and over-pruned rose bushes just as Trevor had planned them, thirty years ago.

'Ask for what, Susan?' I said. My head was spinning with the possibilities.

107

Susan didn't answer. I could see her shoulders were shaking slightly. Was she crying?

I got up, wondering what to do. Should I go over and put a consoling hand on her arm? Hug her? Did I dare?

At last Susan turned round and I realised she was angry. More than that, she was incensed. She looked at me, her grey eyes like chips of ice.

'This is very embarrassing. I don't know what to do. You're the last person I want to have involved in this but I can't think of anyone else to ask – I obviously don't want to involve the police. She wants money.'

My jaw dropped.

'Trudy wants money from you?'

Susan nodded. 'She says she has some personal items of Ian's and also some photographs.'

I stood there, gaping for a moment, not knowing what to say. Just as I was wondering if I dared ask how much Trudy was expecting, Susan spoke again.

'She wants five thousand pounds.'

At that point I laughed. 'She's not serious?'

'She says she is.'

'Or she'll what?'

She made a quick gesture with her hands, her shoulders very narrow and angular under her cardigan.

'That's blackmail, Susan.'

'Of course it is. But what can I do?'

'Ignore her. Tell her to sod off.'

She flinched at my language. 'But Ian's things…'

'A few snaps and a couple of pairs of socks. So what.'

'She says she'll burn them.'

'Then let her.' I couldn't imagine a few pictures of Ian in his leisure moments with his mistress were worth anything to anyone but Trudy.

'But you don't understand, she's got his passport, his birth certificate. She has the album containing his baby photographs. A sweater I knitted for him. Other things. She won't tell me. How could she say she's going to burn them? What sort of woman is she? I can't bear it. I can't sleep for worrying about it. I can't eat anything. I'm just so tired all the time.'

I moved a step closer. Treading carefully in case she lashed out at me. Her skin was pale, translucent, her eyes rimmed with red, flaking skin.

'Have you seen the doctor?' I said.

Susan regained a little of her old venom. 'Her? She's never there. I rang for an appointment a couple of times and she's always off. Her children. Sports day. Half term. I don't know why they employ her at all.'

'You could see Doctor Hawkins? He's very kind.'

Susan pulled a disapproving face. 'I don't want a man messing me about, asking questions.'

'You don't look well, Susan,' I said.

She shot me a poisonous look. 'What do you expect? He was my only child. My son.' Her eyes slid away from me as though she couldn't bear to look at me. 'You never loved him.'

'Yes, I did, Susan.'

'Not like I did.' She began to wring her hands together, her voice rose in despair. 'I don't know why I asked you here. You're as useless as ever. How? How could that woman have his passport and his birth certificate? I don't understand it. Why did he give them to her? His baby photographs!'

I opened my mouth to protest and then some of the depth of her misery struck me. If it made her feel better to have a go at me then so be it. It was blindingly obvious to me why Trudy had my husband's passport and birth certificate but I wasn't going to add to Susan's grief by telling her.

'Do you want me to speak to her? To Trudy, I mean?'

I saw a spark of hope flare in her eyes and then she looked away.

'You? What could you do? Nothing.'

'I can try.'

'Do what you like.'

It was the closest I was going to get to her agreement.

She stood and watched me for a moment while I fidgeted. In the past Ian had been there, taking her attention away from me for ninety-nine per cent of the time. Now she looked me up and down, her mouth pursed in dissatisfaction. I wished I had worn something more formal rather than jeans and a white shirt. But then I had already dispatched a large bin liner of what my sister called my 'middle-aged' clothes to a charity shop. I didn't have a lot left to choose from.

'You've lost weight,' she said.

What does a woman say to that comment? I opened my mouth to thank her for this rare compliment and then she spoiled it.

'You needed to, you were getting very fat.'

'You've lost weight too, Susan,' I replied, 'you look very frail.'

If we were being honest with each other I didn't mind having my say.

She ignored me. 'So will you speak to her? To that woman?'

'If you have no objections I will. It can't hurt, can it? But I'm not going to give her a penny.'

Susan pressed her lips together and nodded in approval. 'I wouldn't dream of asking you to.'

'Right then,' I said, wondering what to do next. How soon could I politely leave, I wondered? Susan's attitude was more straightforward.

'I want you to go now,' she said, 'and don't feel you need to come back if you don't get anywhere. I don't think we need to pretend any special friendship, do you?'

'No,' I said.

It made me rather sad. It's one thing to deal with one's own dislike of someone and quite another to face outright loathing from them in return.

Susan held out an arm and for a moment I thought she wanted to shake my hand, so I held mine out. She curled her lip at me and I realised she was directing me to the front door. I went.

Trudy bloody Stroud.

I had hoped I would never hear that name again. An unlikely femme fatale by anyone's standards. I'd met her a couple of times but she had just been someone Ian complained about a lot, he told me she worked in HR, if anything he said could be believed with hindsight. And then at the last minute, on Boxing Day, Ian had casually chucked out the idea of inviting some of his staff to our New Year's party as though he was doing me a favour. We were sitting around the dining table with Ian's mother who had joined us for Christmas as usual and who was now picking at the re-hash of overcooked food respectfully known as Boxing Day lunch.

'I know, I'll bring along some people from work if you like. We can invite Phil from accounts…'

I raked my memory banks. Ah, yes, Phil, a man distinguished only by his pedantry.

'…and I'd better ask Trudy from HR…keep her happy.' He'd rolled his eyes at this point.

Trudy – short, sullen, with the beginnings of a fine moustache.

I frowned, remembering something.

'Hang on, Trudy Stroud? I thought you couldn't stand her? You're always moaning about her.'

Ian looked puzzled. 'No, I'm not, you must be thinking of someone else. And Julian from IT.'

Julian – tall, with rimless glasses; spectacularly boring.

I could see this was shaping up to be some party.

Ian was warming to his theme. 'And of course—'

'I won't come, if you don't mind,' Susan interrupted before we could beg her to attend. She looked down and fiddled with the linen napkin in her lap. 'Ann is going to call round and we like to be alone with our memories on New Year's Eve. A bit of peace and quiet after all the madness of Christmas.'

Madness? What madness was that then? Perhaps Susan had spent the festive season in a parallel universe. I don't remember any wild behaviour since she had turned up on December 23, unless you count an unusually spirited exchange of views over a game of Scrabble on Christmas Eve. And just for the record, Qi *is* a word.

'Won't people have made other arrangements by now?' I said, ignoring her. I knew I was grasping at straws. 'I mean, it's very last minute.'

It was bad enough spending every Christmas with my partner's mother but after the dullest Christmas since records began, the prospect of spending New Year's Eve with Ian's workforce was too horrible to contemplate. I tortured myself for a few seconds, imagining the regulars at our local pub whooping it up at a raucous party. Perhaps they would form a conga line around the pub car park in the snow while I spent the evening with people ten years older than I who would want to discuss the forthcoming New Year kitchen sale in minute detail.

Ian laughed, confident of his pulling power.

'They won't turn down an invitation from me, will they? Not from their boss. Don't be daft. You wouldn't, would you? If Doctor Hawkins asked you round for a party?'

'God forbid.'

'I'll probably have a quiet supper and read,' Ian's mother continued, looking into the far distance and her perfect life on Planet Susan. Ian rolled his eyes and topped up his mother's wine glass. She didn't seem to notice. 'My friend Ann gave me such a lovely book for Christmas, about debutantes in wartime.'

Ian turned back to me, his enthusiasm growing. 'I'll fetch up some wine for the party from the cellar and you can do some nibbles.'

'Hah! So your part in the proceedings takes ten minutes but

I'm going to be in the kitchen chained to the stove for days!'

'I'll help,' Ian said. He took my hand and stretched his eyes wide in an attempt at sincerity. Then he pulled a funny face and I laughed and slapped his arm.

'You'd better if I'm expected to entertain the dullest workforce in England!'

I stood up and began clearing away the battered remains of our turkey pie while Ian and his mother discussed the weather and tried to trump each other's snow stories. One that Susan would always win because she had lived through the winter of 1963.

I returned with the Boxing Day special, a vast trifle in Ian's grandmother's glass bowl; a thing of unparalleled ugliness. Ian's eyes lit up.

'I think I deserve a dessert,' he said, as he always did.

He took a spoon and plunged it into the soft, custardy depths, lifting out a jelly-bottomed spoonful. It made a slurping, sucking noise as he did so and Susan flicked him a look of exasperation as though he had broken wind.

'I might have had a season, if I had been old enough,' she said mournfully, trying to stop the proceedings degenerating into rudeness, 'such elegance, such gaiety.'

'Would you care for a trifle of trifle, Mother?' Ian said, holding out the spoon to her and trying to stop laughing.

Susan shuddered and reached for the cheeseboard.

'Not for me, all that cream is terribly unhealthy,' she said.

'What do you think cheese is made of?' Ian said.

I think he must have been a bit pissed. Normally he never answered his mother back.

Susan ignored him, took a chunk of Stilton and spitefully sliced the nose off the Brie.

I went back to the kitchen to make the coffee.

It was nearly two forty-five and Susan would want to go home after watching the repeat broadcast of the Queen's speech. Why she needed to watch it twice on successive days I had no idea. Perhaps to reassure herself that the foundations of the Empire were still out there somewhere. And we weren't allowed to set Sky+. She seemed to think that to record the Queen and watch her at a time more convenient to us was disrespectful.

Her little blue suitcase was in the hall by the front door, her taxi had been pre-booked weeks ago. *The Sound of Music* was on at three forty. Ian had marked it for her in the *Radio Times* with a red pen.

I took the coffee tray through and left mother and son grazing through the tangerines and chocolate truffles and bickering about the latest political scandal that had dominated the newspapers over Christmas.

'The man's a damn disgrace,' I heard Ian say in a tone that brooked no argument. 'Got a perfectly pretty wife and sees fit to mess about with a lap dancer.'

'Such a shame,' Susan murmured, 'he always seemed so charming on the BBC. Do you remember that programme he used to do about wildfowl? *Feathered Friends.* Pity he took up shooting. I never quite felt the same about him after that. Lovely thick hair though; I like a good head of hair in a man.'

I went to start clearing up the kitchen. It was quite possible my brain was going to explode with boredom. Still, not long now and we would have done our duty and be free to enjoy the rest of Christmas on our own.

Susan's barbed comments about the possibility of us *getting married next year* would stop.

The taxi was on time and Susan and her little blue suitcase were bundled into it so she could get home in time to watch *The Sound of Music.*

'I'm just going to clear up the kitchen and put the dishwasher on,' I said as we waved her off.

'Oh, can't you leave it for now? We can do it together later,' Ian said.

114

A likely story.

'It's OK, it won't take long.'

Ian came and put his hands on my waist, rocking slightly, and kissed me. He tasted of whisky and smelled of a rather gorgeous aftershave I had bought for him.

He rested his forehead on mine and chuckled. 'We could, you know, have a little, you know, *nap*?'

This was code for sex. I was up for it although I thought it unlikely as we'd already had sex this month. But perhaps we could spend the rest of the day in bed, drinking our champagne as the winter light faded.

Then Ian looked past me and through the door to the kitchen beyond. I looked too; it was one dirty plate away from being a pigsty. It was all very well saying leave it but I was going to have to do it at some point.

I'm sure Ian believed kitchens really did look like the ones in his Lovell Kitchens brochure. Clean, polished worktops, an elegant vase of yellow roses and maybe a pristine child doing its home-work on the breakfast bar. In the background an improbably young and thin mother smiling as she took a freshly baked loaf out of the spotless oven. My kitchen on the other hand was a scene of some devastation and every surface was covered in used pans and food spills. I think Ian realised the extent of the problem and the moment passed. He let go of me.

'Well OK, get cleared up if you want to. Then come and sit with me. We can cuddle up and find something to fall asleep in front of.'

I watched Ian totter over to the sofa and flop down among the cushions with a theatrical sigh. He took the TV remote and fired the buttons at the screen, squinting with concentration. After a moment I heard Julie Andrews burst into song. By the time she got to the bit about the lark learning to pray, Ian was snoring.

CHAPTER 10

Wallflowers – courage in adversity

I didn't hang about after I left Susan's house. A couple of phone calls and I found Trudy. Lovell Kitchens had gone into receivership after Ian died and all the staff had been made redundant. Some of them went to work for the opposition in the form of the usual DIY giant superstores and Trudy was employed by one of them; Ram Builders. They were a booming company owned by a local Sikh family with a predilection for the colour orange and the slogan 'Do It Your Way'.

I tracked her down early one Monday morning out on the shop floor stacking tins of paint in aisle 15. I stood watching her for a moment, marvelling that this short, sullen creature in orange dungarees reminiscent of Guantanamo Bay internees had brought about such a seismic shift in my life.

After a few minutes she looked up from her task, a tin of Herring Gull Grey in each hand.

'Yes? What?' she said, the finer points of customer service still notably absent.

'Trudy,' I said, walking towards her.

She blinked with recognition and held a tin of paint in front of her to ward me off.

'Touch me and I'll have security on you.'

'How are you?' I said.

She narrowed her eyes at me, sensing some trickery.

'I just came to see how you are getting on. A bit different from your last job, isn't it?'

'What do you want?' she said.

'I want a chat.'

'Sod off. I'm working. I've got a mortgage to pay, you know.'

'Lucky you, I'm homeless and broke,' I said.

'Not my fault. You should have looked after him a bit better. It takes two you know?'

'Having trouble paying your bills, Trudy? Is that why you are trying to blackmail Ian's mother?'

Her eyes swivelled away. 'Dunno what you're—'

'Yes, you do. You know exactly what I'm talking about, Ian's personal possessions. His passport, his birth certificate. I assume the pair of you were going to do a flit to Spain or something.'

'None of your business.' Trudy flicked a glance at the CCTV camera overhead and resumed stacking paint cans.

'But you thought you could get some cash out of his mother, didn't you? For his baby photographs. How low are you?'

Trudy fixed me with her curranty eyes and blew out her cheeks.

'Five grand's nothing to her, the old cow. I knew you wouldn't cough up but she will. All that pissing about and pretending she was going to put the phone down. She'd do anything to get his stuff back.'

'She's devastated, Trudy. Her only son has died. How do you think she feels?'

Trudy shrugged and didn't reply.

'You do realise trying to extort money out of people is a criminal offence?'

Trudy flipped me the finger and went to get more paint from her trolley.

Realising it was now back in the land of the living so to speak, my phone rattled with several texts and then rang. It was the annoying tune my sister had chosen as her call tone; the theme music to *Monty Python*. I turned away and answered it while Trudy clumsily stacked tins of paint with a vicious expression on her face. It was a good job she hadn't found work as an egg packer.

'Lottie? Where are you?' Jenny said, strident and annoyed. 'I said I was going to have a lie in. Then I find you gone and there's no milk for coffee and nothing for breakfast that I can see. It's not my fault—'

I cut her off still squawking and fiddled around with my phone, pretending to check the time before I put it in my pocket.

Trudy went to walk past me. I stood my ground.

'Why don't you just give those things back? Susan's been made distraught by Ian's death.'

'So have I! No one gives a flying fuck about me though, do they? I don't count. You get all the glory, you and his bloody mother. What do I have to show for it? Sweet F.A. And he loved me. He loved me more than the pair of you stuck together.'

I gave a short incredulous laugh. 'Glory? What glory? Me, homeless but first of all having to face off to all his creditors who called at the house? Susan, burying her only son? Seeing the family business collapse? Where's the glory in that?'

'I've got nothing to show for it.'

'So you blackmail his mother? Five grand in exchange for his passport and his baby photograph album?'

'She can afford it,' Trudy said stubbornly.

'That's not the point. Ringing her up, pestering her, asking for money or telling her you would burn Ian's stuff. What would Ian have thought of that? What does your fiancé think? What was his name? Ken? Does he know what you are up to?'

She sneered. 'Ken's cool with it. I've told him Ian was sexually harassing me. He was angry, quite keen to make a claim and then, well—'

'You really are the pits. How far is five thousand going to get you, anyway? What about when that runs out? Are you intending to drip-feed Susan bits of Ian's life when you come across them? A hundred pounds for the return of a pair of his socks? Twenty quid for a handkerchief?'

Trudy put down the last of the paint tins and turned to face me.

'Oh, shut it, Lady Muck in the big house. Sneering. Swanning it over the rest of us at the work party. Looking down your nose at us. Well I had one over on you, didn't I? Boss's bit of stuff in your fancy shoes. I know things. Maybe things you wouldn't want to come out.'

I looked at her, really looked into her eyes. They were muddy, nondescript just like the rest of her. I saw a flicker of panic underneath the bravado. My initial impulse of punching her in the mouth faded.

'Trudy, this isn't going to get you anywhere. Give it a rest if you know what's good for you.'

Her expression faltered. 'I'm just saying. That's all.'

'Yes, fine, you say it if it makes you feel better.' I pulled my phone out. 'By the way, I've just recorded our conversation on my mobile. So I think we'll call it quits, shall we?'

There was a pause while her eyes swivelled from my mobile and back to me again.

'You tricky cow!' she shouted.

Further along the aisle I noticed an elderly couple, dithering between Frosted Sage and Meadow Green emulsion, move pointedly away.

'That's rich coming from you. I think we're even now. Unless you want Ken and the police to hear all about it.'

'That's blackmail!' she hissed, indignant.

I rolled my eyes at her.

'Big wow. You don't say?'

She shrank under the brim of her orange baseball cap and aimed a kick at a couple of rawlplugs on the floor.

I waved the mobile at her. 'I've got indisputable proof. It can and will be used in evidence against you in the highest court of the land. How do you think life inside will suit you, Trudy Stroud?' I think I got a bit *CSI Taunton* there. 'This has to stop. I'll be back here to collect all of Ian's things the day after tomorrow. Don't go off sick or mess me about. If you do I'll be going to your boss, then the police, and then I'll be contacting Ken. I don't know what load of old bollocks you've told him but I'm more than happy to put him straight. And the same applies if you phone Susan again. Understand?'

She narrowed her eyes at me. 'Are you threatening me?'

I narrowed my eyes back at her and licked my lips. It was like *Gunfight at the OK Corral*. I swear my trigger finger was itching.

'Damn right I'm threatening you. I've got contacts.' I had a sudden memory of the huge men from RCL standing on my doorstep when they came to repossess Ian's car. I remembered my script. 'And I know other people who won't be as *polite* as me and Susan are, if you get my meaning.'

She didn't answer, but turned and pushed the empty trolley away towards the swing doors and the stockrooms beyond them. I think she was trying to appear defiant but the set of her shoulders under the orange polo shirt was hunched and rather pathetic.

I returned to the car park, heart pounding, threading my way through arguing couples and crying children. Everyone seemed dissatisfied and harassed. The myriad delights of DIY as pictured in Ram's TV adverts were notably absent.

No couples stood laughing with delight at the range of wallpapers and not a single pneumatic blonde was wiggling around in a short skirt looking for a glass hammer or a long weight and giggling when the joke was explained.

I stabbed at the keys of my mobile. It turned out I had been bluffing and worse than that I had been incompetent. The volume control was turned down and I hadn't recorded anything except the fluff inside my pocket.

It was a miserable and thoroughly unsatisfactory day. And it got worse.

I got home to find Jenny standing on the bottom rung of the stepladder, dabbing half-heartedly at the window reveal in the sitting room. She turned as I came in and nearly fell off. There wasn't much paint on her brush and there was a tell-tale gin and tonic flush to her chest and a distinct slick of suntan oil on her cheeks. My guess was that she had sprinted to get in position when she heard my car pull into the drive.

'Did you remember the milk?'

'Yes, will six pints be enough, do you think?' I said, bad tempered.

She turned back and daubed some more. 'You've had a visitor.'

'Who?' I didn't like visitors.

Jenny shrugged. 'I don't know. She turned up at about ten thirty, woke me up – um, I mean she disturbed me, and said she had some stuff to do in Exeter and she would come back at two o'clock.'

'What did she look like?'

'Looked about fourteen, blonde, driving a huge SUV thing.'

'SUV? Honestly, you've only lived in Texas for five minutes. Do you have to speak American too?'

'Sport Utility Vehicle.'

'4x4. That'll be Jess, she owns this place. It was her idea to let me stay here.'

'I wonder what she wants?'

I looked at my watch. 'We'll know soon enough. I hope she's not evicting me.'

Jenny gave a trilling laugh and then, realising I wasn't joking, turned it into a high-pitched cough and investigated the paint pot again.

'I'll make some lunch,' I said.

'I'm starving,' she said, favouring me with an exhausted expres-

121

sion that spoke of many hours up the stepladder, not ten minutes. 'Where have you been?'

'I went to see Trudy.'

Jenny gave an appreciative gasp of horror.

'What happened?'

'I gave her a piece of my mind and said I would go to the police if she didn't bring Ian's stuff in to work on Wednesday. I'll have to go and get it.'

'Wow well done! D'you think she'll take any notice?'

'I threatened her with the heavy mob. And I said I had recorded our conversation on my mobile phone.'

Jenny looked at me with admiration. 'Good for you!'

'Well I recorded the inside of my pocket. The only thing you can hear is when she shouted at me and called me a tricky cow. I don't think that stacks up as evidence, do you?'

'Ah but *Trudy* doesn't know that, does she? Just look knowing and inscrutable like the woman does on *Silent Witness* when she's trying to get someone to confess.'

'How do you do that, then?' I asked.

'Well, how about this?' Jenny pulled a face, her chin lowered and eyes narrowed.

'You don't look knowing or inscrutable, you look constipated.'

'Well this, then?' she tried again, chin up and the corners of her mouth turned down.

I burst out laughing. 'You look like Marlon Brando in *The Godfather.*'

We practised looking knowing and inscrutable for a while, asking each other what about this, and frowning. Or this, and pursing up our mouths and looking out of the corners of our eyes.

I went out and mowed the grass. Bryn had been as good as his word and given the mower a once over. He had done whatever was necessary and now it obediently striped up and down the lawn in a very pleasing fashion. I had to keep stopping and looking behind me to admire the effect.

When I'd filled up the green waste bin and made lunch we did a bit more painting. A short time later Jess arrived, country girl personified in a sweet floral tea dress and snowy white gym shoes. She had a huge bouquet of flowers and a Little Red Riding Hood wicker basket over one arm. She ran to give me a hug, and when introduced to my sister hugged her too.

We went into the kitchen and I made tea while she arranged the flowers and unpacked the treats and dainties she had brought with her in the basket. It felt like I was receiving a Red Cross parcel. Jenny exclaimed with delight over the chocolate truffle cake and deep-dish apple pie Jess had baked and wrapped in a red gingham cloth.

We sat around the kitchen table with tea and goodies. Jess said all the flattering things that could be said about my decorating and cleaning. She was amazed, so pleased, etc. But all the time I noticed that she was giving me nervous little glances, so I wasn't surprised when she came out with what was troubling her.

'I got some news,' she said.

I didn't like the sound of that.

'Oooh, are you expecting?' Jenny trilled.

Jess fidgeted in her chair and rolled her eyes. 'Get out of here! No!'

Jenny wasn't giving up. 'Going on holiday?'

'Um no, I—'

'Discovered a hairdresser Lottie can go to? I mean look at her!'

'Jenny, will you just let Jess speak?'

My sister twittered and made zipping motions across her mouth.

Jess took a deep breath and threw me an apologetic look that froze my blood.

'I told you I was thinking of selling Holly Cottage,' she said. 'Well, I might ask an agent to come round to see the place and give me an idea of what it's worth. I'm going to give you first dibs. I mean, do you wanna buy it?'

I looked into the far distance, a bit shell-shocked by this development.

'I'd love to but I haven't got the money at the moment. And I can't imagine any bank would give me a mortgage.'

'Well no, but y'know, if you had a job?' Jess said.

Well, yes, I supposed that might have made a difference. But not quickly enough. Not with the high security clearance needed by my local supermarket. So I did what I did best under these circumstances, I prattled.

'Will it take long to sell? Stupid question, I don't suppose you know. I mean, gosh, the housing market is a bit…it could go in days, although the legal side might take longer. You never know, it might take a while to sell. But this is a lovely location, unless you don't want to be so isolated. Not much they could do about that. Ha ha!' I stuttered into silence.

Jess pulled a pained expression. 'I'm awfully sorry, Lottie. But I did tell you I was thinking of selling. And the Websters were a wake-up call to me. A real nuisance and they've caused thousands of pounds of damage. Can you see why I want to sell? I do hope you do. Oh dear, I should have got Greg to come with me but he wouldn't come. He doesn't like coming here very much.'

'Of course I see. I do understand, honestly. So, shall I keep on with the decorating?'

'Yes, absolutely, if you don't mind? You're doing a fabulous job. And I still need to do something about that broken wardrobe and I know the loft insulation needs to be increased. I'd really appreciate it, and you still need somewhere to live, don't you? Give us both time to think about things.'

I felt as though I was in limbo, caught between no rock and no hard place.

'Yes, I see. Thanks.'

I realised with some dismay that in the time I had lived there I had grown fond of Holly Cottage. I loved the early morning view from my bed over the hazy hills. I could see the little branch line railway with its brave train heading off into the darkness once an hour. I had got to grips with the plumbing. I knew when the bins went out and what the recycling lorry would and wouldn't accept. Leaving here was going to be a bit of a wrench. And on top of that, where would my sister go?

Jess patted my hand and gave me a sympathetic smile.

'I promise I'll give you plenty of notice. Let's have some cake,' she said, 'there's not much that doesn't look better after a bit of my truffle cake.'

'That's a splendid idea,' Jenny said, apparently not at all disconcerted by these developments.

One thing Jess had said stuck in my mind.

'Why doesn't Greg like coming here?' I asked.

Jess turned round from the cupboard where she had been rummaging for small plates and pulled a face.

'Bryn. They fell out years ago. Before I met Greg. Years before. I never did get to the bottom of it. Something to do with their mum. I can't say much about it because I don't know. Greg won't talk about it.'

'But he was upset by something Bryn did? Or didn't do?' I said.

Jess began carving up the cake into slabs and levering them onto plates.

'I think so,' she said, 'all I know is it was something about borrowed money. And then it all turned very nasty. It never got sorted out and then Greg went to France and after that Spain.'

'Money is the root of all evil,' my sister said piously.

'Actually, it's the love of money which is the root of all evil,' I said. 'There's nothing wrong with money.'

Jenny pursed her mouth and took a slice of cake.

'Smart arse.'

By the time Jess left we were so full of cake and other carbohydrates that we could hardly move never mind carry on painting the sitting room. Outside the afternoon was warming up nicely; the sky rich and blue and cloudless.

We did a bit more painting, then Jenny said she was going upstairs to sort out some laundry but I think she was planning a nap to sleep off the calories. I went out into the garden and pottered about doing a bit more weeding and general messing about. After about an hour, I heard Bryn's truck pulling into the drive and my heart did a little jig of excitement. I shook out my hair in what I hoped was a rumpled and attractive cloud of curls. And not as though I had just pulled off a red elastic band that I had found on the driveway where the postman had dropped it.

Bryn came to call to me over the fence between our two gardens and like a distracted child I dropped my handful of dead roses and went to see what he wanted.

'I wonder if you could help me out,' he said.

He was wearing his CAT boots, jeans and a white T-shirt with an artistic smear of mud across the broad expanse of his chest.

'Sure,' I said, deadheading a barely opened rose bud on the fence between us and trying to appear casual.

'There's a hot tub round the other side of my house. I don't know if you've noticed it. It needs servicing but the only time the chap can come and do it is later on this week, and I'm going to be away for a few days. I'm taking Bonnie back to London.'

The only parts of this I really heard were the words *hot* and *tub*. After that I sort of drifted off. I batted away the thought of Bryn in the aforementioned tub because Bonnie's sleek figure also featured in that particular image. I could almost picture her in a spotty retro bikini, frolicking about next to him in a very irritating fashion.

'So could you?' Bryn was saying. 'Would it be convenient?'

Gosh, his eyes really were very blue indeed. I pulled myself together.

'Could I what?'

He sighed. 'Could you let him into the garden when he gets

here and sign the docket to say he's been round and serviced the tub?'

'Of course.' I casually deadheaded another rose and cut the end off a finger of my gardening glove at the same time. I made a small, shocked bleating noise that I converted into a cough.

'You're a love. Thanks. Here's the key.'

I took it. 'What's this for?'

Bryn shook his head and laughed.

'I told you. I knew you weren't listening. It's for the padlock on the side gate. I don't need to open it very often, but I won't be here to let him in through the house. If you could let him in when he arrives? He drives a blue van with "Tom the Tub Man" on the side. It's a bit of a clue. OK?'

'OK, no problem.' I tucked the key in my pocket.

'So how are you getting on? I haven't seen much of you recently. I've been away doing some work for a client near Launceston.'

'I'm fine! Well, no, I'm not very fine actually. Pretty crap. Well you know. Fine I suppose.'

Bryn looked confused. 'Well which one is it? Fine or not?'

I groaned. 'Mostly not fine, if I'm honest. Jess was here earlier; she came to tell me she's thinking of selling Holly Cottage. It's not definite yet but if she does I'm going to have to move out. I don't suppose many people would want to buy a place with a sitting tenant who doesn't pay any rent. And there's only so many times a house needs decorating. Even I know that.'

He frowned. 'Selling? Where will you go if she does?'

'Dunno. Jess said she was going to think about it and then she might get an agent round to value it, so she came to tell me.'

'That's a shame. I've got quite used to you being here. You're the most entertaining neighbour I've had in a long time.' He smiled down at me.

'I'm used to being here too. You know. Um…'

To my horror I felt quite weepy all of a sudden. I hesitated, shifting from one foot to the other, not quite knowing what to

127

do. I managed to stand on the trailing lace of my trainer and almost fell over. Bryn reached over and grabbed me, steadying me. Was it my imagination or did he hold on to my hand for longer than was actually necessary? No, it was definitely not my imagination. He was holding my hand and looking at me, his mouth curving in a gentle smile.

'You're the most accident prone woman I've ever met,' he said. 'How did you make it this far without serious injury?'

I enjoyed the feeling of my hand in his for a moment. Then I drew breath to tell him about my fall out of an apple tree when I was five. The many trips to A&E with various sporting-, climbing- and glue-related incidents. The time I had both legs in plaster for a week because my X-rays got mixed up with someone else's. Fortunately before I could, Bryn looked at his watch and gasped.

'Blast, I've completely forgotten. I was supposed to be on the other side of Exeter in ten minutes and it's going to take me half an hour to get there. I've been working on a garden plan for Lady Trehorlicks.'

He gave me a brisk wave and left. I listened to the purr of his truck travelling down the hill and wondered why suddenly it took on a rhythmic sound. Then I realised the noise was coming from the open bedroom window. It was my sister upstairs, snoring. Typical!

I went into the kitchen and started making a bit of noise. The odd door slam and I rattled a few drawers, waiting for Jenny to come downstairs. Nothing happened. I opened a bottle of red and sloshed a good measure into a glass. I didn't often set out with the deliberate intention of getting pissed but today I was prepared to make an exception. Still there was no sound from Sleeping Beauty upstairs, so I started bashing a saucepan with a ladle. Like you do.

A few minutes later Jenny appeared, blinking and rubbing her face.

'What the hell are you doing?'

'I'm getting pissed. Care to join me?' I said.

Jenny shrugged. 'Oh, OK, if it's strictly necessary.'

I know my sister can sometimes be a pain but she is also very quick on the uptake when it matters.

'It is.'

I poured her a glass and she sipped it.

'Gosh, this is really nice. I thought you were down to Superfine Bogoff Premier Cru?'

'Ha! One of the few things I came away with when I moved out of Ian's house. His wine cellar,' I said.

'Brilliant, well done. What's this then?'

I held out the bottle. 'Don't know, I chose it because it's a nice label.'

'Very pretty,' Jenny said.

'It's a 1967 Barolo Adriano, I even have the tasting notes if you're interested?'

'Absolutely, go for it.'

I cleared my throat. '*This lovely Barolo from the very good 1967 vintage is sweet and rich with a fragrant bouquet and a lovely lingering length. Drink now – 2020.* I think we'll drink it now, shall we? Although it does say it makes a good anniversary gift.'

Jenny pulled a face. 'Ha! Good joke. Anniversary, we won't be doing that any time soon.'

'No, we don't seem to have much luck with men, do we? Here's to better times.'

We clinked glasses and I knocked back the remains of my glass and refilled it.

'I saw Bryn while you were upstairs,' I said, trying to sound casual.

'Oh yes? How did you get on?'

'I made a complete prat of myself as usual, falling over and jabbering mindlessly. Then he went off somewhere in a steaming rush. Doing some work for someone called Lady Trehorlicks down towards Honiton.'

'Lady Trehorlicks, how marvellous. I can practically imagine her. Six feet tall, built like a battleship, in a cord skirt with a trail of Labradors slobbering all over her.'

I pulled a face. 'Or she could be twenty-six, built like a pole dancer in designer jeans and wellingtons with a trail of men slobbering all over her.'

I refilled Jenny's glass; the wine was slipping down nicely.

Jenny tried to quash my vision. 'Or she could be a Miss Marple type in crêpe de chine, a hand-knitted cardigan and a straw bonnet. She'd be talking about the war all the time and insist on showing you round the ancestral pile.'

'Hmm, or she could be—'

Jenny emptied the last of the bottle into my glass. 'Here's to a nice bottle of wine,' she said, trying to distract me from a slow descent into depression.

'There's another one over there,' I said, nodding at the worktop. 'I've opened it to breathe.'

'A likely tale.'

I looked back at the tasting notes. 'Well, it is ninety quid a bottle, the least I can do is give it some air.'

Jenny spluttered a little. 'Good grief.'

'If Jess is going to sell Holly Cottage then it will be one less thing to move if we knock it back, I suppose.'

'Happy to help, it really is rather splendid.' Jenny took another slurp.

'We should be eating something.' I looked back at the tasting notes. '*This fine wine is a splendid accompaniment for venison, fillet steak and all game.* Fuck that for a game of soldiers. I've got some fish fingers. What do you think?'

'Perfect. Although we should be drinking white with fish, surely?'

I held up a finger. Or it might have been two; everything was going a bit blurry. 'Good point; I'll see what I can find.'

I wandered off into the garage and came back with another bottle and held it up.

'What do you think? It's a 2009 Aile d'Argent Blanc Château Mouton Rothschild.'

'It's got a pretty label,' Jenny said, 'if that's what we are judging it on.'

I carried on reading in a silly voice. '*An outstanding 2009 vintage, this delightful dry white wine from Château Mouton Rothschild exhibits more fat than normal.* More fat than normal? What the fuck does that mean?'

'I'm exhibiting more fat than normal, too,' Jenny said mournfully, pinching a fold of flab above her waistband.

I carried on. 'Listen to this; *Marmalade notes present in this honeyed, crisp, refreshing wine, loads of personality. Drink now – 2022.* What do you think, should we wait until 2022?'

'Oooh, drink it now,' Jenny said. 'After all, you've got the fish fingers all ready.'

'It's not very chilled,' I said doubtfully, holding it against my cheek.

'Well, stick an ice cube in it. Or run it under the cold tap.'

'Fair enough.'

'How much is this one?'

'Eighty quid. No wonder Ian wouldn't let me into the cellar. When we had dinner parties, which wasn't very often in the last year, I'd pick up whatever was on offer at Waitrose. Two for ten quid and some free chocolates.' I held the bottle under the cold water and dropped it with a clang. 'Bugger. Where's the bottle opener?'

I rummaged around in the kitchen drawer until I found one and dug the screw into the cork.

'We don't have to let this breathe though, do we?'

'Deffo not.' Jenny finished off the last sip of red still in her glass and held it out. 'Pass some over.'

I frowned. 'That isn't even a white wine glass, is it? I can tell the difference you know. Ian was really particular about that.'

'Bugger knows,' Jenny said.

'Don't call me Bugger Nose,' I said, throwing the cork at her. 'Do you want a clean glass?'

We looked at each other for a moment before both of us spluttered with laughter.

'I'll stick the fish fingers in,' I said, 'and you can tell me all about Trent and the *Atlantica*.'

'Yes, it was fantastic. A lovely ship too, but miles to walk back to your cabin if you forgot something. We had a butler called Sven, he was rather gorgeous.'

'Sven the butler. Sven. That sounds funny, doesn't it, when you say it a lot? Sven. Good morning, my name is Sven.'

We giggled for a bit and said his name a bit more.

'So does this mean you're not getting married after all?'

Jenny pulled a face and shrugged. 'I don't honestly know. Why – did you fancy being a bridesmaid?'

'I've been a bridesmaid three times for you. That's enough, isn't it? I still haven't forgiven you for the dress I had to wear when you married Crawford.'

'Ah, the one his sister designed? Yes, it was a bit much,' Jenny admitted.

I thought about it.

'A bit much? Which part, the dress, the fringe, the shoes laced up to the knee, the hat or the wide black patent belt around my fat gut?'

We screamed with laughter and I threatened to get the photo album out and remind her but then I remembered there was some dip in the fridge and some pitta bread somewhere so I went to find that instead.

'And, *and*, Crawford – I can say this now, Jenny, because he's long gone – was a complete prat. And his brother…'

I clicked my fingers at her as we struggled to remember his name.

'Um. Tall, balding, with eyes like gooseberries.'

'Gregor, that was it. Gregor the Groper. Well he tried it on with me.'

'Tried what on?' Jenny said frowning.

'Well not my *hat*, dear. Not my wee tartan *bonnet* that made me look like I'd collided with a pheasant on my way to the wedding. He suggested we go outside for a cigarette.'

'Yes?'

'Via the back seat of his car.'

'Really? He always was classy.'

I refilled our glasses.

'I can't taste any marmalade in this wine, can you?' I said.

We did a bit of slurping and sucking as though we knew what we were doing – without the spitting out, of course.

'I can taste wine,' Jenny offered.

'Brilliant. It says this one goes well with samphire and sea bass or the delicious fruity notes are a pleasant accompaniment to own-brand hummus and salt and vinegar crisps.'

We carried on slurping and tasting until the fish fingers were done and then had a mild argument about ketchup or mayonnaise.

'I was fifteen when you married Jeremy and I had to wear the ruched thing that made me look as though I had my skirt tucked into my knickers,' I said.

'It was fashionable then.'

'Yes, if you had a thing for the Spice Girls. Or Bananramarama. You're lucky I'm still talking to you.'

I went to look in the cupboard for chocolate and came back with my 'secret' hiding place box held out in front of me accusingly.

'You've eaten all my secret KitKats,' I said.

'Well, they weren't very secret then, were they? You liked the short dress you wore when I married Paul, didn't you?'

'Dark blue with a white belt. All his friends kept mistaking me for a waitress and ordering drinks,' I said.

'I don't think it was because of your dress, I think it was just the way it was. Do you know, the bar bill was the most expensive thing about that wedding. By a very long way. I remember Paul crawling under a table with a bottle of scotch as the music for our first dance started. I should have made a run for it then.'

I shook my head at my sister. 'Well why didn't you? Why on earth did you marry them? That's what I can't understand. Ian asked me to marry him when we first got together. He asked me four times. It became a bit of a joke really. I couldn't see the point. Especially with your example to follow.'

'Why didn't you marry Ian? He was –' she tried to find the right word '– he was very – he was very…'

I prodded the table with one finger. 'He was very predictable.'

'Oooh that's a long word.'

'I didn't know all about the debts and the gambling. I just knew it didn't feel quite right. And I shouldn't say it but I don't think he was very good in bed.'

Jenny frowned, puzzled.

'Well was he or wasn't he?'

I tried to explain. 'I only ever went to bed with him, so how would I know?'

'Bloody hell. Really?' Jenny said.

We'd finished off the white by now and I tottered to the windowsill to get the other bottle of red.

'Well just 'cos you put it about – how many men have you—'

'More than you, obviously!'

'I'd like to go to bed with Bryn. Oh!' I clapped a hand over my mouth, horrified. 'Did I really say that?'

'Why don't you?' Jenny asked, fishing a bit of sediment out from between her teeth.

'He might not want to. He might not fancy me.'

Jenny laughed and gently banged her forehead on the table. 'There is no such thing as a man who wouldn't fancy you, Lottie. You're lovely. Oh, hang on a minute. Perhaps banging my head on the table was a bad idea.' She reeled slightly and held on to the chair until things settled back into focus.

'So go on, why did you marry them?' I said.

'Because Dad said no one would ever ask me. And they did,' Jenny said at last.

'How absolutely stupid. At least Ian could get me white goods at cost price. And I had two new kitchens in five years. And they were top of the range. And they had Corian worktops.'

I waited for her to be impressed.

'Whoop de doo,' she said. 'So why didn't you marry Ian? Remind me.'

I rested my chin on my hand and thought about it.

'He wasn't the one,' I said at last, and hiccupped. *In vino veritas.* 'I always knew he wasn't the one. And I wasn't prepared to risk it. You know, I've realised something really incredibly important.'

Jenny sat up a bit straighter and looked interested. 'What? The American Electoral system is a fucking joke?'

'No, you twit. I know you shouldn't speak ill but I've realised our parents were the most incompatible pair to ever walk into a registry office. They had a miserable life together, scoring points and squabbling for thirty something years. Arguing about every meal, every twatting holiday. They even used to argue about what was on the conveyor belt on the *Generation Game*. Do you remember?'

'Yes, and?'

I stabbed my finger onto the tabletop to emphasise the point.

'I never wanted to get married if it was going to be like that. And *you* got married to prove it didn't have to be like that. I was scared of getting married and you couldn't stop yourself. See?'

'I suppose so,' Jenny said.

It felt as though I had discovered the secrets of the universe.

'Weird. They fuck you up, your parents, don't they?'

CHAPTER 11

Cherry blossom – kindness

Two days later I was back in the canyon-like aisles of Ram Builders looking for Trudy. Even at 9.30 a.m. on a Wednesday morning it was quite busy.

Customers seemed to fall into two camps. The ditherers wandered around with vacant expressions, picking up leaflets on kitchen design or handfuls of paint colours. The others knew exactly what they needed and had written lists and had a determined glint in their eyes. I found Trudy skulking at the back of the shop in the paint aisles, trying to get away from a couple of ditherers. I stood at a reasonable distance to make sure she could see me, and waited.

Mr and Mrs Ditherer wanted some paint to make their hallway lighter, but wanted it to be a colour somewhere between Plum and Damson. They were about to find out they had picked the wrong girl to help them.

'I don't know. I just stack shelves,' Trudy said, lower lip stuck out.

'But is there a light-reflecting paint that's quite dark?' Mr Ditherer hadn't assessed the situation very well; he wasn't about to give up.

'I shouldn't think so.' Trudy flicked me a sour look. 'How can purple be a light-reflecting paint? You'd better ask—'

'Oh not purple! Maybe not quite Damson, more a—'

'I don't know,' she said, 'and I don't fricking—'

'Light plum? Is there such a thing?' Mrs Ditherer flicked through her colour chart.

Trudy dropped her head back and rolled her eyes. 'Bloody Norah!'

'That's a strange name for a paint. Oh.' Mr Ditherer realised his helper wasn't going to help. 'Well with your attitude, young lady…'

Hands limp by her sides, mouth hanging open, Trudy listened to him voicing his disappointment and threatening to write to Mr Ram, whom he claimed was a neighbour and personal friend.

'You'll have a bloody job,' she fired back with a spray of spittle. 'He lived in Beverly Hills and he's been dead for twelve years.'

'I've been coming to this place since it opened and this is the first time I've been treated like this!'

Trudy pulled off her orange baseball cap and flung it at him. 'Well count yourself lucky you got away with it this long, you bloody nitwit!'

Mrs Ditherer tugged at his sleeve. 'Come on, Arthur, she's drunk or worse. We'll go to Homebase.'

They scurried off and Trudy turned her Medusa stare onto me, full beam. I returned the knowing-but-inscrutable look I had practised with my sister. Chin up, mouth turned down. I hoped I didn't look too much like Marlon Brando in *The Godfather*.

'What?' she said.

'Don't "what" me. You know why I'm here.' I pulled my mobile out of my pocket and waggled it at her.

'Oh for fuck's sake.' Trudy picked her baseball cap off the floor with an ungainly side swipe and jammed it back over her eyes.

'Have you got the stuff?'

She flicked a glance at the CCTV cameras. 'I might have.'

'Hand it over then.'

She stood dumbly, looking at me, and unexpectedly Ken slithered out from behind a rack of masking tape. He was as grubby and as beige as ever, but to give him his due he came and stood protectively in front of Trudy and stared at me.

'Trudy told me what you did,' he said, 'trying to blackmail her.'

I resisted the urge to swipe his filthy spectacles off his nose and clean them.

'What! I just came to get some of Ian's personal possessions back so that I could return them to his mother.'

'My fiancée, Trudy, has suffered enough over all this,' he said, 'not only did she lose her career prospects but she's had to put up with months of sexual harassment from her former employer. Months. She could have put a claim in. It was only her loyalty to the company that stopped her.'

I laughed at that. What on earth had Trudy been telling him?

Ken ignored me and ploughed on.

'And then your precious Ian gave her this stuff to look after. Even though she didn't want to. And when she tries to give it back to his mother, the old cow accuses her of asking for money. Which she never.'

'Fine, Ken, whatever you say.'

'It's Mr Bogle to you,' he said, 'if you don't mind.'

'Well, Mr Bogle, I just want to collect the stuff and then this whole miserable business will be over,' I said.

'Yes, well, I don't want to hear no more about it,' he said.

'Nor do I.'

'Good.'

'Good.'

We stood and huffed at each other for a few minutes, Trudy looking up at Ken with an impenetrable expression. Perhaps she was congratulating herself on how easy it had been to fool him. Maybe she was planning a reward for him, a night of ecstasy involving some Ram special offer jubilee clips and a can of WD40.

The tannoy system crackled and a message boomed out over the store. Not the usual bored woman wanting someone from cleaning to go to aisle 4, but this time a man's voice, annoyed, urgent.

'*Will Trudy Stroud come to the manager's office immediately. Trudy Stroud to the manager's office immediately.*'

Trudy rolled her eyes at Ken and swore under her breath. A few seconds later I saw Mr Ditherer coming back down the aisle towards us. I think perhaps he had reflected on Trudy's sales methodology and complained about it. He stood breathing heavily a few paces away. Angry as he was, his innate good manners prevented him from interrupting a conversation.

'Hand the stuff over in ten minutes or I'll break your legs,' I said to her through stiff lips.

'No more talk like that, please,' Ken said, straightening the greasy cuffs of his anorak.

Trudy stood mute, looking at me, hating me. She had tried to be something. A seductress, an irresistible lover, a blackmailer, and had failed at all three. Suddenly, much to my surprise, I felt sorry for her. I looked at Ken. He might be a bit down at heel and lacking in charisma but he loved her enough to propose and put that unremarkable garnet ring on her finger. I hoped he would stick by her, help her find some level of satisfaction in her life.

At last Trudy spoke. 'You'll get the stuff but I'd better not get a visit from the police neither. Or I'll be phoning up my contact at the *Echo*. I've got private pictures and I've still got the handcuffs and the feather duster he wanted to use on me too.'

I flicked a glance to see how Ken was taking this information. He curled his lip at me.

'Disgusting,' he said. 'He was a filthy pervert. My fiancée has suffered a great deal at his hands. Done things no decent woman—'

'That's enough, Ken, we don't want to go into all that again,' Trudy said. 'Right, I'll go and get it and then you can leave me alone.'

Mr Ditherer turned smartly on his heel, bumping into his wife who was scurrying after him.

'You were right, Connie. This place is a drugs den. I'm going to the papers.'

I left Ram Builders some time later with an Aldi carrier bag filled with the flotsam and jetsam of Ian's affair. As I hurried to the front doors, I saw Trudy being escorted to the manager's office by an enormous security guard. The sort you usually see outside nightclubs wearing dark glasses at midnight, not in a warehouse full of bickering couples where the most intoxicating item was a bottle of white spirit covered in warning stickers. A few paces behind her was dogged Ken.

I drove away, not convinced that Trudy wouldn't come after me with a mole wrench. After a few minutes, when I was sure I was not being followed, I pulled in to a petrol station and examined my haul.

Ian's birth certificate, passport, a photograph album of his babyhood, a Fair Isle sweater hand knitted by his mother for Christmas some years ago, an engraved silver cigarette box that had belonged to his father and a very basic mobile phone with a charging cord wrapped round it made up the contents of the bag. I took out the mobile; Trudy had smashed the screen and removed the battery. I wound down my window and dumped it in the litterbin. There was no need for Susan to see that; it would only make things worse. I would just pass on the things she knew about and would be pleased to get back. Still slightly pumped up with adrenaline, I abandoned my plan to go back to Holly Cottage and resume decorating. Instead I turned the car round and set off for Susan's house. As I pulled up my mobile pinged with a message. I opened it and read it. I didn't think it was good news.

Have been trying to contact you. Can you give me a ring? Speak soon. Jess. X.

'You again,' Susan said.

She was thinner than I had ever seen her, her skin grey with tiredness. The scent of her home floated out into the still air. Air freshener, Pledge polish, fabric softener.

She hesitated for a moment, looking at me with her usual expression of suspicion and distaste, and then she saw what I was carrying. She looked up at me her eyes sparking with hope.

'Is that…?'

'Yes.'

She gave a little gasp and stepped back from the doorway in order to let me in. I wiped my shoes on the mat and handed over my swag. It was strange that something so important should look so insignificant. The writing on the plastic bag was flaking off, the handles stretched and distorted.

Susan left me standing in the hall, not sure what to do next. She went into the sitting room. I closed the front door behind me and took a few steps towards her.

I could see her pulling things out, smoothing her fingers over the photo album, opening and closing the silver box, clenching her hands in the sweater, pulling it up to her face. Inhaling. Perhaps catching the last trace of Ian's aftershave deep in the wool.

I felt the unexpected sting of tears behind my eyes. I had never liked Susan but I could empathise with her need for this last connection with her only son. I felt ashamed of all the unkind thoughts I had harboured against her. The times when I had made excuses to avoid coming here. I realised that I had little to be proud of. I had not raised a child. I hadn't really made Ian happy. I had been selfish. I had been careless.

I remembered her at that last Boxing Day dinner, mellowed by her sherry aperitif, two glasses of wine and a tot of Baileys. She had watched Ian across the table with a level of adoration I would never feel for him.

She had nodded as he explained how he needed to reorganise things at work. Smiled with approval as he outlined our plans to go to France for our summer holidays. We'd been offered the use

141

of a customer's *gîte* near Dordogne; it sounded fabulous. I had been looking forward to it. She frowned when Ian added sugar to his coffee and flicked me an accusing glance.

Ian had opened his new bottle of Highland Park, filled a generous glassful and took an appreciative sniff.

'Sure I can't tempt you?' he said vaguely to both of us.

'God no,' I said, reaching for the wine.

'Oh no, whisky is a man's drink,' Susan said, ducking her chin back into her neck as though he had offered her meth. 'You're just like Daddy; he loved a good whisky after dinner. Only one. He was very moderate.'

'Like father like son, eh?' Ian said, leaning back in his chair.

At last Susan turned, dry eyed, to look at me.

'Thank you,' she said, 'this is the last thing I wanted out of life.'

'I'm glad I could do it,' I said. I took another step forward. 'I'm so very sorry.'

She nodded and looked down at the sweater. 'I'm tired.'

'Can I make you a cup of tea?'

She didn't answer for a moment, but then she nodded.

I went into the kitchen and flicked on the kettle. Everything was spotless and shining. The worktops cleared and cleaned, the tea bags still in the tin decorated with kittens, the sugar in the painted china bowl that Ian had bought her on a school trip when he was eleven; *A Present From Lands End.*

I made tea and took it in to her. She was sitting where I had left her, the sweater still in her lap, her hands folded on top of it. She had wound a rubber band round her finger to keep her wedding ring on now that she had lost weight.

I placed the tea on the table in front of her, and then, noticing her sharp-eyed stare, I put a coaster under the saucer.

'I think you should see the doctor,' I said, 'you look so poorly.'

She gave a dismissive sweep of one hand.

'Perhaps a tonic?' I said.

'Oh, I don't know. What does it matter?'

'It matters to me. I'd make you an appointment and come and get you, if that would help.'

She pressed her hands down into the sweater. 'Suit yourself.'

I got up. 'I'll let you know when.'

'You can see yourself out, can't you?'

'Of course.'

I thought of kissing her cheek but couldn't bring myself to do it. We had been adversaries for too long. A cup of tea and a few civil words weren't going to make much difference. But it was a start.

Back at Holly Cottage, Jenny was walking around in the lane where the mobile signal was sometimes stronger. She was prattling into her phone and she waved as I pulled into the drive.

She ended her phone call with a tinkling laugh and gave a triumphant little skip.

'You'll never guess who *that* was,' she said, her eyes bright with mischief.

'No, I won't.'

'Go on, guess.'

'Oh, Jenny! For heaven's sake!' I was hungry, thirsty and had a banging headache.

'Go on, three guesses.'

I gave an exaggerated sigh; I wasn't in the mood for this at all.

'Barack Obama? Johnny Depp? David Attenborough?'

'Don't be silly.'

'Well you said I wouldn't guess and I haven't.'

Jenny tossed her head, nostrils flaring like a triumphant horse winning the Derby.

'It was Trent. From Houston. Well, he's not actually in Houston, he's in London. He couldn't bear it any longer.'

She followed me as I went into the kitchen and started rummaging through the drawers to find some aspirin.

143

'What? Houston? I thought it was the only place to live.'

'You can be very annoying, Lottie. He can't bear being without *me*! He's come to try and win me back. *Come home, Jenny, I can't live without you.* Marvellous! I'm going up to London on the train this evening. I'll be there by seven thirty. He's staying at Claridges. He's going to take me out to dinner and I'm going to have the most outrageous things on the menu. And a bottle of the most expensive champagne. Even if I don't want it. See how he likes that! And if he complains I'll insist on separate rooms.'

'God, you're childish,' I said, marvelling at my sister's unsinkable optimism.

She hunched her shoulders with delight and wrinkled her nose. 'I know, isn't it super? Anyway I must go and pack.'

'Do you need a lift to the station?'

She thought about it for a moment then snapped her fingers. 'No, I'll leave the car in the car park. If I get a ticket, Trent can pay. He's going to pay in so many ways too. He's going to organise golf lessons for me.'

'And they say romance is dead.'

She looked chastened. 'Sorry, Lottie, I don't mean to leave you on your own but I have to do this for Trent. He did sound so desperate.'

'I don't mind. I have exciting and glamorous things of my own to do. I've got to let someone in next door so he can service Bryn's hot tub.'

Normally this would have provoked a suggestive comment but her mind was obviously elsewhere. Probably prowling the streets of Knightsbridge with only Trent's Black American Express card for company. By this time tomorrow her kitten heels would be striking sparks off the pavement.

Within half an hour she had gone, waving through the sunroof as her little yellow car sped down the hill. I was glad for her, she wasn't a woman who liked being alone, she certainly didn't enjoy the countryside, and male company was almost as essential to her as oxygen.

I did a bit of tidying up and switched on the washing machine. Then I walked to the end of the road and phoned the doctor's surgery.

'Lottie!' Daphne recognised my voice almost immediately. 'How are you?'

'Good, absolutely great,' I lied. 'How are you? Managing OK without me?'

Daphne hesitated and then drew a deep breath. 'Well once we undid your reorganising of the blood test results, we've been fine.'

'Great…'

'And there were a few appointments missing from the computer. That caused some trouble with Doctor Faraday. You know what she's like. One patient in the wrong place and there's hell to pay.'

I wished I hadn't asked now. 'Yes, well, sorry about…'

'And then there was the baby clinic you booked on the wrong day. That was a pig of a day. Twenty screaming babies and no district nurses. Still what doesn't kill us gives us indigestion, so they say.'

'No, absolutely, I mean, yes, sorry. Look, could I book an appointment? Susan Geraldine Lovell. She's registered with Doctor Faraday but…'

'Doctor Faraday is on holiday,' Daphne said with a hollow laugh, 'no appointments with her until – well goodness me, I mean weeks really.'

I took an executive decision. 'Then can you book her in with Doctor Hawkins? She really isn't well. She's looking awful. Lost a lot of weight, I don't think she's looking after herself at all. Since Ian died, you know.'

At the mention of Ian, Daphne drew in a hissing breath.

'Oh yes, of course, I'd forgotten. I'm terribly sorry. Hang on, I'll see what I can do.'

There was a pause and I could hear the computer keys clicking in the background accompanied by some um-oh noises from Daphne.

'As it's you, I'll squeeze her in tomorrow afternoon at three. There's just a short appointment spare. Ten minutes. Would that be long enough?'

'That would be fantastic. I'll make sure she's there. I'll have to bring her.'

Daphne started talking to someone else, her voice muffled as though she had put her hand over the mouthpiece. Then she came back to me.

'Fine, I'll have to go now, Lottie; we're very busy, even if you're a lady of leisure! We'll see you tomorrow at three.'

Lady of leisure indeed.

I phoned Susan and had the briefest of conversations. I barely had time to tell her I would be picking her up just after two o'clock before she hung up.

Almost immediately my phone rang. It was Jess.

'Hi, I've caught you at last!' she said.

'Sorry, the reception is hopeless. I've just been to the end of the road.'

'I know, sorry. Look, I thought I should tell you myself, I think I might go ahead with getting someone round to value the cottage and I didn't want someone to turn up out of the blue.'

'Thanks, I appreciate that.'

'I feel bad about it, honestly I do, Lottie. But…well…I need—'

'Please don't apologise, Jess. I'm getting on well with the decorating, it was only ever going to be a temporary thing, I knew that. I'll be fine, don't worry.'

We chatted some more and then I walked back up the hill and trudged out into the garden.

It was a glorious afternoon, probably the warmest since I had moved here. I suppose I should have been doing the decorating, but instead went to carry on with a bit of weeding and dead-heading in the front garden. After about an hour I was getting very hot and sweaty and I was just going to go in when a small blue van pulled up and tooted its horn at me; Tom the Tub Man, short, stout and energetic, right on schedule.

I let him into Bryn's garden and went to put the afternoon's debris into my green waste bin. How did it fill up so fast? Even a small patch of weeds seemed to produce an incredible volume of stuff, but there was something wonderful about seeing the crumbling red soil in a clean, orderly state again.

I had some orange squash and carried on with my task, working steadily along the flowerbeds. I thought about Jenny and wondered how things would turn out for her. Then I thought about Susan and marvelled how two women could be so different.

Susan was embedded in elderly disapproval of everything pre-1959, where my sister embraced everything with equal enthusiasm. Even the Kardashians. Which did I want to be when I was Susan's age? Old before my time or young for my age?

My reverie was interrupted by the tub man's return to my side of the fence.

He stood in the faintly scented cloud of chemicals that seemed to follow him around; his plastic box tucked under one arm.

'OK, all done. I've changed all the filters, done the pumps and tested the water. Tell him I've adjusted his levels, put in some pH stuff and some bromide crystals.'

'That didn't take long.'

'Ah well, Bryn's very good with his water, see. He might need to do a drain down in a month or so. All depends on his usage, that's what makes the difference. Not like some I could tell you about. You'd think they'd emptied a bottle of Fairy Liquid in. And scum! Don't talk to me about scum!'

'I promise not to.'

'Well if you're going in, leave it for another ten minutes, it's the bromide, see. Makes your eyes sting. I've left the pumps on to give it a good circulate. If you could close the lid up in about half an hour?'

'Of course.'

He scribbled on his paperwork and signed it with a flourish. 'Sign here, will you? Just so he knows I turned up.'

He held out a clipboard and a pen and I signed. Then I saw him out and locked the side gate. I looked at the bubbling waters of the hot tub. I thought how hot and sweaty I was. Then I remembered Bryn was going to be away for a few days.

Now what would my sister do in this situation?

And what would Susan do?

After that it was a no brainer. I went back into the house, found a clean towel, tried and failed to locate a swimming costume, stripped off and lowered myself with many oohs and aahs into the tub.

It was one of those light bulb moments when you realise what everyone else has been saying about hot tubs is true. I could imagine Bryn enjoying an hour or so in here after a day's digging. That was a really nice thought too and I considered it for a while.

Bonnie made a fleeting appearance and I shoved her out of my daydream with a few impeccably witty words. Then I pressed a few buttons and extra bubbles shot out all around me. I switched the lights on and watched delighted as the water changed from purple to blue and all other colours of the rainbow. I tried out all the different seats to see which one I liked the best. I rested back onto the padded headrest and closed my eyes. Total bliss. Everyone should have one.

CHAPTER 12

Honeysuckle – devotion, fidelity

I lay in the water enjoying the feel of the roiling bubbles, and occasionally scooping up insects that had fallen in. The honeysuckle was out sending a wonderful fragrance across the garden and after a while I got out, wrapped myself in my towel and scooted back across the garden to my house to fetch a bottle of Ian's bubbly and a glass. I got back in, toasted Tom the Tub Man, the garden and the golden evening.

I was halfway down my second glass when I heard something.

I wasn't sure what it was because of the noise of the bubbles, but I sat up, on point like a gundog. Nothing. Perhaps it was just farm workers going home down the lane.

I sank back into the water and turned on all the water jets to maximum. Wow they were powerful. My kidneys had never been so surprised. I haven't done three rounds with Wladimir Klitschko, but I expect that's a bit like how it felt. In a good way, of course.

I sipped my champagne and watched the birds flying overhead and then perching like commas on the telephone line at the end of the garden. Swallows or swifts? Or house martins? Was there a bird called a house martin, or was that a pop group? Whatever they were, they were having a lovely time, swooping and diving, catching insects.

I thought about the day I had spent, mainly with the two women I disliked most in the world. And yet somehow I had managed to feel something for both of them other than hatred. I had felt sorry for them. A thing that was very unexpected.

'Enjoying yourself?'

Bryn was standing beside the tub.

I gave a strangled bleat of shock that turned into something resembling a full-blown 'baa' noise. I was momentarily distracted by the choice of remaining hidden under the water or getting out. I decided on the former. I had braced one foot against some part of the tub's moulded interior and of course in my panic it slipped and I sank inelegantly under the water, just managing by some inherent reflex to hold my champagne glass up above the water level. I surfaced a moment later spluttering, my hair over my face.

'OK?' he said. 'Not trying to drown yourself?'

'Yes, I mean no, I'm so sorry, I just couldn't resist it. I got so hot doing the weeding. I didn't think you were coming back tonight. Sorry, that makes it sound worse. What I mean is—'

He held his hands out in a reassuring movement. 'It doesn't matter, Lottie, really. Calm down. I'm glad you did.'

Having established I was not in trouble, I then began to worry about how I was going to get out. Perhaps he would go indoors soon and I could make a run for it. He stood looking at the garden, his hands in his pockets. The lights under the water turned a dazzling blue. The colour of Bryn's eyes. Really rather gorgeous.

Focus, woman, focus.

'It's a lovely evening. Mind if I join you?'

I covered myself as best I could with my hands, forgetting I was still holding a nearly full glass. The champagne sprayed out across my face, stinging my eyes and causing me further spluttering distress. Bryn kindly took the glass away, refilled it and handed it back me.

'Really you should stick to plastic,' he said.

'Plastic?'

'Plastic glasses. Tell you what, I'll go and get a couple. Don't move.'

He went off into the house and just as I was wondering if I could reach the towel and wrap it round me under the water he was back.

'Here we are.'

He put them onto the handy table next to the tub and then, to my shock, horror and – let's be honest – delight, tugged his T-shirt off, pulling it over his head from behind the way men always seem to.

I felt quite faint. He had changed into a cute pair of swimming trunks covered in pictures of camper vans. The golden hairs on his arms glinted in the late afternoon sunshine. The muscles of his chest transfixed me. Evidently gardening did more than just make you hot and sweaty. If I hadn't been in the tub, I would have been a bit hot and sweaty myself.

He stepped into the water, brushing a few grass clippings off his (large) feet and I shrank away from him. The lights turned green.

'God, that's better.' He ducked his head back and water streamed over his shoulders. 'I've had a long, hard week; London *and* Lady Trehorlicks. Remember I mentioned her?'

I nodded, mute with embarrassment.

'She's very old school. Likes things formal. Calls me Mr Palmer. Wants to know the proper Latin names of all the plants so she can write them on copper labels. She likes her borders regimented, whereas I like things to flow, just hang out.'

I wondered if I was about to hang out too. I had been in this tub long enough to know the jets were on a timer and when they stopped I would be revealed in all my glory.

'I don't know why she was so insistent I should do the job except she was at school with my mother.'

Ah, his mother. The rift between him and Greg. I wondered if I could prise some details out of him and then stopped myself. Never mind his mother, I needed to prise myself out of this tub soon and hopefully with my dignity intact.

'You don't look very relaxed,' he said. 'You can always move to another seat if you like?'

'No, no, I'm fine, honestly,' I said, sipping my champagne and trying to look casual. The lights turned to gold. I wondered what colour would make my thighs look smaller.

He leaned towards me. 'Can I adjust those water jets behind you? They look as though they're on full, and they're a bit powerful.'

'No, no, honestly they're fine! I like it really hard.'

I closed my eyes in horror at what I had just said.

Perhaps Bryn didn't have such a filthy mind as I did, as he didn't so much as flicker. The jets continued to pummel my kidneys – they were certainly getting a work out they hadn't anticipated.

Bryn leaned back and sipped his champagne. The sun had set now and the evening was glowing with a glorious sunset. The air seemed to thrum with warmth and light. Above us a single little bat swooped in elegant parabolas. I wondered what time it would get dark. Perhaps I would stay in the water until then, only to emerge as a shrivelled, prune-like figure, my toenails dropping off as I did so.

'So how are you?' he said.

'Fine, I mean, well not fine…'

He clicked his tongue. 'The same old Lottie, never a straight answer.'

'Life's a bit odd at the moment. Half the time I don't know if I'm coming or going. I had a bit of unpleasantness to sort out, as a result I had to see someone who I would much rather ignore. And then of course Jess is selling up.'

Bryn sipped his champagne and frowned. 'Definitely? You said she was only thinking about it.'

'I think she wants to buy somewhere else a bit nearer to home, rather than have a rental property out here. She's planning on getting someone round to value it some time soon.'

'So where does that leave you?'

I shrugged. Then I realised that showed my naked shoulders above the bubble level, something I really didn't want to do. I shrank down a bit further.

'Finding somewhere else to live?' I said.

'Where?'

'I don't know.' I was horrified to hear a tragic little crack in my voice. I cleared my throat and carried on, trying to sound bold and confident. 'Oh somewhere else, perhaps I'll visit my aunt in Croydon? My sister seems to be reconciling with her fiancé in Texas so I could go and stay with her for a bit. Maybe.'

Neither of these prospects sounded the slightest bit attractive to me, and by the look on Bryn's face, he didn't think much of them either.

'Croydon,' he said. 'Hmm, I've never been there.'

'It's OK,' I said. 'But it's not like here.'

'Texas; I visited some years ago. Nice for a holiday, but I don't know if I could live there.'

'Nor me. That's not like here either, I'm guessing.'

Bryn pulled himself up out of the water and over the edge of the hot tub onto the grass in one athletic and impressive movement.

'I'm going in for five minutes,' he said, 'to give you time to get out. I promise not to look.'

'*What?*'

He slung his towel around his neck and grinned. Oh great, so he had been sitting there chatting away as though nothing was wrong when all the time he knew I didn't have a stitch on!

He winked at me. 'That's the second time I've had to look away to preserve your modesty.'

'I promise it won't happen again,' I said, putting my arms across my body.

Bryn towelled his hair until it stuck up in spikes. He fired me a grin.

'That's a shame,' he said, before he went indoors.

The following day I drove to Susan's house and delivered her, still maintaining her glacial silence, to the doctor's surgery.

I went to announce her arrival at the reception desk while she took a seat in the corner furthest away from the entrance.

There was a miserable-looking blonde behind the desk, presumably my replacement, and my name meant nothing to her. She checked Susan off on the computer and jerked her chin at the woman behind me in the queue. Doctor's receptionist customer service at its best.

I went to sit down by Susan but she pointedly put her handbag on the empty chair next to her and ignored me.

I picked up a copy of *Country Life* and flicked through the property pages. They were doing a special on Somerset and there were some glorious properties for sale. It was obvious that what the home-buying experts on daytime TV had said was true. Life was much cheaper in Somerset. If I had 450k for example, I could buy a small manor house with seventeeth-century origins and ten acres of woodland near Curry Rival. If I had 550k there was a six-bedroom house near Milverton with— Ah, of course. Silly me. The magazine was dated February 2003; surely some sort of doctor's waiting room record? I put it back in the wire stand and flicked through a copy of *Hello* celebrating the recent wedding of William and Catherine. If I delved a bit deeper I wouldn't have been surprised to find Mafeking had been relieved.

I was personally very relieved when just after three o'clock Susan was called in to see Dr Hawkins. She gathered her coat around her thin body and scooped up her handbag, somehow managing to radiate disapproval with every step as she went into his surgery. I carried on reading about Carole Middleton's elegant outfit and admiring Pippa's bottom. I didn't know anyone in the waiting room and no one recognised me. Which was something of a relief.

Time passed and a man with an arm in a sling sitting opposite me started to tut and look at his watch. Some irritated fidgeting and newspaper rustling accompanied this before he checked his watch again. Just after three thirty he got up and went over to the reception desk.

'I know Doctor Hawkins is always late but this is getting ridiculous,' he said in aggrieved tones.

The miserable blonde stabbed away at the computer keys and huffed along with him.

'Nothing I can do, Mr Hubbard, if the doctor is late there's usually a reason.'

'Well, I've got to pick Paige up from her friend's house at four and it's going to take me ten minutes to walk there. I can't drive, you know. Not with this hand. And Marge isn't going to be back until five.'

Miserable Blonde gave him a look showing exactly how uninterested she was in his domestic timetable and he went to sit down again.

He looked to me for sympathy.

'It's always the same,' he said. 'I wonder why they bother making appointments at all. He's never on time. Even if you get the first appointment of the day.'

We both looked up as a woman with a pram full of crying twins struggled through the door.

'And this will be someone else who's going to be disappointed,' he said, getting up to hold the door open. 'He's running late, love.'

The newcomer sighed and jiggled the pram handle as an insistent wailing started up.

'I'm three thirty,' she said.

Mr Hubbard rolled his eyes and tapped the face of his watch. 'Three twenty and I still haven't gone in. He's got some old woman in there, not much wrong with her, I'd say. Expect it's just an outing for her. I've got to get Paige in twenty minutes.'

The three of us tutted for a few minutes and the miserable blonde tapped heavily on the computer keys.

Just before four o'clock the surgery door opened and Susan came out.

'Well,' huffed Mr Hubbard, looking at his watch, 'it's about flipping time.'

The wailing from inside the pram increased in volume as Susan, unconcerned, passed her notes to the receptionist and made for the exit.

I trailed after her into the car park.

'OK?'

'Yes.'

'Do you have to come back? Shouldn't you have made an appointment? I don't mind fetching you.'

'No, there's no need. Doctor Hawkins is going to make a house call next Monday.'

'You're honoured,' I said, surprised, 'he hardly ever does that.'

'Yes, well.' Susan patted the back of her hair, tidying away a few strands. 'There we are.'

We got into the car and Susan fastened her seat belt. It was obvious she was not expecting to talk to me but a long period of silence is anathema to me.

'So do I need to stop at the chemist? You know, for a prescription?'

'No, thank you.'

'He didn't give you a tonic or some vitamins or something?'

'No, nothing.'

Another long pause as I tried to think of something to say.

'And he was OK? I mean you didn't really want to see him, did you? A male doctor; I know you had reservations.'

Susan fiddled in her handbag and brought out a brutally ironed cotton handkerchief. She unfolded it and dabbed at the corner of her mouth.

'That's absolute nonsense, Charlotte. He was perfectly pleasant.'

'Good. That's good. And you really don't have to go back?'

She clicked her tongue at me. 'No. Why don't you ever listen? He's going to call on me. Next week. Now please would you just drive?'

I gave up and we passed the remainder of the journey in silence. When we pulled up outside her house Susan got out and was about to close the door without comment when she stopped and ducked her head back into the car.

'Thank you,' she said.

Well you could have knocked me down with the proverbial.

CHAPTER 13

Forget-me-not – remember me, friendship

My sister, from henceforth to be known as the Dirty Stop Out, didn't come back from London until three days later. Her little yellow car barrelled up the drive, skidding to a halt and sending gravel everywhere. She came into the house, humming happily and swinging a large hatbox.

'I've bought you a gift,' she said, placing it on the kitchen table, 'to say thank you for having me visit.'

I noticed her American accent was back along with her good humour.

The hatbox was grey-and-white striped with a pale pink rope handle. It was absolutely beautiful. I looked at it without enthusiasm. I didn't wear hats. The opportunity for wearing hats in the last few months had been zero. The prospect of wearing hats in the near future was the same.

'Is it a hat?'

'Go to the top of the class and give out the pencils! Go on then,' she said, almost hopping from one foot to the other in her excitement, 'open it.'

Inside was a confection of pale pink feathers and netting pinned down with silk roses and forget-me-nots. It was exquisite. Just the thing for keeping the sun off when I was weeding.

'Thanks,' I said, trying not to sound sullen.

'Look properly,' Jenny said, her eyes sparkling.

The crown of the hat was stuffed with pale pink tissue paper and under that was an envelope with my name on the front. I opened it. Inside was a business-class plane ticket to Houston and a substantial wad of fifty-pound notes.

She came towards me and put an arm around my shoulders.

'What do you think?' she said. 'It's open ended. Just come visit when you like. Stay as long as you like.'

'Wow,' I said, not knowing what to think.

'It was Trent's idea. Isn't he a darling? He said you must have been having a rotten time and you could come and stay with us for a bit. You could have the suite of rooms by the pool house if you'd prefer. You'd be quite independent. He thought it might cheer you up.'

I looked at the ticket for several seconds. I couldn't push from my mind the fact that I had the equivalent of at least six months' rent in my hand. Not to mention the cash.

I realised I was being an ungrateful cow. I went to give her a hug.

'It's marvellous, Jenny. So kind, I can't thank you enough. And the hat is – well it's divine. Really lovely. When I will get to wear it is anyone's guess.'

She laughed. 'I know it was a terrible extravagance but it was just so pretty I couldn't resist it. Perhaps you could wear it when you get onto the plane and they'll upgrade you to first!'

'Perhaps I will!'

'Now I have some news,' she said.

She blushed. I think I knew what was coming.

'You and Trent have rekindled your passion and are going back to Houston together?'

'We are,' she said, sounding astonished by my perception. 'Trent says he's been simply lost without me. It made him realise how much he wants us to make a go of things.'

'And you? How do you feel?'

Jenny tilted her head to one side. 'Lottie, I'm not thirty-four like you; I'm nearly forty. I don't feel forty, I don't look forty, I don't think forty and I don't behave as though I'm forty but the fact remains, I am. I love Trent. I've missed our life together. I've missed him. I've missed the fun.'

I picked up my hat and smoothed the feathers. They felt soft and cool under my fingers.

'That sounds very measured and sensible and not like you at all, not very romantic,' I said.

'You're wrong. It is terribly romantic and it's more than enough. Perhaps at last I've learned the value of friendship and companionship in relationships. God knows it's taken me long enough. I'm the first to admit it. It takes a lot of beating. The feeling of coming home, shared interests, being part of a successful team. Of course it doesn't hurt that Trent is so incredibly attractive –'

Whoa! Hang on. Really? *Attractive?* Did she think so? Trent was fifty-eight, slightly overweight, and if the photos Jenny had shown me recently were anything to go by he had the worst dress sense of any man in North America. Bar none.

'– but in the end you have to have something in common other than mind-blowing sex,' she concluded.

My attention was dragged back from remembering a photograph of Trent playing golf in a green-and-pink-striped sports shirt, orange Bermuda shorts, knee-length white socks and black and white golf shoes. *Mind-blowing sex?*

'Far too much information, Jen!'

'Yes. And he's been on his own for long enough. I can't leave him to the mercies of those witches in the golf club. I bet they've been circling. They can scent a vulnerable man just like a piranha smells blood in the water,' she said, patting at her newly highlighted hair. She really had been busy while she was up in London.

'You'll be writing a self-help book next.'

She looked a bit thoughtful. 'Oooh, what a brilliant idea.'

'Don't you dare!'

'Well, we'll see. Anyway *you* should take a look near home if you're looking for fun.'

'Huh?'

'Mr Muscle next door. Come on, Lottie, do keep up. He's nearby, he's solvent, he's attractive and he obviously fancies you.'

'No, he doesn't!'

She gave me a world-weary-older-woman look. 'Are you really my sister? You're hopeless. Yes, he does. I can tell.'

'He's also got an exceptionally attractive girlfriend, or were you forgetting that?'

Jenny made a dismissive noise and snapped her fingers.

'Girlfriend? I don't think so. And since when did that ever stop anyone? Right, I'm going to pack. And then let's open a bottle of champagne!'

Jenny left the following day, swanning off after lunch to return her hire car before boarding the train to London. As she drove away, I stood at the end of the drive waving. There was the scent of new-mown grass in the air, which reminded me I needed to mow my own grass; it was getting really long. I sighed – I was alone again, but somehow it felt different this time. Still, my sister was happy and she couldn't wait to get back to Trent, their wide circle of friends and a life of luxury that she enjoyed and under-stood.

I went into Stokeley to pick up some milk and a new deluge of texts and emails landed on my phone. Most of them unim-portant, one from Jenny telling me she was on the train, a couple from Ian's solicitor asking me to contact him. Several from Sophie wondering when they were going to see me again. Could they do anything to help? After such a long silence it was nice to see I wasn't completely forgotten.

I made a few calls, arranged to see the solicitor and called Sophie's number. It went straight to answer phone, so I left a message explaining, yet again, my problems with phone reception and went home. As I reached the top of the hill, I found I was half expecting to see an estate agent's board outside Holly Cottage. I was dreading it. So far there had been no viewings by any tape-measure-wielding agents, but I guessed it was only a matter of time.

By now I was starting to decorate the last room; the room I regarded as my bedroom. Despite the prettiness of the wallpaper, it was torn and scuffed where furniture had been moved and small fingers had picked at the edges. I was going to strip it off and replace it with a glorious paper I had lusted after for years. A muted botanical thing with tiny birds and flowers. I moved my belongings into the spare room and started work, washing down the paintwork, starting to soak the wallpaper so it would come off more easily.

After a while, I realised again how quiet this place was. I opened the windows and listened, my hands flat on the windowsill. There was an occasional tweet of a bird in the garden and the far off sound of a tractor in one of the fields across the valley. I turned the bedside radio on and listened to the news while I worked. Not much had changed in the months I had lived here. The scandal-hit politician who had provided the hot gossip for our ill-fated New Year's Eve party had resigned from Parliament in order to spend more time with his family and was rumoured to be a contestant on the next series of *Strictly*. The road works on the A303 continued to cause delays and the planning officers still hadn't given the go ahead for a proposed development of two hundred new houses near Honiton.

I moved all the furniture into the middle of the room and covered it in dustsheets. Then I rolled up the rug and started to strip off the old wallpaper. It was a messy business, involving a sponge, buckets of hot soapy water and a fair amount of cursing.

As I pulled the soggy paper off the walls I realised I had done little besides clean this house, decorate it or tidy up the neglected garden for months. It was looking better, I could see that, and I was pleased with what I had done. But there is only so much of this sort of work that I could take before I reached screaming point. And I was just about there. Then a text arrived from Jenny; she couldn't get through to me on the phone but she wanted me to know they were going back to Houston and she and Trent were going to be married. I put my phone back in my pocket and got on with my work.

I finished one wall and then chucked my sponge into the bucket. I went downstairs and out into the garden and sat on one of the rickety iron chairs. Perhaps the plane I could see leaving a pink vapour trail across the evening sky was Jenny's, on its way back to Texas. Trent would have been only too pleased to pay the excess baggage allowance resulting from her three-day shopping spree. I could just imagine them now, settled into first class (window seat for Jenny, aisle for Trent), her hand snuggled under Trent's arm, both holding glasses of champagne as they toasted each other and the future.

I couldn't help it. Suddenly I could feel my chin begin to wobble and I started to cry.

Yes, it was probably seventy-five per cent self-pity but there was also twenty-five per cent fear. I couldn't even get a job with a supermarket. I still didn't know what I was going to do when Jess sold Holly Cottage. I was alone. I'd spoken pretty confidently about being OK if the house sold, but where would I go? I sat and sobbed, went into the house for some kitchen roll, wiped my eyes and started all over again. It wasn't fair. To which the obvious retort is; who said it was going to be fair?

I'd buried all these feeling for months, ever since Ian had died. I realised I hadn't even known how I should feel or how I should react.

I had wandered into the sitting room the day after Ian died to see the tracks from Sophie's careful hoovering still visible in the carpet pile. I looked at the Christmas tree standing in a curly gold stand, jolly and twinkling in the corner. The Christmas cards lined up on the mantelpiece. Robins, snow, Christmas trees, angels. All of them wishing Ian and Lottie a wonderful time.

That was when I really lost it.

I think I made a sound that came from somewhere deep inside me. A gut wrenching cry of terror and misery as I swept the cards off with one arm so they fell into the hearth. There was a smash of glass as two candlesticks broke, the crash of china as a little porcelain bell Ian had bought me as a joke when I had flu broke into fragments. I turned and pulled the Christmas tree down. It bounced on the carpet, scattering peacock blue ornaments and silver tinsel and a shower of dead needles. I stood and kicked it with a howl of rage, thin glass from the broken baubles crunching under my slippers. Slippers; I mean how pathetically middle aged had I become? I kicked them off. One hit the standard lamp next to Ian's favourite chair and it fell over in a graceful arc. The light bulb shattered, the shade fell off and rolled behind the sofa. The other slipper knocked my mug of tea all over the cream carpet. I looked at the devastation, slumped down onto a chair and cried. I thought my heart would break. I was alone and I was terrified.

Trust me, it's pointless doing something like that – having an adult tantrum. After you finish you have to clear it up yourself because your mum isn't there to do it for you. Not that my mother would ever have done so. It took me a long time.

And then I tried to put my feelings away somewhere deep inside me and had not looked at them. Until now.

After a while I stopped crying and calmed down a bit. What could I do but keep going? There was no magic wand to make things right again. There was no one to take away the problems and pressures. I had to deal with it myself. I had been let down by other people, the least I could do was not let myself down.

I went back upstairs and carried on the tedious process of stripping off the wallpaper with vicious strokes of the scraper.

I finished and bundled all the rubbish into some bin liners to take downstairs. I was tired and hungry. It was only half past six but I considered going to bed and pulling the covers over my head.

There was a knock on the front door. It was Bryn.

'I wondered if—' He broke off when he saw my face.

I glanced quickly at my reflection in the hall mirror. My eyes were red from crying, I had mascara stains down my cheeks, my hair was wet and speckled with bits of wallpaper. I looked a proper sight.

'What's the matter?'

He put out a hand and touched my forearm, rubbing gently as one might soothe a miserable child.

'Oh, you know.' I tried to seem offhand. If he was too nice to me I might cry again and I was determined not to.

'Oh dear,' he said.

'I'm fine.' I even tried a laugh, but it didn't come out right. More of a hiccup. 'My sister's gone back to Houston and I don't know what I'm going to do when Jess sells this house. I'm sick and tired of decorating and cleaning and being on my own. I don't know what's round the corner. I don't even know if the bin men will take these.' I aimed a kick at the black bin liners. 'They got very arsey about the amount of rubbish I left out a couple of weeks ago. They left a warning notice on my wheelie bin…'

My voice was now so high pitched that only dogs and bats could probably understand me. I had to stop. I was going to cry. Even the bin men were against me. It was the final straw. I could feel an unstoppable tsunami of misery behind my eyes.

He took the bags of rubbish and slung them in the back of his pickup truck. Then, without speaking, he came over to me and hugged me.

I can't tell you how good it felt. He was tall and broad and warm and he smelled of new-mown grass and wood smoke. I sobbed for a bit against his chest, my tears soaking into his sweater.

I think a lot of men under these circumstances would have tried to get me to stop. Asked me what the matter was. Tried to reason with me. Bryn didn't say anything. He just held me and waited for me to calm down. All the worry and sadness, the hurt and the insecurity and the fear came out. Ian's months of betrayal. The shame of my many failures. The feebleness of my grasp on the future.

Even with all that to deal with, I couldn't cry forever. I had to stop at some point. I made all sorts of snuffling, gulping, incredibly unattractive noises, and fished in my pocket for a tissue. Bryn handed me a blue, spotted man handkerchief and I mopped myself up. I kept my head down. Some people can cry and look tragic and attractive. I'm not one of those people. I go the full gamut of piggy eyes, red nose, snot; you get the picture.

Bryn leaned back and looked down at me.

'Better?' he said.

I made a few more hiccupping, gulping noises and blew my nose as a trumpeting finale.

I held out his handkerchief. 'I'll wash this,' I said.

He laughed. I could hear it rumbling up in his chest as he hugged me again and I relaxed into his arms. At that moment it felt the best place in the world to be. Solid and comfortable. Like I fitted into a shape made just for me.

'Sorry,' I said.

'What for, you daft thing?' He rested his chin on the top of my head.

'All this.'

'Stop it. You don't have to say sorry to me.'

I leaned my forehead on his broad chest and wondered if there was any possibility that I could just stay where I was for the rest of time.

Bryn released me and took my hand. He pulled me towards his house. 'Come on, you're cold. How about that drink I promised you?'

'That was months ago. You don't have to. I must look a sight.'

'Come on. You look fine. I want to. I'll cook you dinner too. I think you need a bit of TLC.'

'That would be nice,' I said, mistress of the understatement.

CHAPTER 14

Azaleas – passion

His house was exactly what I expected. I caught a better glimpse of the sitting room, comfortable sofas grouped around a low wooden table, and the walls painted dark red. Bryn led me through into the pale cream kitchen that was filled with chunky wooden units; solid and smooth with the patina of old age juxtaposed with the new granite worktops I remembered from my first visit. A mismatched selection of crockery interspersed with balls of twine, a glass jar of small change, some secateurs and a few battered cookery books filled the fitted dresser that stretched the length of one wall. There was a mug and plate in the Belfast sink, otherwise the place was immaculate. It was certainly tidier than my kitchen.

'Sit down.' He pushed me onto a chair and passed me a box of man-sized tissues. 'Hang on to those, just in case you're not quite done.'

I gave a weak laugh. 'I think I'm OK.'

'Good. Now then, first things first.'

He pulled out a dusty bottle of red wine from the rack and opened it.

'Red wine's very good for you. Full of iron to give you strength,' he said.

He poured me a generous glassful and I sipped it; it was exactly what I needed. Nothing fancy with medal-shaped stickers on the bottle, just a decent red wine. I sat and enjoyed the feeling as it worked its way down to my cold, empty stomach.

'OK?' He threw me a concerned look.

'Thanks.'

'I'm just going to put a match to the fire in the sitting room. Stay here, I won't be a minute.'

I watched him through the hallway as he crouched down in front of the inglenook fireplace and lit the fire. I heard the kindling crackling and then the smell of applewood logs burning. It made me feel safe and happy for the first time in months. I nipped into the downstairs cloakroom and splashed some cold water on my face. I looked a fright. My hair was all over the place and my nose was all blotchy. I did what I could to sort myself out before he came back into the kitchen, brushing the dust off his hands.

'Right then, what shall I cook? Any requests?'

I shook my head. 'I don't mind. I'm really not fussy. I'll eat absolutely anything. As long as it's not tofu. Or pineapple. And I'm allergic to shellfish. Not proper allergic but I come out in a rash. Ooh and I don't much like tuna. Or rare meat. Or duck. Or blackcurrants.'

'But apart from that you'll eat anything?' he laughed.

'Sorry. I'm being a pain.'

He came over, hunkered down in front of me and took hold of my cold hands in his. He bent his head and kissed them. I felt his stubble graze my fingers; his hands were warm and slightly roughened. It felt very, very sexy.

'You're not being a pain.' He looked up at me again and I caught my breath. I had forgotten how beautiful his blue eyes were. 'And do me a favour, stop saying sorry, OK?'

'Sorry, I mean – oh hell.'

We both laughed and he stood up and went to open a door, revealing an old-fashioned pantry stocked with canned food and

168

dried goods. On a slate shelf was a ham on a china stand. He brought it out and put it on the kitchen table.

'Ham, egg and chips?' he said.

My mouth watered. 'Oh, yes please. I haven't had that for years.'

'Never fails. One of my favourites. Mustard, brown sauce or ketchup?'

'Mustard.'

'Excellent, me too.'

I sipped my wine while he got cutlery and crockery out of drawers and cupboards, his movements efficient and graceful for such a large man. Bryn slid a tray of oven chips into the Aga, sliced the ham with a razor-sharp knife, and then cooked eggs in a bubbling pan of butter.

'Not really into all this cholesterol stuff, I'm afraid,' he said. 'I tend to eat what tastes good.'

'Well you look great on it,' I said, and then I blushed, hoping it hadn't sounded as though I was flirting. Although I probably was.

We sat and chatted for a while, consuming more of the wine. Then Bryn passed me a plate of food and slid a pot of English mustard after it. While I helped myself to a fair-sized dollop, he sliced some hunks of crusty bread, leaving them on the bread-board in front of me with a slab of butter in a glass dish.

'I'll never eat all this,' I said.

'I bet you do,' he said, sitting down opposite me, 'you don't look like you've had a square meal in weeks.'

Did I finish it? Of course I did. I even took a slice of the bread, which was heavenly, and made a chip buttie.

'Enjoy that?' he said, pushing his chair back from the table as we finished.

'Bliss,' I replied.

Bryn came round and collected my plate and stacked it in the sink with his.

'Come on, bring your wine,' he said, 'the fire will be just right by now.'

We went into the sitting room and I sat in one of the huge, comfortable sofas, watching as he added a few more logs to the fire in the inglenook fireplace. Then he closed the curtains against the dark evening outside.

I looked around, noticing the smallest portable TV in the Western world half hidden behind a pile of gardening magazines on a floor to ceiling bookcase; not an *Emmerdale* fan, then. There was an old red leather armchair pulled up next to the fireplace where I guessed he normally sat. Nothing was particularly new or smart, but everything seemed to fit well together. The room was furnished with things chosen for their comfort and quality rather than for style.

Something was niggling at me but it took me a few minutes to realise what it was. There were absolutely no feminine touches anywhere. No flowery tea towels in the kitchen or ornaments or brass bowls of potpourri in this room. There was no evidence Bonnie lived here. No casually draped throws over the sofa, no invitations to friends' weddings above the fireplace. I was desperate to ask but didn't want to do anything that would make him glance at the clock on the mantelpiece with a guilty start or check his mobile phone for texts. Although if he did that I would have wanted to know what network he was on, because I never had any service.

The fire flickered and crackled as the new logs caught the flame. Bryn lit a couple of huge candles on the mantelpiece and then came and sat beside me. He topped up my wine glass.

'Warm enough?' he said.

'Perfectly,' I kicked off my shoes and curled my feet underneath me. 'I'll have to be careful I don't fall asleep.'

'Feel free,' he said, sipping his wine and leaning back on the cushions.

We sat in a comfortable silence for a while, then we made small talk about nothing in particular. It was lovely. It was almost familiar.

We finished the wine and he went to find another bottle. I closed my eyes, content for the first time in ages. Outside I could hear the rain beating against the window. I felt as though we were in a safe, warm nest. Just the two of us. The world and all its problems were locked out.

He came back in and topped up our wine glasses. I watched his hand on the bottle, his fingers curled around the neck of it, his nails short and square. He had taken his sweater off and his shirtsleeves were rolled up. I could see the muscles in his forearm, the small freckles on his wrist, and the golden glint of the hairs light against his tan. I had to say something or I would be lost.

I said the first thing to come into my head. Stupid. Ridiculous.

'How was Lady Trehorlicks?'

Bryn sat down again, slightly closer to me and stretched one arm out along the back of the sofa.

'She's a character.'

'Is she young and pretty? Did she have a spotty raincoat? Or a Labrador?'

Bryn looked rather confused for a moment.

'Um, no, none of the above. She must be in her eighties, but she's the sort who will go on forever. Feisty, you know. The kind of woman who built the Empire. She's delightful. And she didn't have a Labrador but she did have a Border terrier called Nigel. And she's tiny, no more than five feet tall. Wiry.'

'She's probably never had your ham egg and chips,' I said.

'If she did it would be served on a silver chafing dish in the dining room.'

I giggled. It wasn't that funny. I sipped my wine. I was suddenly nervous.

'So,' he said, 'I've got you to myself at last. It's taken some doing, Lottie.'

I looked up at him. The firelight was flickering on his face, candlelight casting shadows across the room. His eyes searched mine with an expression I couldn't read. He looked at my mouth.

171

I've read enough magazine articles to recognise that sign. He wanted to kiss me. And oh God I wanted to let him.

I sipped my drink and with a massive effort looked away. I felt as though I was on the threshold of something. It was no use. I was going to stand and watch myself fall.

I thought I heard a car outside and I stiffened.

'Won't Bonnie be back soon?' I said.

Why? Why did I have to bring her name up at this particular moment? Did I have a death wish?

Bryn gave a short laugh. 'I think you might have the wrong idea about Bonnie. We were close once but we broke up a long time ago,' he said, 'it was all quite amicable but she kept coming back to collect stuff, to see me. We agreed we would be friends. I was like a sort of security blanket, I think. She took one thing at a time to spin the process out for as long as possible. I knew she was hoping we might get back together but it was never on the cards. Not as far as I'm concerned.'

I was confused. 'But I thought she was living here? She was going to organise a party for you.'

Bryn shook his head. 'I put a stop to the party as soon as I found out about it. I hate that sort of thing.'

'I thought you would.'

He smiled. 'Did you?'

He took my wine glass from me and put it on the table with his. Then he turned back and touched my face with one finger, making me shiver.

'I'm sorry for Bonnie. She's had her problems and I'm fond of her. I feel a bit responsible for her, I guess.' He pushed my hair off my face and looked into my eyes. His arm along the back of the sofa slipped around my shoulders. 'But then I saw you. Covered in paint. And I thought, who is this crazy, beautiful, accident-prone woman? Why am I thinking about her all the time? Why does she make my day every time I see her?'

'And there was me thinking you just wanted to get me drunk and have your wicked way with me,' I said.

Never one to miss the opportunity to say something stupid, me.

He leaned forward and kissed me. His mouth was warm and gentle on mine.

'It wouldn't be wicked,' he said. 'I think it would be wonderful.'

CHAPTER 15

French marigold – sorrow, deceit

I woke up the following morning without the faintest idea of where I was. There was an unfamiliar little clock softly ticking by the side of the bed, pale crewelwork curtains at the window. I was expecting to be in my spare room, still faintly scented with my sister's Chanel perfume and crowded with black bin bags of my clutter. Instead I could see a marble-topped wash-stand underneath the window, a deep armchair upholstered in dark red tapestry fabric and – oh yes – my knickers on the window seat.

Hell's bells, what had I done? Where was I? I stretched out a cautious hand and touched someone in the bed beside me.

Then the events of the previous evening came back to me and, just for a moment, I relaxed. I felt a huge grin stretch across my face. I put my hand over my mouth to stop myself from laughing.

I'd been a virgin when I met Ian and our rather predictable sex life was all I knew. I had nothing much to compare it to. The cinematic moans of couples in ecstasy were a mystery to me. Pop songs filled with lust and desire fulfilled went over my head. I had never understood how an act so mundane could inspire such interest. It was something couples did while one of them planned the week's menus, wasn't it?

No, it bloody wasn't.

Now, at 6.34 a.m. on September 14, I knew what all the fuss was about.

I listened to Bryn's steady breathing beside me and I remembered.

He had kissed me more thoroughly than I had ever been kissed in my life. He had kissed my mouth, my breasts, my eyelids, my ears. His breath had warmed my neck and made me quiver. His hands had been tender then firm then gentle again. He had moved over me and round me and inside me, stroking and touching until I thought I would faint. My heart was hammering so hard I wondered if I was having a seizure.

He whispered to me against my hair, my back, my throat. Words of longing and lust and his need for me. He had waited so long for me. He wanted me. He desired me. He watched me as he made love to me, as I felt myself melt into him. He cried out my name and held me against his heart.

What can I say? The earth moved. In fact, it probably shifted several degrees to the right. There may have been some structural damage in Collumpton. I was mad, I was sane, I was saved, I was lost. I had sobbed. Now I knew. And not once had I thought about what to have for lunch on Wednesday.

I began to think more lucidly. What did I do now? I hadn't woken up in bed with another person since…when? Well, since the morning of December 31 to be precise. I'd hardly ever in my life woken up in bed naked with another naked person. In the past, pyjamas featured quite heavily in my bedtime preparations and they were always a birthday and Christmas gift from Susan. Perhaps she wanted to make sure I was nocturnally decent? Well sod that for a game of soldiers. Those days were gone.

I curled and stretched out in the huge bed, enjoying the feel of the cool sheet under my back, remembering how Bryn had held me as I trembled.

Bryn.

I turned and saw he was watching me. Instinctively I pulled the duvet up under my chin.

He raised himself up on one elbow and smiled down at me.

'Good morning, Lottie. And how are you?'

Suddenly I was no longer the wanton, sex-starved woman of last night. I was me again; shy, thirty-four, agonised, waiting to say the wrong thing.

'Fine,' I said in a small voice.

He kissed me and ran a warm hand down my flank, making me quiver.

'Tea or coffee?'

'Coffee.'

He kissed me again, pushed back the duvet and got out of bed. There was a blue cotton dressing gown hanging on the back of the bedroom door and he went to put it on. But not before I had taken a good look at his long legs, the sweep of his smooth strong back, his broad shoulders, his neat bum. Crumbs. I felt like a jumble sale of assembled parts in comparison.

In comparison. That was a horrible thought. What must he have thought of me? How did my rather ordinary body compare with the sleek, toned, exfoliated physique Bonnie would have presented to him in this same bed? How did her titian curls look first thing in the morning? How far did she wrap her long legs around him? Further than I could, I expected. Did she know Bryn had particularly sensitive shoulders? Had he groaned with pleasure as he had when I touched him? Had she run her tongue across his instep as I had?

I'd never even read *Cosmopolitan*, how did I know how to do those things anyway?

My God, was this what my *sister* did with Trent?

Was this what she meant by *mind-blowing sex*?

I went cold with horror.

I wasn't the woman from last night any more. I was back to being Lottie, the girl who fell into flowerbeds and messed things up. The morning was breaking through the bedroom curtains, casting beams of light onto something glittering beside me on the bedside table.

I moved the little clock to see what it was. Bonnie's Koh-i-Noor earrings.

Of course it was.

I believed Bryn when he told me he and Bonnie had split up. Perhaps I had fallen for the oldest line in the Boys Book of Seduction. I felt a bit sick, embarrassed as I remembered what we had done, places we had stroked, kissed, licked, nibbled.

With a small whimper I got out of bed and scrambled to find my things. My bra and T-shirt were in a tangle on the floor, my knickers on the windowsill. There was no sign of my Mickey Mouse socks. My jeans were also nowhere to be seen until I tracked them down outside the bedroom on the landing. Inside out. Then I remembered the frantic way we had pulled at each other's clothes as we went to his bedroom. He had drawn me down against him halfway up the stairs and pulled my jeans off, I was desperate to feel my skin against his. I groaned at the memory and put my hands to my hot face. Then I got dressed as fast as I could.

He appeared in the bedroom doorway with two mugs of coffee as I was putting on my trainers.

'Oh.' His face fell. 'Are you going?'

'Gosh yes.'

'Why? Please don't go, Lottie. Come back to bed.'

'I've got such a lot to do,' I said. 'Things.'

I couldn't look at him. I kept having flashbacks. The faintly spicy smell of his skin. The kind softness, the muscled hardness, the warmth of his breath on my neck, the hollow at the base of his throat where I had tasted drops of wine.

He had gone downstairs to make a snack at 2.30 a.m. when we had both been slicked with sweat, exhausted with lovemaking and yet unwilling to sleep. He had brought back brandy and a plate of toast and he had fed me. I had licked the dripping butter off his body and I had drunk brandy from his mouth as we kissed.

Oh God Almighty, the taste of him.

I felt panic and embarrassment rising up in my throat. What must he think of me? He must think I was a right slapper to do the things I had done. All these months I had kept myself in check, no matter how much I might have fancied him. Then the *very first time* he invited me into his house, I drank his wine, sat in his kitchen, snoozed by his fire and I had ended up in bed with him doing things I had never ever done before.

God I was low. I was the lowest of the low. But then Ian had cheated on me, hadn't he? That made a difference, didn't it? I'd done nothing wrong, had I? I didn't know what the etiquette was on these occasions. I mean, I wasn't going to pretend a depth of sorrow I didn't feel. Was that a sign I was OK? Or was I an insensitive cow?

Ian hadn't been dead for a year and I had lusted after and slept with another man. Although there hadn't been that much actual sleeping involved. Hardly any, if I was honest. Perhaps a couple of hours? On and off. His arm had been round me, holding me close to his side. And all the time Bonnie's earrings were witness to my behaviour, lying next to me on the bedside table.

He had spoken words of desire, of need, of wanting me. He had touched every part of me and melted my cold, lonely heart. He had turned me and moved me and moulded my body to his until the air was driven from my lungs and I had gasped his name, sobbing with the depth of my feelings. Not once had he spoken of love.

He must have lied when he told me that they had split up. Months ago? And yet her earrings were in his bedroom. In my eye line when I woke up, for anyone to see. Perhaps he didn't care? Perhaps she knew? Perhaps they had one of those open relationships? And what about the business with Greg and their mother? Money had gone missing. Suddenly Bryn was a much less appealing character.

'I have to go home,' I said, 'now.'

I pushed past him and fled down the stairs.

Next door in Holly Cottage everything was as I had left it, of course. The decorating had not been miraculously finished off by the pixies; yesterday's washing up remained in the sink along with the stuff from the previous few days. I was a slob. I was both a slob and a tart. A slart.

I had behaved badly, completely out of character. But if that was the case, why was my whole body tingling? Why did I feel as though I could run across Dartmoor? Why did I want to jump and shout and scream at the top of my voice?

Why did I want to turn on my heel and throw myself back into Bryn's arms? For just a moment I allowed myself to imagine myself doing just that. I would meet him as he was halfway down the stairs, his hair still wet from the shower, confused by my sudden departure. I would drag him back into the bedroom; pull his clothes off with trembling fingers...

I did some desultory tidying up. Trying not to remember how Bryn's kitchen looked. Trying to concentrate on removing the congealed food stuck to my plates. How did I know he had a particularly sensitive place at the base of his spine?

Think of something else.

Anything else.

I went back upstairs to my bedroom with the intention of slapping paint onto the walls. I stood looking at the latest tub of white undercoat (there had been several) and remembered the day when I had fallen over and Bryn had pulled me to my feet.

And then I saw you. Covered in paint. And I thought, who is this crazy, beautiful, accident-prone woman?

Think of something else.

I even got as far as tipping some paint into the roller tray and then I stopped. A lump of something slopped out in the paint with a splat. I knelt down and prodded at it with the stirring stick, wondering what it was. After a few minutes I reeled back, revolted. It was a dead rat. How the hell had that got in there, the lid was firmly on. I felt sick. Had it drowned in there?

Then I stood up and made some retching noises. I lifted up the paint tray, nauseated by the weight of the dead animal. I staggered out into the garden and chucked it into the bin. I looked across the garden. Bryn was only next door. Had he seen me? Perhaps he had gone back to bed? Maybe Bonnie had phoned to ask about her chavvy earrings? Perhaps she was coming home and he was changing the sheets, opening the window to rid his bedroom of the reek of sex. Maybe he was thinking about last night's triumph and smirking. I could almost visualise him carving a notch on his bed head with a huge bowie knife.

I retreated back into the house and peered out of the front window to see that his truck was still in the drive. I chucked the roller down, grabbed my handbag and car keys and ran out of the house, petrified he would come out and see me. I drove away down the hill, blind to the beauty of the autumn morning. All I could see were Bonnie's earrings on the bedside table.

He had lied to me. He had told me a pack of lies and I had believed him.

I wasn't even sure where I was going, I just knew I had to get out and away from him.

Away from Bryn with his wonderful blue eyes, his warm tanned skin, his wide white smile, his strong hands, his mouth on mine. I was going to go mad if I carried on thinking about him.

Ooops, too late.

CHAPTER 16

Geranium – determination

I drove aimlessly, listening to my mobile dinging triumphantly with the arrival of the usual cluster of text messages and emails. I ignored them until I pulled into Stokeley. There was a promising array of shops I hadn't investigated before, one of which might well cater for my urgent caffeine deficiency. When I checked my phone there was nothing worth reading. How on earth did we manage in the days before this instant communication of unimportant trivia? But at least my day and succeeding days would be better for knowing that there were new friends waiting for me on the Jolly Bingo website, that there was a fully trained team of concerned experts waiting to help me reclaim PPI and that there was twenty per cent off cruises to the Caribbean. Fat chance.

I found a bunting-bedecked café nestling between a charity shop and a bank. I ignored the latter, examined the array of autumn dresses in the windows of the former and resisted the temptation to go in.

The café was a warm, wonderfully scented haven of coffee and bread products and I found a table in the window and ordered a large coffee and a doughnut. A bored-looking girl with turquoise nail varnish and matching eye shadow brought my order and then stood next to me looking out of the window and grimacing at a group of her friends who had stopped outside. I stirred sugar into my coffee and gazed out of the window too. Although I didn't pull faces at anyone.

I allowed myself to daydream as I bit into my doughnut.

Perhaps turquoise-eye-shadow girl would walk out of her job to join the grubby-looking set of teens sitting on the bench outside. Then the café owner, who would be sweet but ditzy, probably because she had adorable one-year-old twins, would offer me a job. And I would become indispensable and her new best friend. Or maybe not.

Eye-shadow girl went back behind the counter and began re-stacking a perilous heap of Chelsea buns. Chelsea. That rang a bell. Didn't Bryn do something in Chelsea? I had been so busy removing his clothes I had forgotten to ask.

What was it? Tuesday? Outside it was an ordinary day, local people were wandering about, stopping to chat, enjoying the sight of a flustered-looking blonde trying to parallel park. Across the road a harassed mother with magenta hair dragged a buggy and two small children out of the sweet shop. I could hear their shouting from inside the café and I expect much of Mid Devon could too. Feeling slightly better, I ordered another large coffee.

The sun was shining through the bull's eye glass panes, sending a rainbow of light through the crystal vase onto the white cloth. I moved my left hand so that the colours sparkled across my fingers and then I realised something. My commitment ring. I wasn't wearing it.

I couldn't believe it. I gave a strangled gasp and looked around the table, on the floor, in my pockets, turned out my handbag, but nothing. I knew I had lost weight in the last few months, the ring had been loose, the emerald swivelling around my finger like a pea, but this was the first time it had fallen off. I remembered Susan, the way she had kept her wedding ring on her thin finger with an elastic band. But my ring knew the inner secrets of my heart.

It knew what I had been up to. It had rejected me. Where the hell was it?

I went cold at the thought. What if Bryn found it when he went to remake the bed? Would he laugh and put it on the bedside table, pushing Bonnie's Koh-i-Noor earrings to one side to make room for his latest trophy? Perhaps he had a cupboard somewhere with other similar nicknacks. Someone's hair band, a particularly saucy pair of red satin knickers, a lacy bra with tassels attached. Good grief, my imagination was in overdrive.

I dropped to my knees and scrabbled around on the floor, looking for it.

I had a flashback to the day when Ian had put that ring on my finger. He had patted my hand. *You'll say yes eventually*, he said.

I sat back on my heels. What was I going to do? And how could I start to make my life easier instead of always, always mucking things up?

I had an appointment with the solicitor tomorrow; perhaps he would be able to update me on the tortuously slow process of settling Ian's estate and debts. It had been months since he had died; surely it couldn't take much longer? Could it?

I stood up, brushing the dust and cake crumbs off my knees, and sat down again. What was I going to do? I was sick of feeling so out of control. I could always go to stay with Jenny in Houston for a while, but I didn't want to live there. England was and always would be my home. I couldn't bear the thought of living in a country where the seasons were predictable, where Christmas took second place to Thanksgiving and where cafés didn't – as this one had – put little cut-glass vases of lavender heads on the table. I rubbed the space where my ring should have been and finished my coffee. I went to pay.

'Did yew find what yew was looking fer?'

Behind the cake-laden counter, turquoise-eye-shadow girl, identified on her name badge as Gin, took my money and handed over some change. She had been a placid witness to my fruitless search as I grubbed around on the floor pushing dust balls and cake fragments to one side, looking for my ring.

I shook my head. It wasn't that I was tearful or upset, I just felt so hideously guilty.

'I've lost a ring. I've no idea where it could be.'

'It'll turn up,' Gin said, brushing crumbs off the front of her overall. 'I lorst mine in bed once; found it stuck to me old man's bum. Gawd we laughed! And once I found it down the bottom of the bed. Happens if you're a restless sleeper. Expect that's what's happened to yourn. Pop back in a couple of days, I'll let you know if I find it. Have a good look when yew gets home.'

'Yes,' I said, blushing.

It might well have got lost in the bed, but the trouble is it wasn't my bed. Possibly that was too much information for Gin, given our short acquaintance.

I wandered around feeling a bit jittery for a while; perhaps that was my general state of mind – heightened by a huge caffeine and sugar rush.

There was a small farmer's market filling the town square and I meandered through the stalls alternately admiring the quality of the local vegetables and marvelling that someone local was still producing legless crochet dolls to cover the spare loo roll. I noticed a small jeweller's shop, one half of the window filled with second-hand – or as P.D. Smith Esq preferred to describe it, vintage – jewellery. I made a note of the name and phone number and decided that I would return with some of my things. I needed the money after all. And I might just as well sell it as lose it in random strangers' beds.

'Lottie! Lottie!'

Someone was calling my name and I turned to see Sophie hurrying through the stalls towards me. She reached my side and after looking at me for a long moment, threw her arms around me and hugged me.

'Are you all right?' she said at last, suddenly angry. 'We've been worried sick about you. I even phoned up that witch Susan but she wouldn't tell me anything. I asked Jess and she said you were OK but didn't want us to make a fuss. Every time I phoned you didn't answer. Then she and Greg have been away, I think they went to Spain; I haven't seen them for ages.'

'I told you about the mobile reception, but to be honest, Sophie, I didn't want to see anyone. Not after…you know.'

She almost danced on the spot with frustration. 'No, I bloody don't know! We've been friends for a long time, Lottie. What happened doesn't change that, you silly cow!'

I shook my head. 'I know, yes, I know. I should have…oh I don't know, Soph, it's all been such a bloody mess.'

The tears were very near the surface now. Sophie put an arm round my shoulder and pulled me over to the one bench in the square not filled with smoking teenagers. We sat down and I filled her in on Holly Cottage, the cleaning, the decorating, Trudy, Susan, my imminent visit to the solicitor. All the time she gasped and groaned in all the right places and occasionally patted my hand or rubbed my arm in sympathy. It was really nice.

'It's all been pretty shit,' I said as I finished my tale of woe.

Sophie puffed out her cheeks in a sigh. 'What will you do next?'

I shrugged and didn't answer.

'And you're sure Jess is selling the house?'

I nodded. I didn't trust myself to speak any more.

'So have the estate agents been round? You know, to value the place and measure up?'

I frowned. 'No, that's odd, isn't it? And it's been a while. I wonder why not.'

'Perhaps she's changed her mind,' Sophie said. 'Decided not to sell after all.'

'I don't know. Surely she would have told me?'

Sophie pulled out a diary and a pen. 'Write your address and all your bloody contact details here. And don't be such a twit in future. Come and see us.'

'I'm so ashamed, so embarrassed, I've made a complete fool of myself.'

Sophie looked puzzled. 'How? Don't be daft. You have nothing to be ashamed about, nothing to apologise for. We've all missed you. There are still public phone boxes. And if you can't ring you could always write, you know. Postcards, letters, cards. Got the idea?' She checked her watch and then winced slightly. 'Bugger, I've got to go, I've got an appointment with a physio; frozen shoulder.'

I nodded. I didn't tell her the latest piece of the story. Bryn. I'd keep that to myself. But I did feel a little bit better about things. Perhaps I wasn't friendless after all.

She hugged me and made me promise we'd see each other again soon. Then she dashed off down the street.

I got back to Holly Cottage late in the afternoon when the sun had set. The evening was chilly and fog was beginning to thicken in the road between the high Devon banks and in the garden. To my fevered imagination it looked as though Bryn – huge and bear-like – might be lurking in the shadows, although his truck was missing from the drive and there were no lights on in his house. I parked my car as far as possible down my driveway, hoping when he returned he wouldn't notice it, went inside, locked the door and closed all the curtains.

Inside, I wandered around looking for my ring and feeling wretched. I searched everywhere. That way I could pretend that it wasn't next door down the back of Bryn's sofa, or halfway up his stairs, or on the rug under his bed. He might have shaken out the duvet and wondered what had fallen on the floor and rolled out of sight. I expect he would eventually hoover it up and maybe it would block the nozzle, collecting a revolting bouquet of hair and random bits of plastic.

I trudged upstairs with a glass, a bottle of red wine, a bag of salt and vinegar crisps and a bar of fruit and nut chocolate – I tried to convince myself it was one of my five a day, if not two. I was both delusional and fed up. Was it only twenty-four hours ago that I had been in bed with Bryn?

Had we been making love? Or was it just having sex? Or had I been generally fucked in every sense of the word? I opened the wine and sloshed out a generous glassful. I wished I could forget.

The following day I woke still fully dressed in a tangle of bedclothes with a headache, crisp crumbs in my underwear and a square of chocolate stuck to my cheek. The wine had done the trick and knocked me out. Now I could add self-medicating with alcohol to my list of sins. Oh well done, Lottie.

Outside, the weather was dull and dreary. Yesterday evening's mist had thickened overnight into proper fog and the view I had become so fond of had disappeared into the murk. There was still no sign of Bryn's truck. Perhaps he had gone round to spend the night with Bonnie. I didn't even know where she lived. I clenched my teeth in fury. Maybe he had gone to double check which one of us was better in the sack? Or maybe he had gone to return Bonnie's earrings?

I put on my scruffiest paint-smeared clothes and vowed that before I set out to see my solicitor I would make a start on the wallpaper. Sophie had said she thought Jess and Greg were abroad, but they would surely be back sometime soon. I needed to stick to my side of the bargain.

The morning passed quickly and the bedroom (I needed to stop calling it *my* bedroom) started to look better. There had been grubby cotton curtains at the window when I arrived and I had washed them and never put them up again. Why spoil the view? I took a moment out to lean out of the window. The fog was clearing as the sun raised itself above the hills and I realised I would miss this room with its tranquil outlook over the fields. I had never felt afraid in this house, I had got used to the peacefulness of this place, the clear air in a way I would never have believed. The only sounds were birdsong, the occasional tractor going up the lane, a farm dog barking somewhere in the hills, the far distant noise of a plane overhead. Would I like being back in the noisy world of cars and people and shops? I didn't allow myself to think about it too much, but I wasn't sure I would.

I carried on, concentrating on the edges where the sloping ceiling met the uneven walls and parts of the roof beams had been exposed as a feature.

I must try harder to get a job when I finished my task here. If not at the supermarket then somewhere else. I had lived frugally enough but after all these months my savings had been seriously depleted. I couldn't carry on like this for much longer. The trouble was I wasn't trained to do anything.

My novel (*Love at Last*) had stalled into a soggy heap at 44,000 words and my plucky heroine, Amber, was still out there somewhere, torn between handsome but unreliable Jake and stolid, dependable Tom.

By the time I had finished wallpapering one wall I had cheered up enormously and dreamt up a pleasing future for myself where Amber, Jake and Tom were released onto the unsuspecting literary world and made me a fortune. I even thought about which mega Hollywood stars would play the title roles when the film rights were acquired, again at huge financial benefit to yours truly. I would soon look back at this part of my life and – well not laugh exactly, but certainly smile.

I was in relatively good spirits as I washed the paste brush and bucket out, a job I usually detested. I was due to see the solicitor at three so I changed into a tweed skirt and white shirt. Checking my reflection I realised I looked dull and middle-aged. Would Venus Williams have worn such an outfit? Not likely.

I pulled the offending items off and chucked them into the recycling. I spent half an hour doing much the same thing with my other clothes until practically the only things left to choose between were my pyjamas (perhaps not) and a pink dress that I had never worn because Ian had said was too short. I put it on, jammed on some ballet pumps and stuck my tongue out at my reflection.

In my opinion solicitors should, by law, have offices in a rambling, Regency house with piles of documents tied with pink tape lined up on the elegant staircase. There should be worn velvet settees in the waiting room and an elderly receptionist called Janet hovering between the desk and Mr Senior Partner's (on whom she has a lifelong but unrequited crush) office.

Sadly my solicitor worked out of a featureless glass block in the middle of an out-of-town business park. His secretary – or PA, as she preferred to be known – was Leanne, a brusque unsmiling twenty-something with dreadlocks and a penchant for exotic nail varnish.

As I entered the foyer she jerked her chin at me by way of greeting.

'Take a seat, Charlotte, Jeff's around somewhere. He shouldn't be long.'

I sat in the corner on a stylish but uncomfortable chair and thought about picking up one of the obscure magazines on the table, but I couldn't be bothered.

I'd been here in this overheated office before, terrified about what was happening, just after I'd received a visit from the first of the many creditors who were about to come out from the woodwork.

Only a day after Ian died two large men had come to the house in matching black jackets with logos on the breast pocket. RCL. One held a clipboard. I assumed they were canvassing for the local government elections in March, and I was not in the mood.

'Mr Ian Gerald Lovell in, is he?' said the taller of the two, chewing a large wad of gum with obvious enthusiasm.

'No he's not.'

'Are you Mrs Lovell?'

'No.'

He gave me a disbelieving look.

'We've come for the car,' he said. His face flexed into a rictus smile.

I stood and stared at them, my mouth open.

'Car?'

'A silver Lexus.' He shifted his gum to the other side and reeled off the number plate. I caught a waft of cigarettes on his breath, thinly camouflaged with spearmint.

'What about it?'

Had Ian arranged for the car to be serviced?

'We're from Regal Car Leasing.' That would explain the logos. 'The car is being repossessed for non-payment. Six months in arrears. You should remove any personal items from the car now.' The unpleasant smile went as quickly as it had appeared.

I staggered back, grabbing hold of the doorframe for support.

'Do you have the keys?'

'No, I don't have the bloody keys!' I could feel my heart hammering.

The other man, marginally smaller but balder, stepped forward. He gave me a cold-eyed look, reminiscent of a shark waiting outside a diver's cage.

'I realise this must be upsetting, but we're just doing our job, Mrs Lovell. When will Mr Lovell be available?'

'I've already told you, I'm not Mrs Lovell. He's not available and he never will be,' I said. I closed my eyes and took a deep breath. I felt sick.

First man puffed out his cheeks and shook his head. 'There's no need to be like that. We have the legal right to remove the car.' He held out a sheaf of paperwork towards me and shook it. 'See?'

'I have no idea where the car is,' I said.

He gave me a pitying look and then ran his eyes over me with an unpleasant smirk, as though I was also something he needed to value.

'In the garage, is it? Go and take a look, Les. Mrs Lovell, it would be easier in the long run if you told us. Otherwise we've got other people who won't be as *polite* as me and Les are, if you get my meaning.'

I was cold with dread now. I just wanted them and their grinning familiarity with this situation to go away.

My mouth was dry.

'You'd better ask the police. There was an accident. On New Year's Day—'

First man stepped forward, gum clamped between his front teeth, his face furrowed with concern.

'Was the car damaged?'

Was the car damaged? The strange thing was I had no idea what state the car was in. I thought about it for a horrible few seconds while the first man tapped a chewed biro on the clipboard. His fingers were short and stubby, the nails bitten almost to the quick. Well, had the car been badly damaged? Had it been flattened? Had it burst into flames?

I pushed these thoughts away and found my voice at last. I was afraid, vulnerable, and yet suddenly I was angry.

'I expect it was damaged, numb nuts. Ian was killed. And if you are going to come to people's houses, threatening and demanding, at least have the manners to take your bloody gum out first!'

When Leanne took me through into his office, Jeff Bingham was sitting behind a loaded desk, peering out from between piles of documents. I resisted the ever-present temptation to ask how his briefs were, and sat down.

'All well, Miss Calder?'

'Fine, thanks. Never better,' I lied, plastering a smile on my face.

Isn't it funny; a solicitor's offices must see a lot of people for whom the world is close to ending in chaos, but we always say that sort of thing. But then in a crowded doctor's waiting room, ask anyone how they are and they will always say they are well, which begs the question, why the hell are you here?

Anyway I was one of Jeff's least interesting and important clients and last time I was here he obviously couldn't wait to get me out again. Today was rather different.

'I've been looking forward to seeing you,' he said.

Really? Why?

He was young, tall, thin, and nervy, and like last time, dressed in a dark suit and a dull tie. I always had the impression he would rather be doing something else. He looked the sort who would leave his work clothes at the office and cycle in on a very thin bike, with a long queue of impatient motorists behind him glaring furiously at his Lycra-clad bottom.

'Yes, sorry, I'm a bit out in the wilds. Not much phone reception and no Internet.'

He flicked me a glance to convey his disbelief at this state of affairs.

'Hmm, doesn't the postman call either? Would you like a cup of coffee,' he said, 'tea, or chilled water?'

I looked up at him, startled. This was a first.

'No, thanks, but thank you,' I said. I just wanted to get out of the place.

He shuffled his paperwork about and untied a beige folder tied with pale pink cotton tape in a particular way. I'd noticed how all solicitors do this; perhaps they have lessons at university on how to tie them up. Maybe it's a part of their first year exams. *I'm sorry, Mr Sedgwick, but your knots were not of the required standard.*

I realised he was speaking, very quietly, his lips hardly moving.

'So we have disbursed the proceeds of the sale of the property. HMRC have been satisfied. So have the – um – various people

192

and establishments that the late Mr Lovell frequented. There were some outstanding amounts for the services – electricity, gas that sort of thing. And of course our fees.' He ran a finger round inside his collar.

'What else?'

Would there now be a request for a sample of my blood? Sweat? Tears? DNA? Fingerprints? My full educational history? I wondered if I could remember my GCSE grades.

Jeff raised his eyebrows. 'No, nothing else.'

'You mean it's all sorted?'

He shifted in his chair. 'What were you expecting?'

I thought about it. 'I don't know. It's been going on for so long I wondered if it would ever be finished. It's been months.'

He hummed and hawed for a minute and then went off on a minor rant about the delays inherent in dealing with HMRC, how many phone calls he had made that hadn't been answered. The length of time he had been left on hold. Letters that took at least six weeks to elicit any sort of reply. Then he moved on to the problems he had encountered with Mr O'Callaghan (Big Kev) and his unprofessional solicitor. Then the haggling on the part of the house purchasers' solicitors regarding the stained carpets in the sitting room and the broken tumble dryer that had been left at the back of the garage.

He eventually stopped to draw breath and looked at me for sympathy.

I surprised myself.

'I really couldn't care less, Jeff, I'm sure they can afford to replace the carpets and dispose of the tumble dryer. They got the house at a bargain price. I've had other things to worry about. I've been homeless, living on the charity of friends, not knowing what the hell was happening.'

'Ah yes. Of course. Well, hmm. Anyway, Mrs Susan Lovell called in to see me a few days ago with a particular request.'

What would that be, I wondered? Perhaps she had a sack full

of kittens that needed drowning? Or maybe she had discovered the stained carpet was my fault after I'd kicked that mug of tea over it and was going to sue me for the cost of replacing it.

I noticed a backpack on the floor behind his desk, which reinforced my previous assumption he was a bike rider. On top of the filing cabinet was a metal water bottle. I bet there was a quinoa and nut salad in the staff fridge.

Jeff was still talking.

'…the surplus funds will be transferred to your nominated bank account as of tomorrow. Probably before nine thirty a.m.'

'Surplus funds?' I sat up a bit straighter and blinked at him. 'What surplus funds?'

He pushed another sheet of paper towards me across the desk. 'These surplus funds.'

My eyesight went a bit funny at this point. There was just a bewildering set of columns and figures with some things underlined in red biro and others highlighted in yellow. There was a small Post-it note arrow stuck halfway down the page next to a figure. £92,078.76.

I prodded at it with one finger. 'What's this?'

Jeff obviously considered me to be in the slow learners group at this point.

'As I have been explaining, surplus funds,' he said, very slowly and pointedly, 'funds that are surplus.'

'And what has this got to do with me?'

He sighed with exasperation.

'I've just told you, Mrs Susan Lovell wishes these surplus funds to be passed to you. As a gesture of goodwill.'

'Bloody hell!'

I sat looking at the paper for a few minutes, and then I looked up at him.

'Ninety-two thousand pounds.'

'And seventy-eight pounds and seventy-six pence,' Jeff added.

'And that's for me? That's it?'

He took the piece of paper back and looked at it, wagging his head from side to side.

'I know it's not much. I mean, not considering the house sold for over seven hundred thousand. But, well…' He looked up at me and pulled a sort of agonised sympathetic face. He looked even more like Rodney Trotter for a moment and I half expected him to say he felt like a right dipstick. But no. He fell back into the safe territory of legalese.

'You have to realise that we were charged to disburse these monies. HMRC are not an institution to fall foul of. Much as we might not approve of money being squandered at Mr O'Callaghan's casino or his – ahem – line of work, he had a claim on Mr Lovell's estate that we could in no way—'

'It's fine,' I said. 'I mean, yes, it was awful to think that so much money went the way it did, but it's done now. And Susan is quite sure she wants to do this?'

'Absolutely sure.'

'Then I'm free.'

'Free? I don't understand.'

'You've never had large men come to the house and threaten you.'

'No.'

'Or had a car repossessed or phone calls at all hours from people wanting money.'

'No.'

'You've not hidden behind the sofa because there are people at the front door. You've not dreaded the postman arriving.'

'No, of course not.'

'Well I have and it's not a thing I would wish on my worst enemy,' I said. I stood up and reached over for the piece of paper he was still holding. 'Can I have that?'

He looked at the paper as though he was surprised to find himself still holding it.

'Yes, of course. This is for you after all.'

I took the paper and folded it into my handbag. It was the most wonderful moment I had experienced for ages. Well at least since I had found myself gasping, pinned to the bed by Bryn, my world condensed down to throbbing sparks of pleasure.

Shut up! Shut up! Stop thinking about him! For God's sake!

I was horribly aware of the inappropriateness of remembering such a scene while Jeff sat watching me. I must have seemed feeble minded at best.

I pulled myself together, we made our polite farewells and I drove home. I had money at last, from the most unlikely of sources. I had a window on the future. I could stop buying own-brand food from the budget supermarket all the time. I could fill up my car's tank instead of forcing it to limp along on fumes. I could get my teeth checked.

CHAPTER 17

Anemone – have you forsaken me?

That evening I fished out my laptop and fired it up for the first time in months. Not being able to log on to the Internet meant I had given it up as a bad job. My crops on Farmville had long since withered and died.

I read through the first few pages of *Love at Last* and my confidence faltered. Perhaps I should get a day job after all. Chef Jake's eyes were blue and occasionally brown. Stolid Tom's devoted but incompetent receptionist was by turns Liz, Lisa and Louise. In the space of four chapters Jake smashed crockery three times and Tom saved nine kittens and a Jack Russell puppy.

Thinking that perhaps a glass or three of Merlot might help, I went into the kitchen. Approximately nine and a half seconds after I switched on the light, someone knocked on the back door. I shrank against the fridge, clutching the bottle to my heart like a meths drinker cornered in an alley.

'Lottie? Come on, Lottie. Please talk to me.'

It was Bryn. Of course it was.

I weighed up the options and after a few moments of pretending I wasn't in, opened the door. Bryn stood there in jeans, a check shirt and his CAT boots looking so unbelievably handsome that at the back of my mind Stolid Tom changed his entire appearance and character in seconds. I decided to play it casual.

'Glass of wine?' I said, waving the bottle.

Bryn nodded and, ducking his head under the doorframe, stepped into the kitchen and closed the door behind him. He made a move towards me, the sort that starts with a peck on the cheek and ends with a full-blown snog. I stepped neatly to one side and found glasses in the cupboard. I poured wine, taking care to keep the kitchen table between us.

'How are you?' he said, his eyes never leaving my face.

'Oh, you know, busy. I went into town this morning, saw my solicitor and did some stuff. Important things. Met up with an old friend.'

My mouth was so dry my top lip was sticking to my teeth. I did a passable Humphrey Bogart impersonation, took a swig of my wine and choked a little as it went down the wrong way. 'You?'

'Working at Trehorlicks Hall. It's going to be beautiful. I should take you to see it,' he said.

'That would be nice. I love a good gardener. I mean I love a good *garden*.'

God Almighty, is this a Freudian slip I see before me?

'Lottie…'

'Flowers and that. You know. Trees,' I gabbled on.

'Lottie.'

Bryn put his glass down on the table and came round it towards me. I played chase me Charlie for a few seconds.

'Lottie, please.'

'What?'

He put his hand out and touched my arm. I could feel the heat of him through my shirt. I went a bit woozy.

'The other night,' he said.

He was so close now. I could almost feel the warmth of his body. I could smell the faint tang of wood smoke clinging to his

198

shirt. There was a tiny twig caught up in his hair and it too
my willpower not to reach up and remove it.

'Oh that,' I said, and shrugged.

The most staggering experience of my life and I bloody
shrugged?

I saw a flicker of something in his eyes and he stepped away,
picked up his wine and sipped it.

'So you're not...'

Not what? Not bothered? Not in my right mind? Not gagging
for him?

'Oooh, you know. It was great. Thanks,' I said.

Thanks? Was I insane?

'That's OK then.' He reached into his pocket, pulled out my
Mickey Mouse socks and put them on the worktop. 'You left these
behind.'

'Thanks.'

I don't suppose you found my ring too, did you?

He finished his wine and put the glass on the table. I looked
at the shape of his hands, his fingers, a small white scar on the
back of his thumb.

I had the terrible urge to take hold of his hand and kiss his
palm, feel his fingers on my face.

Then I reminded myself of a couple of things. This is a man
who cheated on his girlfriend. This is a man who isn't speaking
to his brother because he swindled his mother. This is not the
man who is going to fix my life any more than Ian did. I needed
to do that for myself.

I spent another night wrestling with the duvet and a headache
courtesy of yet another bout of self-medication. I got out of bed at
about three thirty to get a glass of water and some aspirin. I caught
sight of my reflection in the hall mirror. All this self-medication
mixed with a stomach-curdling dose of guilt, embarrassment and
lust was doing me no favours. My eyes were huge, my face pale and
miserable. Pathetic. I was a grown-up. Well, as good as.

I shouldn't need to resort to such juvenile tactics to:

1) Get to sleep

2) Stay asleep

3) Stop remembering Bryn's face above mine, his blue eyes lustrous in the dusky light as he held my face in his hands and kissed me

4) Stop remembering the feel of his mouth on my body, my throat, my shoulder, his warm breath making me tremble, his tongue coaxing, brushing…

5) Oh shut up, Lottie, give it a bloody rest.

As I lay down in the darkness I wondered how my sister was getting on with Trent.

I should email her. And tell her what exactly?

That now I knew what she meant by the phrase mind-blowing sex?

That I had allowed my next-door neighbour, the bear-like, black-hearted Bryn, to shag me senseless?

That I was about to be made homeless again but I had some money at last?

I dozed on and off until the small square panes of the bedroom window glowed with the dawn and then of course I fell asleep.

When I woke it was half past ten and it felt as though someone had emptied a dustpan onto the floor of my mouth. I padded downstairs and made some tea. The reflection in the hall mirror was no more encouraging than it had been earlier. I needed to sort myself out before my liver exploded.

Following some alternative therapy of toast and marmalade I began to feel a bit better. By the middle of the afternoon I was fully recovered and feeling pretty positive. But my heart sank when I saw Jess pull up outside. I think my face did too.

'Oh, don't look like that! I know I've been such a bad friend,' she said as she hugged me. 'Greg and me went off, spur of the moment, and I never thought to tell you. You must think I'm such a big fat cow.'

She looked anything but. She was wearing one of her artless little frocks, this one in pale blue and white polka dots that probably cost a fortune in some exclusive boutique. In comparison, I must have been the one who looked pretty bovine. None of my clothes fitted properly any more and my baggy brown painting trousers were held up with an old belt. From behind I must have looked like the back end of a pantomime horse.

I reassured her I was quite OK and put the kettle on. I told her my news (well some of it) and then I asked the question that had been lumbering about the kitchen like the proverbial elephant. Was she going to sell the house?

Jess blushed and looked at her hands, fiddling with a rather fine aquamarine bracelet. At last she looked up.

'I'm sorry I've been so indecisive, it wasn't fair on you at all. I needed the money, if I'm honest, to sort something out. But anyway, Holly Cottage isn't going on the market.'

The relief at this was immense and I closed my eyes and sent up a silent prayer of thanks.

'I expect it'll be rented out again at some point, but…' She hesitated and seemed unsure what to say. At last she smiled and looked at me. 'Let's not worry about that for now. Let's have coffee?'

I was happy to agree. It felt as though the weight of the world had been lifted from my shoulders.

We moved on to her news.

'We've been sorting out a bit of business,' she said. She nibbled at a fingernail. 'Something Greg should've done a long time ago. I think it's going to make things better. I hope so anyway.'

'What do you mean?'

Jess shook her head. 'Oh nothing. I can't say. Personal stuff. Just business.' Her face brightened. 'So how are you getting on? How's Bryn? Have you seen him?'

I made a non-committal noise. Something between *um* and *er*. I turned my back on her for a moment so she couldn't see

201

me blushing. I busied myself making coffee and pretending to look in the biscuit tin. Jess looked concerned.

'Has he been a nuisance? I know he's a bit of a loner now, which is a pity because he's very handsome, don't you think? And Bryn's really nice when you get to know him. I'd hate to think he was making your life difficult. I could have a word, if you like?'

'No, absolutely not!' I yelped.

'Well apart from being a friend, you've been my tenant. So I'm not going to let him get away with any nonsense.' Jess looked as stern as she could considering she appeared about fifteen in her cotton frock and pale blue ballet pumps.

'Please don't. Everything is fine,' I said. I pushed a mug of coffee towards her.

She sighed and sipped her drink.

'Such a pity.' She threw me a look. 'I'll be honest, I was hoping he'd fancy you and you'd fancy him and get him out of the clutches of that awful ginger piece.'

My radar crackled onto high alert. Phasers on stun, Mr Sulu. I could almost feel my ears pricking up like a Springer spaniel at a Boxing Day shoot.

'Ginger piece? You mean Bonnie?'

'I'm beginning to think she's mad. She's been phoning me up recently, though how the hell she got my number I have no idea. Have you met her?'

'Several times.'

'She was a friend of his wife. She and Bryn had a – you know – a thing a few years ago.'

Whoa! What? Wife? Bryn has a wife? And he and Bonnie had a thing? Had a thing? Past tense? What sort of thing? Was it a big thing or a small thing like he told me? Has he no decency at all?

I covered my eyes with one hand and tried to concentrate.

'So he's married, but he had a fling with Bonnie and they've split up? I mean they aren't a couple? I thought…'

Jess screwed up her nose. 'Urgh no. You've met her. She's a right bunny boiler. Any other man would have got a restraining order by now. Bryn's fault, he's too soft.'

My head was spinning.

Wife? Bunny boiler? *Restraining order?*

I wanted to bring up the case of the bedside earrings but that would mean admitting I had been in Bryn's bedroom and open up a whole new line of questioning.

Instead I found a packet of chocolate Hobnobs and emptied them into the biscuit tin.

'And? Go on? What's all this about a wife? I didn't know he was married.'

'Well, he's divorced now, obvs. Even Bryn has his limits. Between you and me I think he must have a new love interest. Or at least Bonnie thinks he has. She's been phoning me up, crying down the phone, asking me to help her win him back.'

'Goodness! What did you say?'

'I told her she needed therapy, silly cow.'

I stifled a laugh.

'Have you seen any new ladies around the place doing the walk of shame?' Jess asked. She poked around in the biscuit tin until she found a broken fragment of Hobnob and took it.

I shook my head and tried to look innocent.

'Well, that's very annoying. I would have thought if Bryn was getting a bit of –' she made a rather rude gesture at this point '– you know, bed action, he would have been nicer to you.'

'He hasn't not been nice to me. I mean, he's been fine,' I said, finding a tea towel to fold so I didn't need to look at her.

'Are you sure? I've got to have a chat with him about something else.' She nibbled around the edge of her biscuit then looked at her watch. 'He should be here in a mo. I don't mind giving him a good telling off. In fact, I'd enjoy it.'

I stretched a false but beaming smile across my face and pointed to it.

'Nothing wrong at all. Nothing to declare. See?'

Hang on.

Here in a mo? Did she say Bryn was going to be here in a mo? And how could I get her back to the subject of the wife without seeming too obvious?

I did what I always do and went for the subtle approach.

'So what happened to his wife?'

Jess looked puzzled. 'Whose wife?'

'Bryn's wife. Jess, keep up.'

She made little flapping motions with her hands. 'Sorry, I was thinking about something else. His wife, Helen – we used to call her Hell behind her back, for obvious reasons – ran off with Bonnie's fiancé. I thought you knew? They'd been married for less than a year. Craig was always a bit of a flirt with anything in a dress and a pulse so no one thought anything of it. You know – the way they were with each other? Flirty chat. A bit touchy-feely. Then out of the blue Craig and Hell disappeared together. They surfaced six months later running a dive school in Barbados. Craig was minted, loaded, did I mention that? That was quite funny, wasn't it, what I just said? Surfaced, dive school? Get it?'

I nodded, stunned, as I processed all this information.

'Then, in zero seconds flat, Bonnie honed in on Bryn like a nuclear warhead. She must have caught him at a weak moment. He soon realised his mistake. We all knew it would never work. It all seemed very amicable to start off with. A sort of friends with benefits thing, but Bonnie wouldn't let it run its course. Seemed to think the four of them could just do a bit of a shuffle around and it would all work out. I suppose Bryn felt sorry for her.'

'I suppose so.' I felt a bit wobbly.

'Anyway!' Jess slapped her hands down on her knees. 'Who cares?'

'Well…' I bloody cared, but I knew I couldn't say anything more without raising suspicion.

'I love how the cottage is looking. You're doing such a brilliant job,' Jess said. 'I can't believe how well you've done it. I totally love the wallpaper you're using in the back bedroom; it'll be like sleeping in a garden. And the colours of that chalky paint in the hallway are perfect. So that proved you were right and so was I and Greg doesn't know sod all about anything.'

'Thanks. I suppose it's just about finished now. Not much left to do.'

'Well yeah, but hello!' She waggled one index finger from side to side. 'What about the garden? And that brings me to why I'm here. I won a competition recently for garden plants, two hundred and fifty pounds' worth. Lucky, eh? Our garden is a bit of a mess what with the swimming pool complex not finished yet and the garden office planned for next month, so we can't use it. Greg says he's going to get someone in anyway, once all the builders have left. And this has an expiry date and we'll never get round to using it before then. So...'

Jess paused for breath at last, handed over an envelope and blinked up at me. The picture of innocence. Something wasn't right here but I was darned if I could put my finger on it.

I took the envelope. On the outside was typed First Prize, and inside was a gift certificate for the South West Garden Centre; £250, just as Jess had said.

'What are you up to?' I said.

Jess laughed and finished her biscuit fragment, something that had taken her all this time. I, on the other hand, had eaten three. Can't eat proper meals but never say no to a Hobnob.

'Nothing! Honestly, Lottie! I've just given you a gift voucher to spend on this garden.' She rolled her eyes. 'Just take it there before the end of the month and tell them that you are the prize winner come to spend your loot. They'll help you.'

'Well OK, but...'

'There are some tools in the shed. You can use those.'

'But...'

205

'God, is that the time? I must fly!' Jess stood up and shook out her skirt. 'I have to see Bryn. I thought he might call round. I mean he must be able to see my car in the drive. Oh well.'

She hurried out of the back door and over to Bryn's garden. After a few minutes I heard his familiar laugh and I closed the door and sat down to think.

Greg didn't get on with Bryn, but Jess did.

Bryn had been married.

Bryn's wife had run off with Bonnie's fiancé.

Bonnie wanted to carry on a relationship with Bryn.

Bryn didn't want to. Or did he?

What had he said? Bonnie was a lovely girl, but…

So it looked as though he had been telling the truth after all. So how would he explain those bloody earrings by the side of the bed?

I rested my chin on my hands and closed my eyes.

There was only one way Bonnie's earrings could have got to that side of the bed and that would be when she put them there. Was there any reason other than she was sleeping with Bryn? I couldn't think of one. And I knew those earrings hadn't been there for months, forgotten after their latest tryst, because I had seen her wearing them only recently.

Horrible images of her in bed with Bryn flickered behind my closed eyelids. She wouldn't be worried about cellulite on her bottom. She didn't have much bottom to start with. She wouldn't be self-conscious, pulling the duvet over herself when she woke up as I had. She would probably have pranced about the room stark naked. Did I have it in me to prance? I wriggled about on my chair for a moment, trying to visualise it.

No. I sighed and took another Hobnob.

CHAPTER 18

Yellow carnations – disappointment, rejection

I crept around Holly Cottage like a burglar over the next few days, hoping to avoid Bryn and yet at the same time longing to see him. When one morning I found myself crouched, peeping out from behind the bathroom curtains to catch a glimpse of him as he got into his truck, I realised I was being ridiculous.

Even if he did look rather gorgeous in jeans and a cream Aran sweater.

He had made no further effort to contact me.

Which surely put him in the wrong. Didn't it?

Yes, it did. Even though I had behaved like an idiot when he came round to see me. I mean, it wouldn't have hurt for him to come round *again* would it? Try one more time? If he was really keen?

I thought about this all morning, carrying on the imaginary discussion as I dug out ground elder from one of my flowerbeds that morning and worked myself up into what might be called a Right Old State.

If he had meant half the stuff he had said to me – all that longing and desire business, my lovely eyes, my hair, etc. etc. –

surely he should have come round to see me? Brought me flowers? Suggested a date? I don't know, written me a poem? Perhaps that was pushing it a bit. And yet there had been nothing. No apology for treating me like that. Not the faintest suggestion that he wanted to establish a relationship with me. Other than one based on random, mind-blowing sex.

I stood up from my digging, indignant. Flaming cheek of the man! Well if he could carry on with daily life and not give a second thought to it then I could too. I'd been wrong, hadn't I? Ian had warned me about this but I hadn't wanted to believe him.

'Look, Lottie, it's a fact of life. All men play around a bit if they get the chance. You know that. Any man who says he doesn't is a liar.'

Perhaps Bryn really was no different? Maybe there were dozens of delusional women around the South West all thinking we were something special to him.

Perhaps Lady Trehorlicks was not as I had been led to believe, an eighty-year-old Empire builder but a young trust-fund babe in ripped jeans, Joules wellingtons and a spotty Seasalt raincoat. I bet she didn't have a Border terrier called Nigel either.

What a complete and utter shit he was.

I picked up a clod of earth laced with ground elder roots and slung it over the fence into his pristine borders. There! Have that for starters.

I carried on in this vein for some time, until I had to stop for a rest and some squash. As I glugged it down I saw the gift voucher propped up on the windowsill. A good reason to go out. A good way to not hang around listening for the roar of Bryn's truck as he came home. I trudged upstairs, washed most of the mud off and changed into some cleaner clothes. Then I set off.

First I called in at P.D. Smith Esq with my jewellery box and my grandmother's little clock. It turned out that P.D. Smith Esq had died in 1976 but a very charming assistant took everything from me, gave me a receipt and promised that young Mr Smith would value it and get back to me when he returned from the jewellery auction in Okehampton later that afternoon. They would agree a price, sell things on my behalf and keep ten per cent of the sum involved. Was that satisfactory? Yes, it was. Did I still need to sell the stuff? Maybe not but there was something about owning jewellery bought with other people's money that repelled me. And my grandmother's clock had stood on my dressing table in Ian's house. It just reminded me of the past now and they weren't happy memories.

I mentally ticked off another job done with considerable satisfaction and headed for the South West Garden Centre. There was a handy map printed on the back of the gift voucher and it was only twenty minutes away.

Autumn was now well and truly here and the trees had steadily turned all sorts of seasonal colours. The valley below Holly Cottage looked so beautiful that afternoon. A thin autumnal mist lay over the little river softening the brightness of the sunshine and there was crispness in the air that encouraged me to open my car window, letting in the faint evocative tang of bonfires. Soon it would be Halloween, Bonfire Night and then another Christmas.

For the first time I wondered how I was going to spend it. On my own? I had spent the last five years fussing around Susan and her uncertain digestion. Maybe I would fly to Texas to see my sister kicking up her heels at the golf club? Perhaps I would drop a few desperate hints to the friends I had neglected. I had sent an email to Sophie telling her I was OK and would call in soon, but apart from that I had resumed my isolated lifestyle.

I wondered what Bryn was going to do for Christmas. I could picture his sitting room decorated with holly boughs along the mantelpiece, perhaps a tree in the corner scenting the air with pine. The warm darkness brightened with candles in glass jars, the light from the fire reflected from baubles and pictures. Or perhaps he didn't bother at all. Did any man cook Christmas dinner for one? Saddest of meals – a cartoon turkey leg, instant gravy and some frozen roast potatoes and parsnips.

My jaw tightened in annoyance; perhaps he did none of those things. I expect he just landed on the Friend with the Most Benefits of the moment and spent the time charming her into providing him with yuletide treats and festive sex.

Perhaps Bonnie would welcome him back into her arms and her bed if there were nothing better on offer. I bet she had a Mrs Claus outfit somewhere at the back of a cupboard and would continue her prancing, stocking tops showing, on Christmas morning. Perhaps she would tease Bryn, standing with his beautifully wrapped present just out of reach at the end of the bed until he lunged for her and—

Bastard.

I reached South West Garden Centre just after three o'clock, found a space in the busy car park and took a trolley. Inside the vast shop was busy with a coach load of elderly ladies admiring scarves and jerseys in the women's wear while their husbands plodded around with their hands in their pockets looking wistfully at the petrol strimmers and battery-operated cat repellers.

The café was full of couples enjoying afternoon tea. It looked like a well-stocked place and outside there was even more to see. Rows of winter pansies nodded their little cat faces in the air and there were plants, wooden troughs of onion sets, spring bulbs and all sorts of seed packets begging to be scooped up. There was any amount of paving, decking, sacks of decorative stones and hundreds of bags of compost stacked in rows. There were plenty of staff too, dressed in bright green polo shirts so they were easy to find.

I saw two in a corner opening boxes of Christmas decorations and complaining that Christmas seemed to be coming earlier than ever as they investigated the contents. I went up to one, an elderly man with more than a slight resemblance to Santa Claus who was looking with some bewilderment at a tree decoration made out of twigs tied with red tartan ribbon.

He held one out to me. 'Wouldn't you think people could tie their own twigs and save themselves two pounds fifty?'

'Um, well I suppose so...'

'I mean it's not exactly difficult, is it?'

'No, I can see that.' I didn't really want to get drawn into this discussion, so before he could start on anything else I introduced myself.

'My name is Charlotte Calder; I was told you were expecting me. I've come to use up this voucher. It's a prize. My friend won it and said I was to come here to spend it.'

I held it out in front of me and after dusting off his hands he took it and read it two or three times. After a while his face lit up.

'Ah yes,' he said, and he threw me a look. 'You're right, we've been expecting you.'

'Shall I just fill a trolley with stuff or...'

'Certainly not!' he said, offended. 'Come with me. I'm to take you to the office.'

He led me through the shop towards the back of the building. We passed an impressive display of wellingtons of all sizes and colours, wheelbarrows, a huge selection of ceramic pots and troughs then some rather ghastly gnomes and flowerpot men made from flowerpots of course. At last he stopped outside a door and knocked. Someone called for him to come in and so we did.

I should have guessed.

Why was I not surprised?

It was a small room filled with crates and boxes of random gardening stuff, books, balls of twine, piles of catalogues and at least one bird table in pieces. In the middle of all this chaos was Bryn.

He looked up from his laptop and his face relaxed into a smile.

'Here she is, boss,' the old man said, sounding rather pleased with himself. 'Do I get a finders fee?'

Bryn laughed, 'Thanks Malcolm.'

Malcolm ambled off and Bryn came round the desk towards me.

He stood in front of me and, for a mad moment, I thought he was going to hug me, but then he folded his arms and leaned back against his desk.

'So, here you are, Lottie.'

'Here I am.'

Could this be just an incredible coincidence? Or had I been set up? By Jess? By Bryn?

'Jess – she said I had – that she had won a voucher in a competition.'

'Yes.'

'And I had to come here to get stuff for the garden.'

'Yes.' He looked at me steadily, waiting.

A shaft of late afternoon sunshine came through the window, highlighting his tawny head.

'So?'

'So?'

'Are we going to stand here all afternoon saying *so*, or do you want to help me?' I said. Perhaps I could cover my unease by being forceful.

He was still watching me. 'Oh, I'd like to help you, Charlotte.'

Why did I love the sound of my name when he said it? Did I suddenly turn from being paint-splattered, mud-smeared, accident-prone Lottie into sensible, grown-up Charlotte?

He looked at me. I looked at him. The tension between us was palpable. I don't think either of us knew what to do. Bryn took one step towards me and I felt myself sway in his direction as though he was magnetic.

He was going to kiss me, I knew he was.

I knew he was and I wanted him to. Why was I finding it hard to breathe? Perhaps he would sweep the paperwork off the desk onto the floor with a clatter of bulldog clips and lift me onto it. He would hold me against him, his arms a vice. I would know again the feel of his warm skin under my fingers, the taste, the scent of him.

Just as I was about to pitch myself at him the office door opened.

'Sorry to bother you, chief, but the man from Parsons is here with a delivery of rotted manure. Shall I tell him to bring it round the back or do you want to have a word with him? We don't want no more split bags after all, do we?'

It was Malcolm, back again at just the wrong moment. I looked at his cheery, honest expression as he stuck his head round the office door and silently wished him all sorts of indiscriminate harm.

Bryn turned away and looked through a pile of letters on his desk, pulling out one and scanning through it before handing it back to Malcolm.

'Just tell him to put it round the back by the decking area. I'll take a look later.'

'Righty ho. And there's a box of Christmas stuff that needs to go back. Half of the stuff smashed. It looks like someone drove over it with a fork lift truck, not moved it.' He gave a wheezing chuckle. 'I'll get Dawn to sort out the paperwork.'

Malcolm closed the office door behind him with a bang. I could hear him whistling as he went away. I hoped the roof would fall on him, or that he might be run over by a posse of the elderly ladies with their sweater-laden trolleys.

Bryn opened the office door for me. 'Look, I'll get one of the chaps to give you a hand. Any idea what you want?'

'Not really, I was hoping you might advise me.'

'I'm a bit busy, to be honest.'

'I thought you wanted to help me a minute ago.'

He turned with an exclamation of annoyance and picked up a walkie-talkie. After a few minutes it crackled into life.

'Malcolm? Can you come back and help Miss Calder?'

There was a crackle of static in reply and some unintelligible but obviously irritated words from Malcolm.

Bryn turned his back on me and spoke more quietly. 'Yes, I know, but I need you to do this now. Just get one of the others to help him and I'll send her down.'

He ushered me out, his arm around my shoulders but not touching me.

'Malcolm will give you all the advice you need,' he said, and he closed the door behind me.

What was I to make of that? One minute it seemed as though he might drag me onto the desk, the next he could hardly be bothered to speak to me.

I trailed miserably after Malcolm who seemed just as irritated with my company as I was with his.

Once he realised I wasn't interested in buying Christmas decorations or in vegetable gardening he steered me in the direction of the spring bulbs, cyclamen tubs and the winter hanging baskets. It was obvious that £250 would take a lot of spending. After fifteen minutes he was getting very fidgety so I made a grab for the nearest ornament and heaved it onto the trolley. Malcolm's eyes widened in horror. Perhaps a resin statue of a grotesque, evil-faced pixie firing a bow and arrow wasn't his idea of money well spent but I thought it would serve Jess right for putting me in such a hideous situation.

Between us we lugged my haul to the tills and I presented my voucher. The assistant hid her feelings very well but she and Malcolm exchanged a knowing glance as she searched for the pixie's price. For the first time I noticed there was a great deal of red biro scribble on the label and a considerable price reduction.

'Cheerio then, Pixie Pete,' she said, scanning the bar code, 'we never thought we'd see the back of you!'

I felt a right fool.

Malcolm loaded the statue into the back seat of my car and

with a humorous twist of his mouth fastened the seat belt across it. As I drove out of the car park a woman pointed in open-mouthed astonishment as we passed her, the pixie apparently aiming its bow and arrow towards her small son, who promptly burst into tears.

CHAPTER 19

Morning glory – love in vain

Back at Holly Cottage, the autumn sky was darkening into evening. I dragged my swag into the garden and arranged Pixie Pete so that his bow and arrow were aimed directly at Bryn's back door. It seemed highly appropriate. Then I dumped the sacks of bulbs outside the kitchen, aimed a kick at them, and in a more than filthy temper, slammed the back door and locked it. Bloody men. Bloody Bryn.

To add to my mood I had somehow managed to leave the fridge door open. The milk carton had fallen over and the contents were sloshing around in a revolting mess of salad leaves and plastic cheese wrappers. A carton of six eggs had fallen out and smashed on the floor. I cleaned up the mess, gagging. How on earth had that happened? Just what I didn't need.

I sat at the kitchen table and tried to understand. I had begun to think things were going to be OK between me and Bryn, but now it was all going wrong and I didn't know why. What had I done? Perhaps Ian had been right after all.

'Look, Lottie, it's a fact of life. All men play around a bit if they get the chance. You know that. Any man who says he doesn't is a liar.'

Blast. Why did I keep remembering that particular sentence? It was thumping through my brain on a loop.

And at last I stopped making myself think about something else and allowed myself to think about that moment.

That awful moment during the party when I was looking for Ian. Wanting him to open the champagne for our guests so we could toast the New Year. Then I noticed the door to the study wasn't closed properly. And I found them. Ian and Trudy locked in an unappealing embrace. His hands halfway up her skirt, her hands on the back of his head, the hairs on her arms glinting in the light from Ian's desk lamp, as they clamped lips together on the red leather Chesterfield.

The breath had been driven from my lungs. I stood shocked and silent for a moment and they were so absorbed in each other that they didn't notice me.

'I can't go on with this. Ken suspects something. You've got to tell her,' Trudy panted, coming up for air.

'Soon, soon,' Ian gasped, his hands navigating the many folds of her dress.

I stepped forward into the room, my head dizzy. 'Tell me what? What the hell do you think you're doing?'

They sprang apart like repelling magnets and Ian struggled to his feet, tucking his shirt in and almost falling over.

'Lottie!'

'Ian, what the hell are you doing?'

'Nothing, it's nothing,' Ian said. He hiccupped and turned to Trudy, spittle at the corners of his mouth. 'Why didn't you shut the door?'

Trudy got to her feet and patted her dress down modestly.

'It's not nothing, Ian,' she said. She turned her muddy gaze towards me. 'It's time you knew. We're in love.'

In the distance our guests were shouting.

'Three minutes to go till the New Year, where's Ian?'

'I want some champagne!'

'Trudy!' Ian said, his voice cracking with the horror of the moment. His eyes were wide as they swivelled between Trudy and me.

'Well, we are, aren't we? We're in love. That's what you just said.' Trudy turned to face me, quite composed, her mouth spewing out horror. 'We're in love and have been for ages. We've been having an affair for over a year. That week you thought he was in Northampton at the builders' conference? Well he was with me in Torquay. The weekend he said he was in Liverpool? He was with me; we went to Paris. Ian loves me. It's time you realised. I wanted you to find out.'

I couldn't catch my breath for a moment. The whole thing seemed utterly ridiculous.

'What? Paris? But, we've been together for years,' I said. 'He said he would take me! He loves *me*!'

Trudy sneered at me and tucked her hair behind her ears.

'Really?' she said. '*Really*?'

I think it must have been the wine but I began to laugh. Not the sort of laugh you do when something is funny but a disbelieving, almost hysterical sound.

Somewhere in the distance I could hear our guests.

'Five, four, three, two, one. Happy New Year!' and then there was a cheer.

I could imagine people embracing in my sitting room, in the village, all over England and still I stood in the doorway and laughed, the tears springing into my eyes.

I felt a hand on my arm and, thank God, Sophie was there.

'Champagne?' she said.

And then she must have realised something was happening. She took in the scene and then hiccupped.

'Oh bugger. What's the matter?'

I wiped hysterical tears from my eyes. Trudy put one hand on Ian's arm and he seemed to change in front of me. He became someone else, a smaller man, he suddenly looked his age. I couldn't quite recognise him. I turned away.

I staggered to the kitchen and Sophie put her arms around me. I stood very still, the tears running down my face. I didn't seem able to stop them. How could Ian do this? It couldn't be true. I could trust him with my life. He wouldn't do a thing like that. Had he been having an affair with her? With *her*?

I was aware of the noise from the party fading. Someone had switched off the television. I could hear people starting to talk in quieter voices, the *what's-going-on* sort of conversation people had at moments like these, I suppose. Someone laughed and another person shushed them. It was as though someone had died.

I tried to focus; the whole room was starting to move. I was hovering in that dangerous place between intoxicated and being seriously pissed.

OK, I wasn't exactly Ellie Goulding in the looks department, but I was damn sure I was more attractive than Trudy. She was short, miserable, dumpy. She had facial hair and no dress sense. What the hell did Ian see in her?

A horrible thought struck me; for all her shortcomings she might have advanced bedroom tricks that would leave me for dust.

I began to gulp for air. I was ill. I was going to throw up. The bile hit the back of my throat. All the party food and wine churned in my stomach, mixed with my disgust and absolute shame. I pushed Sophie to one side and ran for the utility-room toilet where I was violently and humiliatingly sick. After a few moments I pulled myself up to sit on the loo. Hot, dizzy, shaking. I wiped my face with a damp J Cloth that smelled of lemon bathroom cleaner and leaned on the edge of the sink, my head spinning.

Next to the mirror I had placed a card Ian had sent to me on the first anniversary of our meeting. I had liked it so much I had kept it and framed it.

To my darling, the love of my life.

My Heart, my Soul and my Love is Yours Forever.

I realised for the first time that it wasn't true, it wasn't even grammatically correct.

I sat at the kitchen table at Holly Cottage dunking one of the herbal tea bags my sister had left behind in a mug of boiling water. It said on the label it was camomile and raspberry. It tasted like compost smells.

Perhaps having had me, Bryn had decided I wasn't worth the bother. I felt a cold shiver of fear. Maybe he, like Ian, had found me substandard in the sack.

I sat up a bit straighter and thought about this more seriously. Maybe that was the problem.

It was my fault.

I was no good in bed. Ian hadn't thought I was, and nor did Bryn.

How absolutely shaming.

These days when the mildest mannered women's magazine gave helpful advice about pelvic floor exercises and how to keep a man happy, there was no excuse. Perhaps I should have read a few more instead of laughing at the letters from women who worried that they were too fat, too old, too flat chested to keep their man happy.

How did you get to be good in bed anyway?

By reading special books? Erotica? I'd have to get them on Kindle to avoid embarrassment and I didn't have one.

Therapists?

Evening classes?

I pictured a dusty room in the FE College in Stokeley with a group of self-conscious women on a circle of wooden chairs, a bearded tutor giving us breathing exercises and talking about Hubby. Maybe his partner would come in on week three, encouraging us to buy her organic massage oils. He would encourage us to talk about erogenous zones and fantasies and I would probably die of embarrassment. I didn't think I had either, actually. Although if I'm pushed I'll admit my feet are very ticklish and I've always had a bit of a thing for Melvyn Bragg.

I think I might have been getting a bit lightheaded at this point.

Perhaps I should watch some porn?

Hi Bryn, I've brought over some breadsticks and some hummus, shall we watch Debbie Does Dallas?

No. Not a good idea on any level.

I finished my tea and averted my gaze from the half bottle of red wine that was posing seductively on the worktop. Instead I picked up my laptop and went into the sitting room. I would work on *Love at Last* for a bit and try and at least get the colour of Jake's eyes consistent.

I flopped down on the sofa and opened my laptop. After a moment I wriggled, realising something was wrong, and began patting around me. The cushion by my hand was damp. It was too dark to see properly. So of course I did the stupidest thing I possibly could, I switched on the lights.

There was a threatening crackle of electricity from somewhere in the ceiling, followed by an explosion as the bulb blew up. I screamed and all the lights went out.

CHAPTER 20

Lily-of-the-valley – returning happiness

I stood, not daring to move. There were fragments of glass every-where. I could feel it in my hair. I had no shoes on; I was probably going to cut my feet to ribbons. I whimpered in the growing darkness, not sure what I should do. One thing was certain – I couldn't just stand here for the rest of my life.

I shook the glass out of my hair and took a cautious step back, wincing as a glass fragment bit into my toe. I vowed to the gods of health and safety I would never sneer at slippers again. I would buy some and I promised I would wear them in future. Second step, another crunch, another stab of pain. I gave a strangled cry of rage. Bloody hell, how was I going to get out of this?

'Are you OK? I heard you scream, have you had a power cut?'

A voice shouting through the back door, it was Bryn. I bit my lip to stop from crying with relief.

I brushed the glass off the front of my sweatshirt, cleared my throat and tried to sound normal.

'I think it was me. I put the light on and I've blown everything up,' I called out. 'I'm a bit stuck.'

I heard the door handle rattle as Bryn tried to open the kitchen door. Of course I had locked it.

'Can you unlock the door?' he called.

'No, I'm surrounded by broken glass and I haven't got any shoes on. Well I could try…'

A second later he must have put his shoulder to the door, and it burst open. Hardly worth locking it if it was that easy to get in. He stood in the doorway looking at me. I could see his eyes, bright in the gloom.

'Are you OK?'

'I turned the light on and the bulb blew up. There are bits of it all over the floor. Please be careful. You know what you're like with blood…'

He took two steps towards me, his boots crunching contemptuously over the glass fragments, hooked one arm under my knees and lifted me up in his arms.

'Hold tight. I'll have you out in a jiffy.'

Obediently I put my arms around his neck, resisting the impulse to bury my nose in his neck. He carried me out into the garden and then he paused, looking down at me.

I met his gaze in a moment of almost unbearable honesty and there was a second when I had a choice. I could have struggled for him to put me down. I could have said something stupid. I could have made a silly comment about my weight. I did none of those things.

I just looked at him, taking in his face as though I wanted to memorise it; his dark blue eyes framed with thick lashes, the smooth clean lines of his jaw, the texture and colour of his skin. I knew what was going to happen. So did he.

Without a word he carried me down to the end of the garden where the evening air was chill and clear and scented with autumn. The first stars were coming out above us as, still holding me in his arms, he bent his head and kissed me. My hands moved up to his head, my fingers deep in his warm hair. He walked on, kicking open the gate to his garden. I looked up at the heart-breaking sweep of his cheekbone and knew that I was lost.

He carried me into his house and sat me on the kitchen table.

I curled my legs around his waist and he kissed me again. He pulled my sweatshirt off over my head and unhooked my bra, his hands warm on my breasts. Then he lifted me up, his hands under my bottom, and carried me through to the dark hallway where the grandfather clock ticked softly at the bottom of the stairs. He kissed me again, pulling me hard against his body. In the dim light his eyes glowed as he looked at me. A question was asked between us that needed no answering. Then he carried me upstairs and into his bedroom.

He laid me on the bed and pulled his shirt off over his head. He lay down beside me, stretching himself out against me, watching me as he traced my face with his fingers, smoothed my hair back from my face, outlining my lips with his thumb.

He spoke at last. 'Lottie. Oh, Lottie.'

I couldn't speak. I could hardly breathe. I was back where I had longed to be. I hadn't realised just how much I had wanted him. I was alone with him at last in the quiet twilight of his house, my hands touching him, feeling the muscles of his back, the lovely indent of his spine, his mouth on mine.

I remembered him, I knew him. He knew me. The slow way we undressed each other was sweet and familiar. The sound of his sigh above me, the weight, the feel of him – all of him – along the length of my body, pressed close and then closer still. Soft nips and gentle kisses on my naked shoulders. His breath against my back, his mouth on my body, mine on his.

He was breathless. His heart beating against mine. Mine against his. He kissed my forehead; he tangled his hands in my hair. He looked at me. Really looked at me as no one ever had before.

I wanted him. He wanted me. I wanted all of him in great gulping mouthfuls, taking his very essence into my heart with his sweat and his scent. I cried out in the warm darkness. No longer two. We were one. Two heads, two hearts but one soul. I pushed my hands against his chest. It was too much. God help me. Too much. He was compassion, he was everything, he was pitiless. He sought me and found me. The universe and everything else in it was meaningless and unnecessary. My world started and ended with him. Our need for each other. Now, yes, now. And again. There I was. Only him.

A gasp from him, a long groan of pleasure. He dropped his face into the hollow of my neck. Still he did not release me. He rolled onto his side, my legs wrapped around him. Time passed. Seconds? Minutes? Days?

I looked at him at last, his head on the pillow beside me. His eyes were closed. My sweat on his face. His on mine. I ran my fingers over the beautiful curve of his lower lip and he kissed them. I could feel the strength of his pulse inside my heart. I breathed in his breath. He breathed in mine. His skin smelled of me.

This then is what has kept the world turning. Poems written. Songs sung.

We lay together, quiet and spent. He lifted his body a little so I could pull my arm out from under him, but still he held me. I curled around him, his life flowed into me and mine into him.

After a while I thought perhaps he was sleeping but then he turned his head and looked at me. He pulled me yet closer and spoke against my hair.

'I'm not letting you go until I know you won't run off. If you promise not to I'll get you something to eat.'

I smiled in the darkness. 'I promise I won't run off.'

'What do you want?' His hand traced a warm, slow path from my shoulder to my waist and back again.

I closed my eyes and stretched out my spine like a cat under his fingers. 'You.'

'Anything else?'

'Just you.'

He pulled his head back and I knew he was looking me.

'You're so beautiful, Lottie. So brave and beautiful.'

He kissed me and at last he let me go. The movement of his

body away from mine was a little death, a loss.

He rolled onto his back and pulled me in against his side. He pulled the quilt over me to keep me warm.

'Toast and brandy?' he said. I could tell he was smiling.

I nodded. 'Don't be long.'

'Don't go away. Stay here,' he said, and this time I did.

He put on the bedside lamp and I watched as he pulled on the blue robe. I listened as he went down the stairs and I heard him in the kitchen crashing about. I think I must have dozed off for a few minutes and I woke as he came back into the room. There was a delicious smell of toast in the air and I pulled myself up against the pillows as he put the tray on the marble-topped washstand under the window. I could see the same glass butter dish and a pile of toast. He put the tumbler of brandy on the bedside table and then got into bed and pulled me into his arms. I ran my hands over his shoulders and down the muscles of his back until I found that particular place at the base of his spine and I traced my nails over it.

He gasped, his eyes closed for a moment.

'I've been thinking about you, Lottie,' he said against my hair. 'I've missed you.'

He looked at me again and his eyes told me everything I needed to know. He lost his breath in a shaking sigh.

He drew me down underneath him and kissed me.

'Will I ever get enough of you?' he whispered. 'Will you ever get enough of me?'

'No, no, never.'

I could feel myself dissolving into him. I was hungry for him, thirsty for him, desperate for him.

He pulled off his robe and threw it on the floor and then he made love to me again and it was wonderful, just bloody wonderful.

I woke up the next morning just as confused as the first time. But this time I did not scrabble to find my clothes and dash off.

The little bedside clock was still ticking away; it was just after eight o'clock.

I was glad to see there were no flashy earrings this time, but to be honest I don't think I would have cared if there had been. He had explained the situation to me. Bonnie had deliberately left her earrings there, Bryn had found them, given them back to her and she had admitted it. She had the feeling there was someone else. And of course, although I hadn't known it at the time, there was someone else. There was me.

We had stayed up through most of that night, eating toast, sipping brandy, kissing, talking, making love. At about four thirty we had slept.

I pushed my hair out of my eyes and turned my head to look at Bryn. He was still asleep, his head burrowed deep into the pillows. I reached out one hand and touched him. Not to wake him up, just for the pleasure of touching him. To feel his smooth, warm skin. I kissed his shoulder and felt the muscles in his arm move as he woke.

He stirred and turned over, reaching for me, and spooned in behind me even before he opened his eyes. He held me close, my back against his chest. I could feel him breathing.

'Good morning, Lottie,' he said, his voice rumbling against me.

'Good morning.'

'What time is it?'

I checked the clock again.

'Quarter past eight.'

Bryn thought about this in silence for a few minutes while he stroked me.

'I think I'm ill,' he said at last. 'Very unwell indeed. I think it could last for a while, to be honest.'

'Oh dear, are you?' I turned my head to try and look at him. 'What's the matter?'

'Nothing.'

'Then?'

'I'll phone Malcolm in a bit and tell him I won't be in today. Or tomorrow. I think I might have to stay in bed, certainly for the rest of the day.'

'Hmm. I might need to stay here with you. In case.'

'In case of what?'

I looked at him and laughed. 'In case I want to do this.'

I rolled up on top of him and kissed him. He reached down and his hands smoothed my bottom.

'Or this.'

I bent to kiss his body, teasing, flicking with my tongue, making him gasp with pleasure.

'Or this.'

We made morning love, quickly, urgently, him silencing my cries with his kisses until I trembled in his arms.

'I don't think there's anything the matter with you,' I said a long time later. 'I think you're skiving.'

'You're an excellent nurse,' he said. 'I'm beginning to feel better already. I'll go and make some coffee and phone Malcolm. I'll be back in three minutes. Don't move.'

I didn't.

CHAPTER 21

Gladiolus – courage and strength

We stayed in bed all day, something I hadn't done since a few years ago when I had flu. I mean proper flu, not just a bad cold. The sort of flu when you feel so ill you couldn't pick up a fifty-pound note on the pavement if you saw it. That's supposed to be a diagnostic test. But I digress.

Staying in bed all day with Bryn was a zillion squillion times better than having the flu, even so I think I might have ignored that fifty-pound note for quite different reasons.

First we had breakfast in bed, scrambled eggs and toasted bagels, with a cafetière of coffee and a glass of freshly squeezed orange juice. Then we brushed all the crumbs out of the bed, straightened the sheets and got back in again. We had a snooze and then elevenses. Bryn had some Danish pastry things in the freezer. More coffee. Then I spilled mine all over the sheets so we had to change them. We both had a shower. I mean at the *same time.* That's something else I'd never done and I can highly recommend it. It took a long time though, all that soaping and rinsing and snogging, and then one thing led to another and – well, it was amazing.

After we got in between the clean sheets we had another snooze, and then it was time for a very late lunch and Bryn made some

229

vegetable soup and we took that, a bottle of wine and a very crusty loaf back up to bed and got butter everywhere, which was more fun than you can possibly imagine. And we had more wine and more food and dozed and we talked and held each other and sometimes we didn't speak at all.

We talked to each other about our lives and from time to time one thing would lead to another and we seemed to be in a state where making love to each other was an ongoing thing, like a conversation between us that occasionally involved his body speaking to mine.

We tried out different positions, some of them quite tricky, others rather inventive, and I didn't care if I had cellulite or wobbly bits. And if I did it was obvious Bryn didn't care. We drank wine and ate chocolate. We looked at each other. We got through a tub of raspberry ripple ice cream in a new and unusual way.

I sat between Bryn's legs and he pulled me back against him and brushed my hair, pulling it to one side and kissing my neck, running his tongue up behind my ear and whispering what he was going to do to me, what he was thinking. He seemed absolutely absorbed in me, penetrating my needs and giving pleasure until I thought I would faint.

We lay in each other's arms and watched the afternoon fade. Just the rosy glow from the sunset sent a gentle, flattering light over us, so that the many imperfections of my figure disappeared. His face, half in shadow, had the look of mystery, of a Renaissance artist, maybe. I looked at him and he smiled, pulling me onto his lean, hard body. We fitted together so well, like one person divided into two. And for the first time in my life I felt beautiful and valued and content.

We were almost drifting off to sleep in each other's arms, my hand on his broad, warm chest, when I stretched up to look at him and he bent to kiss me. He took hold of my hands and pinned them on the pillows for a moment. Then I broke free and ran my fingers over his wide shoulders, remembering our shared shower.

The steam lacing the shower screen, his soapy hands on my breasts, my back forced hard against the cool tiles on the wall, his face above me, his gasping cry of pleasure. The way the water had run down his body into my mouth.

And then I remembered.

I prayed it wouldn't be too bad. I wanted to open the door and perhaps find things were as I had left them. Just some broken glass on the floor, some unspecified damp on the sofa. In my heart I knew it wouldn't be like that, and it wasn't.

Part of the sitting-room ceiling had come down.

There were chunks of plaster dropping onto the furniture, the ceiling horribly bowed and bubbled with the weight of water. There was water pooled on the floor, dark stains on the walls, a cold musty smell of mould and damp. I screamed and burst into tears.

'Oh no,' Bryn said. He put a comforting arm around my shoulders and hugged me.

'How? How could this happen?' I wailed.

'It might be a burst radiator upstairs. But it's not been cold enough for the pipes to freeze. You stay here and I'll go and look. Don't go into the sitting room, the ceiling might collapse.'

He went upstairs and I could hear him moving around. Then distantly a muffled exclamation. And he came downstairs again.

'The bath was full and overflowing. You must have left the taps on.'

I shook my head. 'No, I never have baths, I always use the shower. I haven't tried to use the bath in all the months I've lived here.'

Bryn shook his head. 'The plug was in, the cold tap was turned on just a trickle, hardly anything but there was a pink flannel blocking the overflow pipe.'

'That makes no sense at all. Why would I run a cold bath?

Pink flannel? I don't own a pink flannel.' I ran my fingers through my hair. 'Bloody hell, Jess is going to go mad when she sees this.'

Bryn put a comforting arm around my shoulders. 'Don't worry about Jess. Accidents happen. She'll understand.'

'I bet she doesn't! Oh sodding hell! What a bloody mess!'

What on earth should I do? Was Jess insured? Would her insurance cover this? It almost looked as though I had deliberately flooded the place. She'd wonder what the hell I had been doing.

I'd have to admit to her I had noticed the damp cushion, that I must have realised there was water coming from somewhere. But what had I done? I'd switched on the light, fused them, blown a light bulb then apparently skipped off to spend the day in bed with Bryn.

I covered my face; I couldn't bear to look.

'I'll have to ring her, tell her what's happened,' I said at last.

Bryn took my hands and put them around his waist so that he could hug me.

'Leave it for now. There's nothing you can do.'

'I can't just leave it like that! It's not going to magically get better!'

'No but…' Bryn hesitated. 'Look, I'll ring her in the morning if you like.'

Oh, I was tempted. The prospect of him taking this burden away was very appealing. Should I just pass the buck?

I straightened my shoulders. No, this was the sort of thing I needed to sort out myself. I was a grown up now. This was the sort of thing they did.

'No, Bryn, it's OK. Thanks, but I really should do this myself.'

'Please, Lottie, let me, I don't mind. I'll drive over there in the morning, and tell her it wasn't your fault.'

I hugged him, remembering the bad blood that existed between Bryn and his brother. It was sweet that he would be prepared to do this.

'It's OK, Bryn,' I said. 'I need to stand on my own two feet. I can deal with this.'

His face fell. 'I just want to help you. Protect you.'

'I know, and I appreciate it, but I'll manage. I can't phone from here, I've no reception. I'll have to go into town and ring her. Unless I can use your land line?'

He looked away, awkward. 'I'm not sure if the handset works. I never use it anyway.'

I frowned. 'But that's not true. I've heard it ringing before now.'

'Yes but – oh, Lottie. Please just let me deal with it?'

I began to wonder what all this was about and my stubborn streak started to surface. I'd grown used to being independent now; I wasn't going to pass the buck.

'Bryn, I know you want to help, but it's my responsibility. If she is covered by the insurance then she needs to get a claim in as soon as possible. I need to tell her what happened.'

He sighed. 'Well, come back over to my house, we'll sort something out. You can't stay here.'

Bryn took my hand and pulled me away from the devastation. We went back next door and I began to look through my phone for Jess's number.

'Do you want coffee?' he said. 'Or tea?'

I shook my head. 'I'm fine, I just want to get this over and done with.'

I found Bryn's landline in the sitting room and lifted the handset. There was a perfectly clear dialling tone; there was nothing wrong with it at all.

'Look, I think it could have been Bonnie,' Bryn blurted out. 'Think about it. She could have run the water, put the plug in, blocked up the overflow.'

I turned to look at him. 'Bonnie? Why on earth would she do that?'

'She's jealous, possessive. She wanted us to get back together. She accused me of having someone else the last time I saw her.

233

She freaked out when she first found out you were coming to stay in Holly Cottage. You know that dose of vandalism we found when you arrived? The rotten fish behind the radiator? The water and the ashes from the fire dumped on the carpet? Well I have a sneaking feeling it was Bonnie not Mr Webster. I can't prove it and Bonnie denied it. I told her if I did have someone else it was none of her business. But then she must have worked it out. She left the earrings by the bedside. She wanted you – or whoever – to see them and feel uncomfortable.' He put his arms around me. 'And it nearly worked. I nearly lost you. I warned her off, told her I was going to change the locks.'

'But how could she have got into Holly Cottage?'

He wiped his hands over his face. There was a dry rasping noise as he rubbed his stubble.

'I think that's my fault, I've always had a spare key; Jess gave it to me in case of an emergency. I'd forgotten all about it but Bonnie must have found it. She could have taken the key ages ago – to be honest I wouldn't have noticed. I'm guessing she let herself in, mucked around with the bath, turned the tap on a little so that no one would hear the water running.'

'So she suspected something but how would she have known about me?' I wailed. 'About us?'

Then I remembered. That first night when Bryn had invited me over for a meal and I had fallen into bed with him. I thought I had heard a car. Bonnie's car. Of course.

'Yes,' I said after a moment.

Then I remembered the open fridge door. The spilled milk, the digestive biscuits, the times when I felt someone had been in the house. The dead rat in the paint pot. I shuddered.

'It all makes sense. I think you're right. What a shitty thing to do.' I felt like crying. 'I wonder if Jess's insurance covers malicious damage?'

I picked up the phone again and Bryn took the handset from me.

'Bryn?'

'Will you let me sort this out? Please, Lottie?'

I began to feel a bit annoyed. Didn't he think I could cope?

'No! I've told you, I'm quite capable of dealing with this, give me the phone back.' I held out my hand to him. 'Please.'

Bryn looked at me for a long moment and then he took a deep breath.

'You don't need to phone her,' he said.

'I do! She's my landlady, it's her house, her insurance policy, it's up to her to sort it out.'

'No.'

'Bryn, stop making life difficult!'

'Listen to me.'

'What?'

'Will you sit down?'

I sat down and he came to sit beside me. He took hold of one of my hands.

'There's no point phoning Jess because she doesn't own Holly Cottage.'

'Yes, she does! She said she decided not to sell after all!'

'No, she doesn't.' He squeezed my hand between both of his. 'I do.'

There was a moment when I didn't process this information properly and I started to laugh. Then I looked at his face and realised he wasn't joking.

'When? How?' I stuttered.

'I bought it because Jess did want to sell up. She was on the point of getting an estate agent round and he told her he already had a buyer lined up. It would only have taken days to sell Holly Cottage.'

'And?'

Bryn swallowed hard and didn't answer. At last he gave a shrug.

My mind was spinning. 'You felt sorry for me, didn't you? Pity? Or was it something else?'

I stood up and pulled my hand away from his.

'No, Lottie, it wasn't like that at all. But your sister said you'd had such a difficult time. I didn't want to lose you.'

My hearing seemed odd, the blood pounding in my ears. It was as though I could hear Ian from somewhere very far away.

Look, Lottie, it's a fact of life. All men play around a bit if they get the chance. You know that. Any man who says he doesn't is a liar.

'You thought I was just another stupid woman in trouble? Like Bonnie when her engagement broke down. I knew you were too good to be true. You can sniff out a vulnerable woman at fifty paces, can't you, Bryn? That's the way you work. You stepped in. Didn't you?'

'No, that wasn't it.'

'Didn't you think for one moment that I might have wanted to stand on my own feet? That I was trying to manage my own life without interference? No, you just assumed that I wanted a big strong man to sort me out, take away all my problems and fuck me senseless in the process.'

He winced. 'No!'

'You weren't going to even tell me, were you? You would have pretended to get in touch with Jess. Pretended to contact her insurance people. Pretended she still owned this house.

'When would you have told me, Bryn? Would you *ever* have told me? Or would you have kept on pretending – lying to me? Another handy little friend with benefits next door? Just like Bonnie? How can I ever thank you. I know, I'll take my kit off and you can shag me into the middle of next week.'

I was shaking with anger and disappointment.

Bryn held out his hands to me.

'Please, Lottie, please listen. You're wrong.'

He tried to put his arms around me but I turned away.

'I think I'm going to go now. And by the way, Mr Palmer, there's been a flood in Holly Cottage. You might like to get on to your insurance people and tell them. Your crazy girlfriend has wrecked months of cleaning and redecoration, not to mention a lot of the furniture. Whether you tell them that is entirely up to you. The ceiling has come down. Some of my things are spoiled. I meant to tell you, I have a little money now. I'll find somewhere else to live as soon as possible.'

'You can't go back with the house like that, Lottie!' he said.

'Don't tell me what I can't do, Bryn. And by the way, you haven't "lost" me, Bryn, because you didn't have me in the first place.'

My voice shook and I stopped to take a deep breath. I was crying; I couldn't see him properly. I didn't understand what had happened. I just knew I couldn't bear it.

I ran back to Holly Cottage, dashing away my tears, the sobs choking and hard in my throat. I tried to lock the back door behind me but it had broken when Bryn forced his way in. He had picked me up, kissed me, carried me outside into the garden, taken me to his bed and – and then what? What had he done? Had he made me fall in love with him, and then dashed all my hopes in one conversation?

I went upstairs to my bedroom and lay down on the bed, deathly sick.

Somehow I fell asleep and when I woke it was the middle of the afternoon. My face was puffy and sore with crying. I had a pounding headache. I couldn't stay here. Apart from wanting to get away from the damp, the smell and the damage, everything I saw reminded me of Bryn. He had walked with me in the garden, talked to me, kissed me, carried me into his house, touched me and undressed me. He had stripped away my sadness, had given me a glimpse of how things might have been. It was hard now to close the door on that. I wished it had never been opened. I liked being in charge of my own life, that was the big thing I had learned. I wasn't a fool, I wasn't anyone's pet.

I got up, washed my face and collected a few things together, and then I got into my car, not looking around, not looking at his house, and drove away.

CHAPTER 22

Purple lilac – first emotion of love

I don't know what I was thinking, but I drove to look at my old house.

I parked outside the gate and stared, recalling how it had felt to live there. The gravel drive that defied all my weeding attempts. The space in front of the garage with the splodge of an old oil spill where Ian used to park his car, until that time. That last time when he had driven away.

I had put out a hand and grabbed his sleeve but he shrugged me off.

I had tried to grab the car keys out of his hand but he turned his back on me.

'Don't be stupid, Ian. Give them to me. You're drunk.'

'Oh, shut up! Get off me!'

'Please! Ian!'

He opened the front door and slammed it behind him without another word. I ran out after him and banged on the car window to stop him. He didn't even look at me as he drove away.

I had waited, waited for him to come back. But he didn't. I had shivered in the cold night air that brought with it the first few flakes of snow and the bitter chill of failure and then I went back into the kitchen to make a cup of tea.

The ugly remains of our party cluttered every surface. Broken food remnants, half-empty bowls of crisps and smoked almonds, empty wine bottles on the windowsills lined up in neat rows. An opened bottle of celebratory champagne fizzed apologetically, untasted on the draining board.

I found my cigarettes and lit one. Then I made some tea and drank it, sitting on a kitchen chair sticky with spilled cream. The oven was still purring away, diligently warming through a tray of cremated sausage rolls. I switched it off and shut the door on them. And then I smoked one cigarette after another until my head was dizzy. Where had he gone? When would he be back? What was I going to say when he did return?

I put on some bed socks and my new pyjamas that were fetchingly decorated with Christmas trees and got into bed. I had expected to be cold. I hadn't expected to be numb. I turned my face to the pillow. I didn't think I would sleep, but I did.

I woke some time later to hear a noise. I lay in the darkness and listened. Had I dreamt it? It was the front door. Someone was knocking to come in. Ian? He should have his keys and I hadn't put the chain on.

I ignored it for a few minutes and then I heard it again. A steady, determined, persistent knocking. I looked at the bedside clock. It was five to three.

I got up and pulled on my dressing gown. My head began to ache. My mouth was foul. I would have to find some aspirin and a long drink of water.

Looking down the stairwell I could see the front door. A dark figure was visible through the glass panel. Of course, the porch light was still on.

I went down and put the door chain on before I opened it. I peered through the gap.

'Yes?'

I nearly fainted.

There was a policeman outside. A tall, dark-haired man, and beside him a small neat policewoman.

'Mrs Lovell?' she said.

'No, my name's Calder. Charlotte Calder. I'm Ian's partner.'

She held out some sort of identity card.

'Could we come in?'

I could still remember the feel of the carpet in that house under my bare feet in the morning. The way the curtains on the landing stuck a little and had to be jiggled into place. The crack in the en suite sink that I had made a few days after Ian had died. I had been cleaning; I had dropped a bottle of bath oil, my hands cold and shaking.

After a few minutes I saw the elderly owners looking out of their upstairs windows, clutching on to each other, obviously wondering if I was casing the joint.

The front door had a new brass letterbox, there was a hideous stone donkey by the door with winter pansies filling its panniers and the hanging basket brackets were empty. Apart from that nothing much had changed. I wouldn't have been surprised to see Ian come out of the house with his short, impatient stride, hurrying off to work. Or going wherever it was he went when I thought he was going to work.

I gave a half-hearted wave at the house, to apologise for being there? I started up the car and drove to Sophie's. I turned off the engine and unfastened my seat belt. Then I sat and thought for a good few minutes. Maybe she was out? Should I go in? Should I just drive away?

I saw her move past the window a couple of times. I had spent so many evenings in that house drinking wine, eating scratch suppers when Ian was away on business. Or at least away. I could have navigated her kitchen blindfolded. I knew where the mugs were. How her coffee machine worked. Where the wine rack stood. Where she hid chocolate for emergencies.

I tried to think it through. What would I have done if she had turned up at my door like this? I would have welcomed her in, of course. I would have done all I could for her. I had tried to be independent, self-sufficient, but I still needed friends and company.

Sophie opened the door and stared at me for a moment.

'What on earth has happened to you?'

Always tactful, that's Sophie.

'I'm sorry. I'm sorry, I didn't know where else to go,' I said. I took a step back, stumbling on the uneven ground.

'For the love of – come in!' she said, grabbing my arm and pulling me inside. 'What the hell's going on?'

'Soph, I'm sorry. I'm sorry. I've made such a mess of things. I thought things couldn't get any worse, but somehow I managed it.' I started to cry. Loose easy tears, as though my tear ducts were faulty.

'Look, I was just getting Tabitha to sleep—'

'Oh shit, I'm sorry!' I sniffed and fished in my sleeve for a tissue.

'Stop apologising, it doesn't matter. Jack's out playing squash with Bruce, he won't be back for ages. I'm going to settle you with a glass of wine and I'll be no time at all. If there is one thing my daughter can do, it's sleep.'

'You're so lucky.'

'I know. Now then…'

She poured me a large glass of red wine, led me into the sitting room and pushed me down into a chair.

'Sit there, shut up, drink that and don't move. I'm just going to check she's OK.'

I sat and sipped my wine, looking blankly out at the garden that was strewn with brightly coloured plastic toys. I tried to remember how old Tabitha was. She must be about a year old. Had I been so self-absorbed I had missed her first birthday? I felt thoroughly ashamed of myself.

My phone pinged with a text message. I felt my heart flutter. Could it be Bryn?

Superfine Supermarkets. We love your food as much as you do.

241

This is to advise you that seasonal vacancies are now available. Please contact Mr P. Phillips at your local store. Superfine Supermarkets.

I almost laughed. A job? How did this work, then? I thought it meant weeks of waiting for clearance? Christmas wasn't far off.

Sophie came back downstairs and hurried over to hug me. I put Superfine Supermarkets out of my mind for a while.

'Now then, Tabitha is out for the count. Tell me what's happened,' she said.

'I've been a fool,' I said. 'I thought I was going to be OK. I was sorting out the cottage. You know Jess let me stay there for nothing in exchange for cleaning it and decorating it. Well it was going well. My sister came to stay for a few weeks, then she went back to Texas.'

I sipped my wine. Sophie waited.

'Yes? And?'

I tried to put into words everything that had happened. Bonnie. Bryn. I closed my eyes for a moment and I had a searing flashback. Bryn whispering in my ear as he made love to me.

You have no idea how much I want you, I need to…now, now.

I gave a strangled sob and hid my face with my hands.

I said the first thing that came into my mind.

'Oh Sophie, I've fallen in love.'

'What?'

Why did I say that? I took a deep breath. Saying it was almost a relief. It made sense of my reaction. I had fallen in love with someone who was a cheat, a liar, untrustworthy.

'I've fallen in love. With Bryn, Greg Palmer's brother. He lives in the house next door to Holly Cottage. I didn't want to, Sophie. I didn't want to, but I did, and then I had a flood – a bath overflowed – I didn't have any slippers, you see? And he took me back to his house and we went to bed.'

'Calm down, breathe, Lottie. We've got all night. And what happened then?'

242

I bent forward, my arms clasped around my knees, trying to dull the pain in my heart.

'Oh, Sophie, I can't tell you how it was. I didn't know. I didn't realise…I can't tell you how wonderful it was. How he made me feel.'

Ah, Lottie, you're so brave and beautiful.

Sophie got up and went to get another glass and the bottle of wine from the kitchen.

'I feel so guilty,' I said at last.

Sophie topped up my glass and filled one for herself.

'Lottie, I hate to break it to you but you're allowed to have sex with another man, you haven't taken Holy Orders, as far as I know.'

I gave a shaky laugh. 'No.'

'Ian's been dead for nearly a year…' she said.

'Ten months.'

'OK, ten months, whatever. You're a young, single woman, Lottie. You're pretty. You have a nice figure. You're intelligent. You have the rest of your life to fill. Meals to cook, books to read, countries to visit, men to screw.'

'I didn't think it was just screwing. I thought he loved me,' I said. I gulped, realising how unutterably stupid I sounded. I'd thought I'd loved Ian, but had I? I'd thought Ian had loved me too. But had he?

'Well, perhaps he did?' Sophie said.

'No. I was just one of his friends with benefits. There was Bonnie – an ex of his on the scene. She was obsessed with him. I expect I am as well. And then some other woman he kept mentioning. Lady Trehorlicks. He said she was in her eighties but how do I know he's telling the truth?'

Sophie screwed up her face. 'If it's the Lady Trehorlicks who was on *Gardeners' World* the other day, she's a classic battle-axe and definitely in her seventies. Christ, I can't believe I just said that. You can see what my life is like these days, can't you?

Watching *Gardeners' World*. Anyway I remember her because she tore a strip off Alan Titchmarsh. He annoyed her. Something about sitting on her husband's bench. I can't believe she would be a friend with benefits. Not unless Bryn's got very unusual tastes. God, Lottie, come back to the real world with the rest of us, it's much easier. You'd like it here.'

I know you like this. And this.

'We spent a whole day in bed. There was a flood at Holly Cottage but I didn't realise how bad it was. I managed to blow the fuses, all the lights went out, and Bryn came to help me out. He took me back to his house and by the time I remembered about the cushions being a bit damp, the ceiling was down. The place was wrecked, there was plaster everywhere. I don't know what I'm going to do.'

Sophie looked at me in silence for a second and then she burst out laughing. She actually laughed. I'd just told her a catalogue of disaster and she laughed. Then I thought about it and realised that it might seem a bit funny. Sort of. The water had been dripping through my sitting-room ceiling and I had been naked in bed with my neighbour doing some pretty amazing things.

Sophie wiped her eyes and tried to catch her breath, holding one hand over her chest.

'He must be quite something. Count yourself lucky. Jack can't raise more than a smile with work and the miles he has to drive now. He hardly touches me these days.'

And here, do you like it when I touch you here, Lottie?

I wished my mind had an off switch so that I could forget.

'I'm going mad, Sophie.' I suddenly felt so tired. Perhaps it was the wine. 'I'm sorry to ask, but can I stay here tonight?'

'Christ, yes! Of course you can, you daft cow! The spare bed is made up, there are some of Tabitha's toys over the floor, but you could just kick that out of the way. I've been having a bit of a clear out.'

'It really doesn't matter. I'm so grateful.'

'Food first,' she said. 'I've made some soup, will that do?'

'I don't think I could eat anything.'

'Well you can watch me then. Come on. Jack will get something to eat in the pub with Bruce. You can tell me all over again. And don't leave anything out. Especially the good bits.'

She took me into the kitchen and put a bowl of chicken soup in front of me. It smelled wonderful, rich and slightly spicy. Despite myself I took a small spoonful and then another. Sophie passed me some French bread and we sat and talked and ate. I felt myself relax and I told her everything that had happened. The deliberate flood, losing my ring, the earrings by the side of the bed, the hot tub incident.

Sophie couldn't help herself. These things, which when I was on my own sitting in the cottage and worrying had seemed so awful, made her roar with laughter. At one point she had to find a tissue and wipe away her tears.

'I know I shouldn't laugh. I'm sure it was awful, but you've had a bit of an adventure, haven't you?' she said at last. 'It's a bit different from your life with Ian. Think of it like that.'

'I suppose so. It's not what I wanted though.'

She put a hand over mine. 'I'm sorry, Lottie; I know it must have been terrible for you. But what do you want?' she said.

What do you want?

You. I want you.

'I think I'll probably take up Jenny's offer to visit her in Texas. Just take the opportunity to get away.'

'Ha! Cowardy custard!' Sophie jeered.

'I'm not!'

'You are so!' Sophie went to get another bottle of wine.

'Not for me,' I said, my hand over the top of my glass.

'This isn't for you, it's for me,' Sophie said, unscrewing the top. 'You know you might be wrong about him. About Bryn.'

'I know I'm not. I'm sure I'm not.'

She shrugged. 'If you're not going to ask him what he's playing

245

at you could always ask the other people who might know?'

'Who?'

She slapped my hand out of the way and topped up my glass.

'The people who know him, the people who might be able to shed some light on things; Jess and Greg Palmer of course.'

Jess took one look at my face, caught hold of my sleeve and led me into the conservatory. She didn't even ask me why I was there. I had a feeling she knew.

'Sit down,' she said, encouraging me towards a heavily cushioned wicker chair. She had been doing what passed for strictly indoor gardening in Jess's world. She was dressed in tiny denim shorts over thick tights, pink Joules wellingtons and a T-shirt printed with pictures of trees. She had been busy planting bulbs in pots in one corner of the room, her French-manicured nails protected with suede gloves.

She sat down next to me.

'What's been going on, babe?' she said. 'You look terrible.'

'It's all gone wrong, Jess,' I said. 'So very wrong.'

She seemed surprised. 'Has it? Really?'

'You have no idea. There was a flood, an overflow of the bath...'

'Yeah, I know.' She pulled off her gloves and smoothed them down on her bare, brown knees.

'I thought, well I didn't know what to think. Bonnie, Bryn, all that stuff.'

Jess waved an impatient hand. 'But I know all this. I told you, remember?'

'Then there was the business of the house; I didn't know you'd sold it to Bryn. And he wasn't going to tell me.'

'I'm sure he would have done. He said he was going to.'

'No, he was pretending all the time. Lying to me about Bonnie.'

Jess reached forward and touched my hand.

'Lottie, I know some of what happened between you.'

'How?'

''Cos Bryn has been here. He was looking for you.'

'He's been here? Looking for me?'

'Bryn is a big guy, he's tough, but he's been through a lot. First Helen and then all that stuff with Bonnie. And you gotta trust me; she's poisonous. I've seen how she works, takes advantage of people, and because she's cute she gets away with it. I've worked with girls like her. They expect to be the centre of attention everywhere they go. They expect treats and favours just because they're gorgeous. And when they come up against someone like Bryn it drives then nuts. They can't believe that they've lost their touch.'

'Someone like Bryn? I thought he was taking full advantage of the situation!'

Jess shook her head. 'Bryn loved Helen, why do you think he married her? When she went off with Craig it broke his heart. He was in a state of shock for months. Bonnie moved in on him like a piranha. She's one of those women who have to win, all the time. He was fond of her, sorry for her. I mean, the four of them had been good friends before it all kicked off. You know, when Craig went off with Helen, Bonnie really went to pieces. She was in bits. Between you and me I think she might have tried to top herself. She said it was all an accident but I'm not so sure. She was a bloody nightmare for months and Bryn took the brunt of it. I think they propped each other up for a while but it was no more than that. And Bryn is honourable, he's honest.'

I couldn't accept that. 'Ha! What about the money?'

Jess frowned. 'What money?'

'All those years ago. You told me about it. The money he took from his mother and never paid back.'

Jess shook her head and looked away. She stood up and walked to look out of the window. There didn't seem to have been much progress on the swimming pool at the end of the garden. The diggers had gone but there was a portaloo and a metal storage shed in their place. It was some time before she answered me.

'You've got the wrong end of the stick. That was Greg, Lottie. Greg took the money, not Bryn. It was years ago, before I met him. Greg was struggling and he got some money out of their mother. He behaved badly, she said it didn't matter, he didn't have to worry about paying it back straight away, but the years went past, and it never happened. Bryn fell out with him over that, not the other way around. Greg got all stubborn. They had a fight…'

I sat with my mouth open.

'Why didn't you tell me? Why didn't you say something?'

'I didn't know for a long time. I told you as much as I found out. Anyway it's private stuff, Greg doesn't talk about it. Like I said, it all happened before I met him. But it was something you said that made him finally sort it out.'

'Something *I* said?'

Since when did I come up with meaningful sayings?

'It was that day when you showed him all those awful letters, d'you remember? The debts and the bills Ian had been hiding. You were in such a spin you didn't know what on earth to do. You said, I want to do what's right, even if it's too late.'

'Did I say that?'

'You did. It stuck in Greg's head, he couldn't get it out. In the end he went over to France, sorted it all out with his mother. Apologised to her. Paid her back what was owed. It made a big hole in our cash flow but that's not the point. I needed to help him do it, to show that I supported him. That's why I wanted to sell Holly Cottage.'

'Flip.'

She came back to sit in the chair next to me and leaned forward, her face very serious.

'You mustn't breathe a word of this to anyone, OK? It's not something Greg's very proud of. And then he went to see Bryn. After they had the chat, well, they sorted it out between them, but he said Bryn was in a hell of a state. He kept saying it was something to do with Bonnie's earrings. He looked a bit like you do now.'

'When was this?'

'Oooh let me think. A couple of weeks ago, maybe?'

'Oh God.'

'That's when we came up with a plan. Greg being Greg wanted to do something to sort everything out in one mighty sweep, and we hatched it out between us. And before you ask it was nothing to do with Bryn. The two hundred and fifty pound voucher to spend at Bryn's garden centre. That was just a way to get you two back together.'

'I guessed it was something like that.'

'What have you done to each other?' Jess said, shaking her head.

'I don't know. I don't know,' I wailed. My stomach was churning so much I thought I might be sick. I put my arms round myself and bent over to try and ease the feeling.

'Where have you been, anyway?' Jess said.

'I'm saying with Sophie, a friend in the village. If nothing else I can babysit for her so she and Jack can have some time together. Where's Greg?'

'He's gone over to Holly Cottage to start sorting out the repair work.' She jerked her chin out at the building site at the end of the garden. 'That's where all our builders are now. That bloody pool's never going to be finished.'

'I'm so sorry,' I said, feeling that the words were barely adequate.

Jess shook her head. 'It's not your fault, it was Bonnie who flooded the place. But –' she looked thoughtful for a moment '– what I don't really understand is how so much damage was caused in such a short time. I mean Greg says it looks as though that bath was overflowing for absolutely ages.'

She looked at me, waiting for me to say something. I could hear my pulse pounding in my ears and feel the hot blush spreading across my face.

'Um.'

'I mean Greg says if the tap was only just turned on a tiny bit, the damage caused must have taken a day or two, not just a couple of hours.'

'Er.'

'But you were around, weren't you? And Bryn was too. Didn't you notice anything?'

Couldn't Jess see how uncomfortable I was? I must have been puce with embarrassment by then.

'And Bryn said he came and got you when the fuses all went. So when was that?'

'Oooh, I really – um. You'd be better off asking him.'

Jess gave me an odd look. 'Yes, he said exactly the same thing. I should ask you.'

I stood up and pretended to be interested in the empty garden.

Jess started to look thoughtful, tapping the arm of her chair with one finger.

'And then you two fell out. He said you were annoyed about him buying Holly Cottage. But then what did Bonnie have to do with it? How could she have got in to turn the bath on in the first place? And *why* would she do it? That's what I don't understand.'

I started to babble on about keys and spilt milk and rats in the paint until Jess fixed me with a pained expression and I stuttered into silence.

After a moment she fished in the pocket of her shorts for her mobile and started stabbing at it.

'Never mind, I promised I would let Bryn know when you turned up. He'll be ever so pleased.'

'No!' I said a shade too loudly.

Jess looked at me, eyebrows raised.

'I mean, no, don't bother. I'm going to head back there now. I need some time to think, Jess. I've almost got it straight. By the time I get there I think I'll be OK. And another thing, I saw my

250

solicitor the other day. Susan wanted me to have the balance of money left when the house was sold. I have some money at last; I can afford to find somewhere else to live.'

'Susan did? Gosh, did she? Well knock me sideways and call me Mabel! Bet you weren't expecting that?'

'Hardly. If the cottage belongs to Bryn then I owe him some rent, surely? And all the money you spent on the fancy paint and the carpets and the new curtains? Oh, Jess, what a bloody shame.'

'Look, it's a complete arse ache, but the insurance will cover it, I'm sure. And if it doesn't I'll go and beat Bonnie up.'

'Oh, please don't! I don't mind contributing—'

'Joke, Lottie! Keep your hair on! Just a joke!'

I stood up. 'Well, look, I'm going now, I'll be in touch.'

'OK, but I did promise I'd let him know when I saw you. Bryn will be really cross with me if you disappear again.'

'I'm going to go straight back there.'

She looked at her watch. 'It's half past three. I'm going to try and ring Bryn at five o'clock. If you haven't turned up I'll kill you. Well I won't actually kill you but you know what I mean.'

'I do.'

She walked to the car with me and hugged me.

'I think you're pretty important to Bryn,' she said. 'I've never seen him quite so upset about anything.'

'Really?'

'Really. Don't hurt him, will you?'

I shook my head; I couldn't seem to speak. Hurt him? I wouldn't do that for the world.

'Take care,' she said, 'and let me know what's happening.'

CHAPTER 23

Chrysanthemum – cheerfulness and truth

As I drove towards Holly Cottage I saw Greg's white van pass me in the other direction. He and two other men were crammed into the front seat, smoking and laughing, and I don't think they can have realised it was me. I was rather pleased to see them go. I didn't want to have yet more complicated and potentially embarrassing conversations. My phone rang and I pulled into a lay-by to answer it, almost wishing I still smoked too so that I could open the window, have a leisurely cigarette and calm down.

'Miss Calder?'

'Speaking.'

'This is Paul Smith from A.J. Smith Jewellers in Stokeley, I've been trying to contact you about your jewellery and the clock you brought in.'

I thought for a moment and then the penny dropped.

'Yes. It's rubbish, is that what you're going to tell me?'

'Not at all. I mean, as a rule the value of contemporary jewellery is little more than scrap value. Unless there is an exceptional provenance. Connections with royalty, famous historical personages. Even so there may be a few hundred pounds that can be realised if that's what you wish? But there is a jewellery and *objets* auction coming up in a couple of weeks at Bonhams in Exeter which might be of interest. Could you spare a few minutes to come in to speak with me about it?'

'Yes, of course. When were you thinking of?'

'Now would be simply perfect, madam.'

I knew he was known as *young* Mr Smith, but really he spoke like a country gent from the 1950s. I imagined him tall and very spare, in a tweed suit with a checked Tattersall shirt, a spaniel fidgeting at his side waiting for an evening walk.

I turned the car round, drove into the town and parked. It was late afternoon and mild for November. The school buses from Exeter had just arrived in the main square and school children were meandering towards me, bashing each other with their backpacks and calling abuse across the street.

I made my way to the jewellers, reassuring myself with the thought that no matter how bad things had been, no matter how bad things might get, at least I didn't ever have to go to school again. Then I remembered about the seasonal vacancies in Superfine. Damn, I bet they would have all been filled by now. I should call in and find out.

As I passed the café where I had first noticed the loss of my ring, I looked in through the window. Through the steamed-up glass I could see Gin was still there, wiping a table with her usual ineffective style. Although to be accurate it looked as though she was just encouraging the scraps from the tables onto the floor. I wondered if somewhere in a dusty, crumb-filled corner my ring was becoming part of a tumbleweed of fluff. Perhaps I should go in and ask if she had found my ring, but at the last minute I decided not to. I don't know why; it would have been as though I was dragging something from my past into my future and I didn't like the feeling. I started to walk away.

At that moment my attention was drawn to the door of the café as the bell pinged and an elderly couple stepped out onto the pavement.

The man spoke, his voice strangely familiar. 'You stay here, dear, while I get the car, it's far too cold for you to be out in this awful wind.'

'Oh, Simon, really, it's fine…' The woman laughed indulgently as he strode away down the street.

My head swivelled round in astonishment to look at her.

'Susan?'

Susan turned and our eyes met.

'Ah, Charlotte. How are you? Thank you for your letter and the flowers. I hope the money will help?' She didn't seem half as bothered as I was. In fact she seemed almost to be preening herself.

I looked down the road, rather incredulous.

'Yes, yes, of course it will, I'm very grateful. That was Doctor Hawkins, wasn't it?'

She pulled on her leather gloves. 'Simon? Hmm, yes it was.'

My mind was in a spin. The woman in front of me looked like the younger, healthier sister of the woman I had known. Susan had put on some much needed weight and was dressed in a smart, dark red coat with a fur collar, a vivid silk scarf at her neck. Her eyes were bright and she looked odd. What was it? No, she didn't look odd, she looked happy.

I stood in front of her, unable to think what to say. Susan saved me the bother.

'We've become such good friends,' she said. 'He's been looking after me. Since that day when you took me to see him.'

Ah yes, the house visit. Good grief!

A dark car pulled up and Susan moved towards it. Dr Hawkins got out of the car and stepped smartly round to open the door for her.

'Little Lottie! Well, what a coincidence!' he said. He grabbed my arm and gave me a smacking kiss on one cheek. 'How lovely to see you. How are you?'

'Fine. Fine thanks.'

'In you get, Susie, the heated seat is on,' he said.

Susan got into the car and favoured me with an almost mischievous smile as she fastened her seat belt and Dr Hawkins shut her door.

'A wonderful lady,' he said. 'I'm so glad you brought her in that day. Means the world to me. I must be off. Lovely to see you.'

As he skipped around to the other side of the car, Susan lowered her window.

'Well, all the best, Charlotte,' she said.

She gave me a little wave; it was like confronting Dame Helen Mirren in the high street. I watched open mouthed as they drove away. Flipping heck.

After a moment I carried on to the jeweller's shop where an assistant was starting to take the glittering trinkets out of the window display and packing them into a plastic box.

Young Mr Smith was waiting for me, and his face lit up when I introduced myself.

'Come into my office,' he said. 'I've made tea.'

He was nothing like I had expected. He was about sixty-five, short, very stout and had a faint tinge of blue about his mouth that spoke of heart problems. He poured tea, investigated the biscuit tin with some enthusiasm and then got to the point.

'As I said, the jewellery you brought in might realise a reasonable sum, but it would be largely scrap value, except the necklace which has some pretty stones in it. There's a quite nice Ceylonese sapphire in this ring. No, it's this clock that interests me,' he said. He had it on the desk next to him and he touched it with a gentle hand as he spoke. 'It's very exciting.'

'Really?'

'Could I ask where you got it?'

'My grandmother left it to me. She died when I was a baby. But she wasn't wealthy. I mean, she didn't have a house full of treasure.'

'No connection with France at all?'

I thought about it. 'My grandfather went to Italy during the war, but nothing apart from that.'

'And his parents? Not known to go to France?'

'My great grandfather fancied himself an artist. He might have gone to France I suppose. My mother had a couple of paintings he had picked up on his travels. Montmartre, a ghastly sentimental one of a girl with some ducks, you know the sort of thing. They weren't very good though.'

'Yes,' young Mr Smith puffed, 'that might explain it.'

'Explain what?'

'This clock is French. Hadn't you noticed it's by Cartier?'

'Yes, but I thought it was a fake.'

He shook his head and picked up my grandmother's clock. It looked small and delicate in his pudgy hands.

'Art Deco, white enamel, onyx base. 1924 or 1925? It's filthy, of course, it needs a good clean. I hate to ask, but was this left to you in a written will? I mean, you have proof that it is in fact yours?'

'Yes, my sister received a painting and I had the clock.'

He turned back to look at the clock and smiled at it rather fondly. 'But it's lovely. Just lovely. It's a fine example; I think it should be sent to Bonhams in Exeter. I'd like them to take a look at it.'

'I had it on the mantelpiece for years, and since I moved here I've kept it in my sitting room. It's a good job I brought it in to you. I've just had a flood and the ceiling came down.'

He gave a sharp intake of breath. 'Yes, that is a happy coincidence.' He coughed and reached into his pocket for a handkerchief. He wiped his mouth. 'Not happy that your ceiling came down, obviously, but that this little tinker wasn't damaged. It may be worth a fair sum.'

I bit my lip. I felt like laughing. 'What do you mean by a fair sum?'

'Well nothing's ever certain and of course the piece needs some investigation and some judicial cleaning. But certainly in excess of forty. Fifty with a fair wind behind it. Particularly if the Internet gets wind of it. Which of course they will.'

'Fifty pounds? Well that's nice. But I can't believe Bonhams would be interested in that.'

Young Mr Smith interrupted me. Patting my hand.

'No, Miss Calder, my dear lady. Fifty thousand.'

CHAPTER 24

Holly and ivy – domestic bliss and faithfulness

I took a quick look around the cottage. There was an almost full skip by the back door filled with the remains of the ceiling and a large number of water-soaked wood beams. Indoors, there was a great deal of mess and muddle and several dehumidifiers were on.

It was obvious I couldn't stay there. I would have to go back to Sophie's house later on. Then maybe I would go and stay with my aunt? Or Jenny? But first I had to see Bryn. I couldn't put it off any longer. I didn't want to.

I walked to the end of the garden. The trees were shedding their golden leaves all over the lawn and there was a smell of a bonfire somewhere. It had been an unusually warm and beautiful autumn afternoon, and now the sun was setting behind the distant hills and the sky was fading to palest lavender.

I took in a deep breath and closed my eyes. I would leave this place soon and not return but I would never forget it. I would miss it and I would miss the person I had become here. I could move on now. Do something.

Maybe I would keep up this way of life. Perhaps now I had

money I would buy a tiny place in the middle of nowhere and become a hermit, wearing organic clothes I had woven myself on a loom, and sell my car and walk with a wooden cart to the local shop once a week and become best friends with the woman who worked there.

Or maybe I would return to my old ways.

Perhaps when I went to stay with my sister I would be seduced by the climate and the lifestyle in Houston. I might take up with one of the young men at Trent's golf club. I could just imagine them; hideous plaid trousers, wide white smiles, mahogany tans. Perhaps it would be easy to live in a gated community behind high fences and manicured lawns and never again think of Holly Cottage. Maybe I would forget about the crystal clear air here and the sweeping views of the gentle hills.

But Bryn? Would I forget him? Could I ever forget him? Would some hard-headed businessman in oil and gas who needed a decorative companion at golf club dinners but who left me to my own thoughts suit me better after all? I didn't need to do this to myself, I'd realised that. I didn't need to be unhappy in order to prove my independence. There was a difference between being alone and being lonely.

My heart seemed to hurt at the prospect, my stomach flipped and I felt nauseous. Would I forget Bryn, could I?

No, not while I lived. Not while I breathed and thought and remembered.

Not while there were inglenook fireplaces, English gardens, the taste of red wine on a dark evening. Not while there was candlelight.

Not while I could still think and feel and know.

I opened the gate to Bryn's garden. He had carried me through and into his house just a few days ago – I wasn't sure exactly how many. When had I fallen in love with him? Was it just the other day? Was it the day he found me floundering on the floor covered in paint? Was it that magical day, September 14, when I had

259

woken up in his bed knowing what all the fuss was about? That date was one I would remember all my life.

I went in under the trees, kicking up the drifting leaves in front of me. All the lush foliage had gone now, the flowers had faded and died. The garden was settling down to sleep through the winter. Just the evergreens, the holly and the ivy bringing little sparks of colour to the hedges. I found a conker on the grass, still in the half case of its prickly shell. I pulled it out, smoothing my fingers over the glossy surface. Its secret beauty made me want to cry. Why was I so emotional these days? What had happened to the person I had been, who had tried to be so sensible? Instead the real me was back, clumsy and impetuous and silly. I might still be idealistic and I might have realised what the phrase 'mind-blowing sex' meant, but I was also somehow stronger. I didn't want to be alone, but the prospect didn't frighten me. I could look after myself.

The evening air was mild and still. The garden was quiet; dusk was beginning to thicken around me. Above me one star winked in the sky, dark wisps of cloud lingered in the last light of the sunset.

Then I saw him. The hot tub lights were on. And Bryn was in it, his back to me, his arms spread along the edge, his head bowed. The water jets were turned off; he was just sitting in the still water.

I hesitated wondering what to do. Should I retreat, pretend I hadn't seen him?

I took a deep breath. No, I bloody well would not. If I was leaving, if I was not to see him again, then I would take this chance to see him alone one last time.

'Hello,' I said.

He didn't turn around at first. His back stiffened, he dropped his arms and was very still for a moment. I walked around so that I could see him.

'Hello,' he said.

'I wanted to see you.'

We looked at each other, I felt immeasurably sad to think that I was losing this wonderful man.

'Jess said she'd seen you. I'm so sorry, Lottie,' he said. 'Sorry I wasn't straight with you about the cottage. It was the wrong thing to do. I panicked.'

'It's OK. I think I understand.'

'Greg's been here. He's been great. They'll have the cottage sorted in no time.'

'Yes, I saw him leaving as I got here.'

'Just a few days to dry the place out.'

'I saw the dehumidifiers or whatever they are called.'

I walked towards him and rested my hands on the edge of the hot tub. I was so close I could have reached out and touched him. I knew how he would feel, the smooth warmth of his skin, the hardness of the muscles underneath. I knew the scent of him now, the taste, the sound of his laugh, that little place at the base of his spine. September 14. A day that nagged at the back of my mind. I couldn't bear it.

'Are you OK?' I said.

'I don't know. Are you OK, Lottie?' He was watching me, his beautiful eyes filled with sadness.

'I don't know.'

No, I'm not OK. Bryn, I'll never be the same again. I'm lost. No one will ever say my name like you. No one will make me feel the way you do.

'What are you going to do?'

I looked down and kicked at the grass growing up around the edge of the hot tub.

'I don't really know. I'm going to see Jenny in Houston soon, she's let me know she's getting married. She gave me a plane ticket when she left. I can go any time and stay as long as I like. I expect she'll want me to be a bridesmaid again.' I gave a small, choking laugh.

'That might be fun. Would you like that?' His voice was very gentle.

'I've no idea. I shouldn't think so. What does it matter? What are you going to do?'

He turned in the water towards me. The tub was flooded with dark blue light. I could see the outline of his body under the water.

'I'll keep going,' he said. 'What else can I do?'

I was going to cry. My eyes filled with tears and everything blurred. I wanted to die, for this terrible pain to go away.

Everything was very tranquil, the garden was quiet, and the only sound was the water moving.

'Oh Bryn.' I turned my head away from him. 'I just had to come back. I had to see you. To say goodbye I suppose.'

'There's only one thing worse than seeing you so unhappy, Lottie, and that's knowing it was my fault.'

Then in one swift movement he reached out towards me and grabbed my arms. And pulled me into the water with him.

Gasping, spluttering and shocked I found myself on his lap and he was kissing me as though he never wanted to stop. I started to complain and then I started laughing and so did he. And then, then of course he kissed me again.

'Lottie, Lottie, don't go,' he said. 'Please don't go.'

'I don't want to go. I don't want to go anywhere.' I was breathless.

September 14.

'Stay here. Stay with me. We can have so much fun together. I know this isn't the most romantic way of doing it but please stay, please, Lottie. I love you so much, I can't bear to lose you.'

I pulled back in his arms and looked at him. I could feel a smile spreading across my face.

'You love me?'

'Of course I love you. Didn't you guess?'

'I don't know. Yes, I suppose I did, but I didn't want to believe it. In case—'

'There is no "in case",' he said. 'I'm never going to let you down or hurt you. You have my word. And I don't want to interfere or tell you what to do. But while the cottage is being dried out and repaired, you could start by moving in with me?'

Suddenly the idea seemed a good one. Instead of my mind shying away like a startled pony from the suggestion, I felt a warm certainty that it would be all right. I could place my trust in him, I would be happy with him. We had a future together.

'So?' His arms tightened around me, around my soggy clothing, around my sadness.

I gave a huge sigh. One that seemed to come from my soul, cleansing out all the doubts and unhappiness of the past year.

'Oh yes. Yes, Bryn. I've been so miserable thinking about never seeing you again.'

He let out a shaky breath. 'I don't know what I would have done if you'd said no!'

'What's the date?' I said after a moment.

He frowned. 'Date? I think it's the 20th November. Why?'

'I just wondered. It's my birthday in two weeks.'

'I know what I'll be buying you then. I always want to make you happy.' He kissed my ring finger.

I hugged him, all my previous misery forgotten, and we kissed again. He held my face in his hands and looked into my eyes and I could almost read his thoughts. He pulled me on top of him in the water and my body felt almost weightless, it slid over his as though we had been made for each other.

'Tell me something,' I said, 'something that's been bothering me.'

'Anything.' He kissed my neck,

'Were you a footballer?'

Bryn frowned. 'I've been known to have a kick about. Why?'

'Jess said something about you going to Chelsea. I wondered if you…'

Bryn began to laugh, his head thrown back.

Then he hugged me to him.

'Chelsea *Flower Show*,' he said. 'I entered for the first time this year. Artisan Garden. I didn't win, but it was a great experience.'

'Oh,' I said, feeling a bit silly, 'of course. I am daft.'

'You're a sweetheart.'

'You'll have to help me with Holly Cottage's garden, I have some ideas but I'm not sure where to start.'

'We'll start by pulling the fence between the gardens down. We'll do it together.'

We just looked at each other for a few moments. I would never get tired of his wonderful face, of the love I saw in his eyes.

'Can I ask just one thing?' he said at last.

'Anything. Of course. What?'

'Can you move that blasted pixie so he's not aiming at me every time I go outside?'

I laughed. 'Consider it done. I'll banish him to the bottom of the garden.'

'That's a great relief and it would make me very happy.' He ran his finger around the neck of my sweater and I saw the expression in his eyes change. 'I want to make you happy now, Lottie,' he said. 'And part of doing that involves getting you indoors and out of those wet clothes. You'll catch a chill.'

I pulled off my sweater and started unbuttoning my shirt. 'I wouldn't want to catch a chill.'

He began to laugh again and after a moment I joined in.

It's a jolly good job Ivy Cottage was on top of a hill with no other neighbours. Making love in a hot tub, another first for me, was amazing. Jolly cold when we got out afterwards but sexy, sensuous utter bliss. Gradually the lights changed from blue to purple and red and gold. I could feel myself dissolving into absolute pleasure. It felt almost as though I was Bryn and he was me.

As he held me I dropped my head back and looked up at the first stars in the velvet sky and knew that at last, at long last, I was home.

I never did find my ring. Nor did I realise at this point that I was pregnant with the first of our four sons, perhaps the nausea and the dates nagging away at the back of my mind should have been a bit of a clue, but then I had other things distracting me.

And Jenny's wedding? And Christmas? Oh they were just magical. But that's another story.

ACKNOWLEDGEMENT

Thanks are firstly due to my agent Annette Green of Annette Green Agency, who loved this book and is obviously very wise, totally brilliant and the best agent anyone could hope for.

Secondly to my editor Rachel Faulkner-Willcocks of Avon who is delightful, dedicated and insightful.

Thank you to Joanne Gledhill for her great copy editing work shovelling away all those commas and picking up the things I missed.

There are of course many others who have supported me, encouraged me and poured me drinks during this process.

Most importantly Jane Ayres, my best friend – without whom life wouldn't be nearly so much fun.

Debi Alper – author, editrix extraordinaire and stalwart champion of all novice writers.

Chris Manby, who said the right thing at exactly the right moment and taught me to plot properly too.

Claire Dyer, who is filled with talent, kindness and good ideas.

A very special shout out to the Literary Lovelies: a group of writerly friends I met through Twitter who provide invaluable advice, riotous lunches and fabulous support. Jane Ayres, Chris Manby, Susanna Bavin, Catherine Boardman, Karen Coles, Christina Branach, oh and Kirsten Hesketh.

And of course David, Freya, Claudia and James and the rest of my family who I think are probably rather surprised.

Printed by RR Donnelley at Glasgow, UK